ANAMNESIS

- A NOVEL -

ELOISE J. KNAPP

If only we could forget.
This one is for you, David B.

CHAPTER 1

The concrete wall sent a bitter chill through my jacket, but I leaned on it anyway. I was tired. An hour gone and not a single hit. I took a drag on my cigarette—fucking tobacco tax was almost bad enough to make me quit—and savored the nicotine. I blew a smoke ring. It hung in the air, gray and thick, before disappearing into the night. Even if I didn't make another sale, at least I had a nice smoke.

Christmas lights set the street ablaze even though it was only the end of November. The Westlake Center tree lighting was yesterday, and the thing towered in front of the mall entrance. Hordes of people posed for photos in front of it, giant overpriced coffees in hand. It was hard to believe people came to Seattle from around the state just for the tree.

"Hey, E!"

Skid emerged from the crowd to my left. His baggy pants dragged on the ground, the hems muddy and ratted. A navy blue knitted hat was pulled low over his forehead. Despite being a street kid, homeless since I met him, he always had a goofy smile on his face and an attitude that didn't match his circumstances. I had at least ten years on him but we got along.

"What's up?"

Skid leaned on the wall next to me. The passing crowd gave us an extra breadth. Two shady guys loitering was scary business. "Got someone for ya. Looking to get some rope."

"He at the spot?"

"Yep."

"Been a slow night, thanks." I tossed my cigarette on the ground and crushed it with my heel. "Come on. I'll give you your cut after. Then I gotta bounce."

We crossed the intersection and walked to the alley where Skid's guy waited behind an overfilled dumpster. He was exactly what I expected. Beady eyes set deep in their sockets, greasy skin. Dressed nice enough to look respectable at first glance, maybe even good if you were drunk. I fucking hated these guys.

Skid hung back while I handled the guy, keeping watch.

"What do you need?" I asked.

He shifted, glanced down the alley. "Uh, roofies I guess? Two of them?"

"Two huh?" I shoved my hands in my pockets and grinned. The guy was a dabbler. Easy money. "Forty bucks."

"That seems like a lot. Google said they'd be less." When he frowned, his nostrils flared wide. I gave him the silent treatment and, as dabblers do, he reached into his wallet and took out four crumpled tens.

I plucked them from his grubby fingers and handed him two small plastic baggies from my jacket. "Best there is."

The second he had the packages he hightailed it back to the main street. I had to take advantage of a guy like that. They were bastards, nasty and despicable. I wasn't supposed to care about what I sold, who I sold it to, or what would happen after. All these years in the game, I still did. Maybe it was because I still believed this life wasn't mine. That one of these days, I'd remember. I'd remember everything. And get out.

Skid wandered back to me and we headed farther down the alley where it exited on the other end of the block. The smell of fresh bread from the sub shop nearby mingled with trash. My stomach rumbled. Fuck I was hungry.

The cash from the rope was still in my hand. I gave thirty bucks to Skid and pocketed the rest.

"Shit, E, thanks. That's a lot."

"Don't worry about it. You're a good steerer," I told him. "Call it a Christmas bon—"

A woman in a short pink cocktail dress rounded the corner into the alley and slammed into me. She stumbled backward then fell on her ass on the sidewalk. People navigated around her, going out of their way not to look at the scene.

"Jesus, watch where you're going lady," I snapped. My voice faltered once I got a good look at her.

She'd been in the dress more than a day. The rumpled fabric had a dried stain down the front and flecks of something dark across the hem. There was a sweaty sheen to her skin and her hair flew in all directions. She was on a bender. I'd seen it before. Good girls got bored, maybe had an addiction in the past. They squeezed into a little number from the back of the closet. Had a nice little breakdown with lots of booze, sex, and drugs. I bet she had a gaggle of friends at a bar somewhere who wondered where she'd gone off to. No doubt they were sending text messages furiously, asking if she'd hooked up with someone.

Then I saw bruises on her neck. Her knees were scraped

and bloodied. Makeup was smudged around her eyes and mouth.

She got to her feet. The heel on her right shoe was missing, setting her stance off kilter. She pushed past me and continued down the alley.

"E, should we do something?" Skid's nose and eyebrows scrunched together.

Doing something meant sticking around, and sticking around was dangerous. You didn't hang around the last place you sold. But the look of concern on Skid's face made me go against my gut.

"Hey, lady," I called out. "Are you okay? You need something?"

She stopped, already twenty feet away, and turned around. "I need somewhere to hide and something to put me to sleep." She wiped her mouth with the back of her hand, then reached into the purse dangling from her elbow. "I have money. I'll give you everything I have. I don't have much time. They're looking for me."

"Who's looking for you? The cops?" I used my arm to gently push Skid back. "Get out of here, now."

Skid nodded and booked it out of the alley without question. He disappeared into the crowd.

"Please," she begged. "I'm going to wake up soon and I won't know where I am."

Someone had taken a sledgehammer to my chest. My heartbeat came to a stop then raced so hard I felt my pulse throbbing in my ears. The bottomless panic in her eyes tore through me. The dark voids of my memory spilled into the foreground of my mind.

I won't know where I am.

My mouth went dry. Any thoughts of running disappeared. "What do you mean?"

"I-I don't know exactly. They took me and *did things* to me. I escaped, but I know they'll find me. I'm remembering things. I remember more every time and—"

"Who took you?" I interrupted. I closed the distance between us and grabbed her shoulders. "What are you talking about?"

Suddenly her body tensed. Her chin tilted up and she scanned her surroundings. Something shifted in her. She brought her hand to her neck and felt the plum colored bruises. She winced and swayed. I tightened my grip on her to keep her upright.

"Where am I?" Her voice was hoarse. She slapped my hands off her and took a wobbly step back. "Who are you?"

The world was expanding and it hurt my brain. She was acting like I did seven years ago when I woke up from my missing time. I was totally alone, the chaotic storm of consciousness fighting to make sense of where I was, who I was.

And with no results. It had been years since I'd fully given up hope of discovering who I was. Years since I stopped looking for answers, since I let the streets suck me under.

"Tell me what happened to you." I demanded. "Were you drugged? How much time have you lost?"

"No. *No!* I don't know why I'm here." Her confusion veered into hysteria. "I don't know how I got here! What did you do to me?"

Tires screeched at the head of the alley closest to us as a black town car came to a halt. Two men sprang out of the back seat and ran straight for us. The dim amber streetlight cast ugly shadows on their faces. Once they entered the cover of the alley, one reached into his suit jacket. I knew that motion. He was going for a gun.

The woman burst into tears. I took her hand and tried to pull her into a run. I wasn't letting her go. I couldn't. "Move, dammit! Come on!"

She took two steps, then her knees buckled and she crumpled to the dirty ground. Her breaths were short and frantic. The two men were seconds away.

Every part of me screamed not to let go. She knew something. She'd help me. She was my only chance.

A bullet pinged off the dumpster beside me.

What good were answers if I was dead?

I let go of her and ran.

CHAPTER 2

By the time I stopped under the viaduct on University Street, my lungs burned and my throat was covered in phlegm. I couldn't remember the last time I ran more than a block. I hoped I'd never have to do it again. Every breath of air I gulped down brought on a sharp pain in my left side.

Across the street, the water in Elliot Bay glittered as it reflected light from the gaudy Ferris wheel built a few years back. Once I caught my breath, I crossed the street and leaned on the railing of the waterfront, watching it spin. The Puget Sound lapped up against the docks.

My hands shook as I retrieved my cigarettes and lit one. There was a wild animal inside my chest, thrashing and trying to crawl out. I needed something harder to make that feeling go away. My self-help books called my drinking problem "self-medicating." Fucking self-help books. I had hundreds of overdue library books in my apartment, all of them offering reasons why I was the way I was. They didn't improve my life but I ate them up and hoped one day they'd click and I'd be better.

None of them ever helped me remember. No effort I ever made to unearth my past paid off. The woman in the pink dress gave me more in the space of minutes than I'd ever gotten on my own. She told me I wasn't alone.

I wanted to tell myself what just happened was a

freakish, unconnected event. Whatever happened to me was a mystery and would stay that way. But she wasn't acting. She wasn't high. She honestly didn't know where she was. Just like me seven years ago when I woke up from four years of missing time. Memories of my life before that moment were missing or jumbled. I didn't know what happened to me during the four years. All I could dredge up were fragmented visions of torture and experimentation.

Whatever chance I had of gleaning information was fucked now. I shouldn't have let go. I should've dragged her with me. I should've fought.

My phone buzzed. I didn't recognize the number. Skid got a new burner every month so I answered anyway.

"E, you okay?" Skid asked. I picked up on cars in the background. He was back at the overpass. "What happened to that lady?"

"I'm fine. Are you?"

"I'm good, yeah." He paused, waiting for me to answer his question.

"She left," I lied. A couple stopped at the railing nearby. I took a few steps away and lowered my voice. "I think she was drunk or high or something. Don't worry about it."

"All right. I just wanted to make sure the po po didn't get you. You wanna push a bit more tonight?"

"I'm fine," I said again. "No, not tonight. I gotta crash. Meet up tomorrow though, okay?"

"You got it. Later."

Before I went back to my apartment I stopped by the alley. There was no sign of the girl or thugs. Not like there should be. I stared at the spot where I had her right in front of me. The spot where I let her go.

I merged into the horde of Seattlites, my unsold package of benzos and roofies feeling heavy in my pocket. I should've stayed out another few hours. I should've done a lot of things. What I was going to do was drink myself into oblivion and make myself forget.

CHAPTER 3

My legs are under ice water. They've been numb for a while, but I want to keep them there for some reason. There's a reward if I keep them under longer than anyone else, or beat my own record. But I've never done this before, so how could I beat my own score? And there's a nagging in the back of my mind that no one wins. I've never seen anyone win. I think of anything but the tingle climbing up my thighs where the ice water stops, the stabbing that will follow when they haul me out and prod at me. They give me pills with tepid water to wash them down. It's never enough water and they feel like stones in my throat.

What is your pain level on a scale of 1-10?

Does this pain feel familiar to you in any way?

It does. Yes, it does. I've been here before, but my whole body is under ice water. A tube down my throat. I can't breathe. I'm going to die. I'm going to freeze to death or choke on this plastic tube down my throat.

Blood on my hands. Screaming. I see the face of a girl with red hair and she's smiling at me. Half her face is burned and her teeth are white against the charred remains. I try to tell her I can't breathe, get this fucking tube out of my throat. She tells me it's okay, she's going to get me out of here. Both of us out of here. But it's too late.

I'm suffocating. I'm going to die.

My heart thundered in my chest when I woke up from the nightmare. I untangled myself from the sweat soaked bedding and brought my legs over the edge of the mattress. They hurt. They always hurt after that dream. A phantom pain that tingled. Sometimes I expected to look at my toes and see them blackened from frostbite. If I was still high from the night before, I'd hallucinate that they were.

I tried to stand. My head swam. I sat down and took a deep inhale. The smell of my apartment comforted me. It meant I was home—or at least as close to a home as I'd ever have—and safe. Cigarette smoke, old pizza. Curry from the neighbors next door. Piss and garbage wafting in from the open window.

I didn't say it was a pleasant smell, just that it meant I was home.

Much to my surprise, the nearest bottle of alcohol was on the folding table by the window, lit by the dying sun outside. I mustered up as much energy as I could and walked to it. Focused on the matted carpet under each footstep, my body moving through space. Sometimes that's what I had to do; hone in on each small motion in order to get somewhere. You know you're fucked up when walking ten feet to a bottle of booze was a daunting task.

It was worth it. I sat in the lounge chair, one of the only nice things I had, and took a swig. Whiskey ignited my mouth, burned my throat as it went down. It was cheap, not something you'd drink to savor. I waited as warmth spread through my core into my limbs.

Like many people, I drank to numb myself. At least I knew it. I wasn't in denial about it. When my mind was clear, I panicked. I was forced to face who I was, what I'd lost, and what I didn't know. If I drank, all that became gray and fuzzy and something I didn't have to think about. When all the memories of your life were Swiss cheese or gone all together, you didn't want to think about it. You did anything you could to make it blurry.

My phone buzzed from somewhere below. I took another swig and slid to the floor to rifle through the scattering of clothes and empty food containers. I felt it in my jeans pocket, where I left it from the day before, and pulled it out. I expected Skid, but it was Donovan. Sometimes I wished Donovan treated me like the other hundred dealers under him. If he did, he wouldn't care about me unless I was right in front of him. Being someone's personal project was tiresome.

I could hear the low thud of bass in the background. I imagined him outside of his strip club having a smoke as he called me.

"Hello?"

"Been calling you all day!" Donovan's Russian accent always sounded heavier over the phone. "Where were you?"

I glanced at the digital numbers on the stove. One advantage of a studio apartment is that everything is in eyesight. It was 3:46pm. I'd been out since 10:00pm the night before.

"Here," I said, letting that word be answer enough. Donovan didn't care. He had me now.

"Lazy bitch. Why were you calling me?"

I wandered to the fridge and opened it. All food went in the fridge. Kept it safe from the roaches. It made searching for food easy. I settled for a package of saltine crackers. They were stale, but edible. Coffee sounded good but I didn't have the energy to make any yet.

"Call you?" I asked. I slumped into the chair again as the sawdust crackers sucked the moisture from my mouth.

"Ten times last night. You get wasted?"

The more I thought about it, I vaguely remembered calling Donovan. I couldn't get the pink dress lady out of my head. My brain kept turning it over and pulling it apart until I had myself convinced I should start looking for answers again. If anyone knew if there was a new drug on the streets, it would've been Donovan. Then I hit my limit and the balm of alcohol depressed me. It dulled the determined vigor. I gave up calling and fell asleep.

But since he was on the phone and I was a glutton for punishment, I owned up to it. "I did. I wanted to know if there was anything new on the market."

Donovan laughed. His voice was all gravel. "Did you sell all your shit already? Nice work."

"Sure," I said. Happy Donovan would tell me what I wanted to know. Mad Donovan? Whole other story. "So, anything new?"

Donovan's voice escalated and he didn't bother to pull the phone away as he yelled. "Angel, get the fuck back in there, your shift isn't over yet!"

He was definitely at the strip club. I waited for him to finish laying into one of his girls.

"Sorry about that. Anyway, funny you ask. There is, but I don't have any. Some new rope. Don't really know much about it, other than a small batch was released in the city two days ago."

My hands were sweaty. I gripped the whiskey bottle and took another sip to steel myself. "Who's dealing it?"

"Not sure. My buddy heard from his brother's friend it wasn't anyone already in the game. Gave it to some low end independents."

"What's the price tag?"

"Free if you can believe it. Whoever's dealing just wants to test it out. You ask me, they're testing the waters. They're getting people on it, then will send another wave out to see how much they can get for it."

When the doorbell rang my heart almost stopped. My whole body jerked, sending a splash of whiskey onto the already soiled carpet.

"Ethan, you there?"

"Someone's at the door. I gotta go."

"Stop by tonight and we'll restock you."

"Right. Bye."

I snapped the phone shut and set it on the card table. Maybe the doorbell was a figment of my imagination. I waited, staring at the door and willing the bell not to ring again. The only people that ever came to my apartment were a few pesky clients who found out where I lived, but they came in the dead of night. Donovan stopped by occasionally to get high together, but he was at the club.

A knock this time. Three hard, fast raps on the door.

My palms started to sweat. I stood and walked to the kitchen, retrieving the one gun I owned. It was a Glock 45 I accepted as payment from someone years ago. From there I padded over to the front door and looked through the peephole.

It was a girl and she didn't belong in my neighborhood at that hour. Her clothes were perfectly coordinated. Spotless. All creams and blacks. She had a mane of wavy auburn hair splayed around her jacket. I relaxed. I knew her type. Overachiever looking for some Adderall. I just wondered who pointed her my direction. Some of the homeless outside could've. Kind of a quid pro quo deal.

I opened the door a crack, keeping the gun behind me. "You looking to get amped?"

"W-what?"

Sometimes they played dumb. It might've been her first time. Coworker or classmate suggested it, the girl said no. Then she came by herself later. I sighed. I didn't want to deal with another dabbler. "Do you want some bennies or not?"

"I just want…"

"I don't take brand requests."

"I'm here to talk to you."

I frowned. Cop? Landlady's kid? I said nothing. Make her do all the talking. That was the trick to keeping the high ground; never say anything until you're certain you know what's going on. All my time on the streets, I learned that the hard way.

She shifted. Glanced left and right, checking the hallway. "Can I come in?"

"No."

"Oh." She reached into her bag. "Just give me one minute. I swear, if you just—"

I shut the door. Jesus peddlers were getting mighty desperate. Didn't they watch the news? People got shot and mugged around here.

The girl hit the door once. "Are you Ethan Knight?"

My full name. Not even my street name, E. Who was this girl? I looked through the peephole again. She'd retrieved a stack of papers bound with a plastic spiral from her bag. There on the front were the words "Memory Loss Experimentation."

I breathed deeply, fighting the sensation of complete emotional flooding that threatened to hijack me. Those words would mean little to every person on the planet but me. They were a physical emblem of why I was a drug dealer living in a shitty studio apartment in Belltown, living off cigarettes and booze. Between pink dress yesterday and this, I almost wanted to believe the universe was trying to tell me something.

"I want to talk to you about your missing time." A pause. Then, softly, "Please let me in."

I opened the door again, enough for her to see me.

"Why are you here? How did you find me?"

"The internet is a magical place, plus your full name is on that blog. You talked about your drug connections so I just started asking around for 'Ethan'. Probably not a smart move on your part. Please let me in and we can talk." She cleared her throat. It was a girlish sound that suited her. "It took a lot for me to come here. Please just hear me out."

There was a desperation on her face I couldn't say no to. That and, since she was so high strung, if I was nice enough maybe she'd buy some benzos. I opened the door completely and waved her in, directing her to sit on the folding chair by the card table. She sat down gingerly, her butt on the edge of the seat. Her handbag—real leather I guessed—in her lap. She was uncomfortable. I was good at reading people based on how they interacted with their environment. Most people were too inside their own heads to see what was going on around them, but if they looked they'd see a lot.

When I closed the front door the apartment went black, barely lit by the streetlights. The last of the sunlight was gone. Now having company, I realized how dark I kept the place.

"What's a bennie?"

"Learn the lingo. We have it for a reason." I collapsed into my big chair. "Start talking."

"Well, I'm not sure where to start." Another cough. She wiggled and the chair creaked. "Now that I'm here it's a lot harder to talk about this."

"You'd better start trying."

"I'll start with my name I suppose. My name is Olivia Holloway. I'm a campaign manager. I put on charity events as well."

I knew the name. Unlike every other fuckup dealer out there, I wanted out of the game someday. It was a fantasy, but one I was serious about. For years I'd hijacked forgotten newspapers on the bus and in coffee shops, kept up on the world outside my own. I even looked for jobs when I felt particularly optimistic.

Olivia Holloway's name showed up next to the mayor, Lewis Ward, often. I'd seen it in dozens of news articles, especially in regard to Ward's recent announcement he was running for a Senate seat. She was a pristine do-gooder. Socialite. Threw great parties and got lots of donations. What the hell was she doing in Belltown with printouts of my blog? It only existed because Donovan hated hearing my incoherent ramblings about my lost time and I had to vent somewhere. There were a few reasons why I gave up on it, but one of them was that I simply ran out of things to write.

"So?" I stared at her expectantly.

"I've never spoken about this to anyone before. Not a soul." Her voice was softer. "You have to understand, for months I've been on the computer for hours a day researching what could be happening to me. When I happened to find your blog, I knew your loss of time was the same as mine. The way you described it was like you pulled it straight from my mind. The strong aftertaste when you wake up, the complete obliteration of memory. All of it."

Any other day, I would've been skeptical. With the previous night fresh in my mind, I was willing to keep going. "I believe I was a victim of illegal pharmaceutical or government experimentation. You're saying that it's happening to you?"

"Not experimentation. Whatever they were testing on you, they're now using in the open. So in a way, yes, it is. I tried to email you through the blog but you never responded. That's why I tracked you down." She looked around the apartment. Her eyes flashed to the messes on the floor. "Trust me, I wouldn't be here if I wasn't desperate."

There it was. The insult to me, to my life, to everything. It was what I expected from her and she delivered. It was easy to be jaded when everyone around you validated your opinions.

As much as I wanted to defend myself, I was curious, too. If the girl in the pink dress was drugged, this one could've been, too. There was something new on the streets. It all added up. "I don't go on it anymore. Haven't for years. Tell me, why do you think our experiences are the same?"

"I've been having memory lapses, like how you describe in your blog, only for shorter durations. I'll be at an event and at some point, my brain switches off. Memories stop recording. The next day I wake up and have no idea where I was or what I was doing. When I wake up, I…"

"You what?"

"I've been violated." One hand began to drift to her chest as she said it. She caught herself and returned it to her purse. "I don't feel comfortable going into the details yet."

"Getting roofied is a far cry from what I'm talking about in that blog. You're sure that's not what's happening?"

Pink dress had been messed up. Went out of her mind. The girl in front of me was in nowhere near the same state as her. Looking at myself, my fucked up self, she wasn't anything like me. I doubted her 'missing time' was the same as mine.

Olivia bolted upright. The booklet dropped from her lap with a hard *thud*. Without a word, she picked it up and put it back into her bag. She pulled a large envelope from her bag and set it on the table. Her hands shook.

"Hey, I'm sorry," I said. "You come in here saying this shit, you have to back it up. I'm not saying you're lying. I just want to be sure."

"I'm here because I believe what you've written in your blog, Mr. Knight, and I believe it is happening to me. I came here to talk to you about your experience because I don't want to be alone in this." She held her head high. "But I will *not* stand here and listen to you make accusations like that. I knew this was a bad idea."

Olivia walked to the door and left. She didn't slam it, didn't curse me. As quickly as she was there, she was gone.

All that remained was a trace of her perfume.

I was stunned. It took a few minutes before I picked up the envelope. Inside were a dozen handwritten notes on lined paper. On the top was a name of an event with the date. It was an account of what she did during the entire day, who she talked to, what she ate, and other details. The earliest notes were vague, but as the dates continued they became more extensive.

They were logs of her memory lapses. Similar to the ones I had on my own blog, but much more cohesive.

I scanned the most recent one. It was a fundraiser ball for Seattle Children's Hospital. She described, in extreme detail, every moment of the party. Olivia didn't eat or drink any food given to her during the event. She had a protein bar and bottle of water beforehand that she bought at a market approximately one mile away an hour before the party. There were lists of times she remembered. The last time was 10:42pm. She danced with an associate named Hugh Raven. That was the last thing she recalled until the next morning.

She described the kinds of pain her body was in and other symptoms. One caught my eye.

"I woke up groggy. The feeling is similar to when I was taking Xanax for my panic attacks. As usual, I taste something metallic. It's not blood. It's like I've been sucking on rusty nails. There's no signs of damage inside my mouth. Last time it took two days for it to go away. Hope it goes faster this time. I can't stand it."

My fingers hovered over my lips. Even after all these years I knew that aftertaste. Just thinking about it made me sick.

I shoved the notes back in the envelope and set them on the table, my thoughts drifting. I didn't have anything new to tell her. Everything about my blackouts was on that blog. I had nothing more to add unless she wanted tips on self-medicating and how to fuck up her life.

Or maybe we could throw ourselves a pity party. Complain about it over a bottle of whiskey. Hey, I lost all of yesterday. Cool, I had that dream again, the one about the guy using a scalpel on my arms.

I wasn't sure what to make of Olivia Holloway yet. I'd find her when I was ready, at least see what she thought I could do for her. I glanced at the clock. 4:30pm.

In the meantime, the world kept moving. I had work to do.

CHAPTER 4

I finished the last bite of my food truck taco and tossed the wrapper in the trash beside me as I walked to Skid. He was waiting for me at the corner of 3rd and Bell. From a distance, he could've been twelve or forty. Wearing so many loose layers of clothing, age and gender were indistinguishable.

I met him on the street a year earlier. He was panhandling and a couple cops were hassling him. I came over and stood behind him. *Is this police brutality?* I'd asked. To emphasize my point I held my phone out as though ready to snap a photo. That was a trigger for Seattle Police Department these days. Always under media pressure and hype, the last thing they needed was a scene. They sauntered off leaving me with Skid.

When I did that, it was because I wanted to piss off the cops. It was an opportunity to stick it to someone, so I did. Protecting Skid wasn't on my agenda. After they left, Skid broke down while he thanked me. He tried to hide the tears at first, then they came in waves. In a world where no one looked out for him, what I did meant something big.

The appeal of having a child was beyond me until I met him. It made me feel good to be needed. To be looked up to. Skid thought I was near godlike and I enjoyed that. I kept him around, and while in the beginning it was for my own ego, the kid grew on me.

When I first met him at thirteen, Skid had just started

smack and was getting hooked. Before the smack he'd just smoked some weed now and then. I got him off the hard stuff. It was sad to see a kid that young get lost to something like that, especially once I got to know him. Sometimes he lapsed and would take pills when times were tough. He was the exception to my sell-to-anyone rule. I'd never sell to him.

His story was a mystery to me. A kid his age on the streets could be there for dozens of reasons. I suspected his parents were druggies, now dead or in jail. Or maybe he just ran away. He'd always seemed familiar with the street.

I tried to give him a purpose and that helped. He was my steerer. The deal was, he found people who were looking for drugs. Led them to me. I gave him a few bucks. I think he mostly saved the money because I rarely saw him high. Unfortunately, my supplier and his buddies thought Skid was hilarious. They'd offer him drugs when they saw him, sometimes even a job working his own corner. He told me he said no every time. He gave me the pills as proof.

I felt bad for him. I knew what it was like to be alone, begging for money from people who walked by like you didn't even exist. Or worse, when the occasional nut stopped to interrogate you about what you'd do with the money if they gave it to you. Like they cared. Like it was any of their fucking business.

"Sorry, E. Got nothing so far," he said as soon as I neared.

Despite the turmoil inside, I shrugged and tried to stay casual. I hadn't stopped thinking about Olivia or pink dress. Coming out to push seemed like a good idea. Now that I was there, I regretted it. "Happens. No worries."

Skid and I retreated to the steps of an apartment building and sat. Those kind of alcoves always smelled the same; urine soaked cement and musk. It was raining and the steps were damp from castoff. But it felt private. Down the street a flood of people exited The Crocodile music club. The street got a lot louder as the group dispersed into it.

A group of well-dressed women, much like Olivia Holloway, passed us. They watched me and Skid from the corner of their eyes. With their hands clutched tightly on their purses, they picked up the pace.

Skid and I looked at each other and shared a laugh. I nudged his shoulder with mine. "Got any plans tonight?"

"I want to keep pushing. It's still early." Skid ground the tip of his shoe into the ground, watching it intently. "Could use the money."

"What for? You need something?"

Skid shrugged. "It's getting colder. I wanted to get some stuff at Goodwill. I don't *need* to, my stuff is still pretty good. I dunno."

"I'll spot you. Let's catch a bus up to the Goodwill on the hill, okay?"

"Goodwill on the Hill. Funny, E." He smiled. "Yeah, let's do it."

It didn't take long to hop on a bus that went up to Capitol Hill. I paid Skid's fare and we sat on the bus making fun of people on the sidewalk all the way up.

"Walking pole people at the intersection. Man, why do they use those? They look so dumb."

I found the couple Skid was looking at. Sure enough, both had walking poles that belonged on a hike, not Downtown. I wasn't sure if they were useful or a local fashion statement. "I guess they can't handle walking like the rest of us. Check out the goths by the Taco Del Mar."

"Those aren't goths, those are candy kids. Big difference."

"Candy kids?" I laughed. It fit. The kids looked Goth to me, but all their clothes were neon and rainbow. They looked a hell of a lot happier, too. The bus jerked into motion and the candy kids fell out of sight.

"Ruby told me about it. She said they are like, really happy ravers who are all about being positive and stuff."

"Ruby, huh? She hanging around again?"

Skid had a crush on the girl. From what I understood, she was in and out of foster care. When things were bad, she hung around the overpass. I'd never seen her, but Skid's face lit up when he talked about her. And he talked about her a lot.

"Yeah." Skid trailed off. He had something more to say. I could feel it but didn't pressure him.

The giant blue Goodwill sign came into view. I pulled the cord above me and minutes later Skid and I were engulfed in florescent light and the smell of dusty thrift store. The Goodwill on Capitol Hill was dominated by hipsters and college students since a popular rapper glorified it. They mostly got in the way and didn't buy much.

I trailed behind Skid, pushing the cart as he browsed for winter gear. My cell buzzed. I pulled it out and stared at the name, surprise and irritation swelled inside me. Trisha. Why would she be calling me?

"Hey, E, I was thinking about school again."

I hit ignore and returned my phone to my pocket, then gave Skid my undivided attention. Any distraction from Trisha calling me was appreciated.

Just because my life was fucked to hell, didn't mean I wanted Skid's to be, too. We'd talked about school the month before, also maybe getting him into the system. Foster care. He wanted a better life but was afraid of trying and being rejected. It didn't help matters that many of the kids he knew chose the streets over foster care and had plenty of horror stories about it. His friend Ruby a perfect example.

"Cool," I said carefully. Interested, but not overly enthusiastic. Don't scare him. "You want to do it?"

Skid pulled a puffy orange winter jacket from the rack, studied it, then put it back. "Yeah. I think. That outreach lady came by the overpass again yesterday. I talked to her for a while. Might be something I want to do. Might be good."

"It *would* be good," I agreed. "What changed your mind?"

"Lots of stuff. I mean, talking to Ruby for one. She says school is the one thing in her life she's good at that's good for her. And it's cold out and I'm sick of sleeping in a tent on cardboard." It came out in a rush. This is what he'd been holding back on the bus. "And that lady last night. That freaked me out, E. She was messed up and then when you told me to run. I don't know. I was freaked."

I clenched my jaw and tried to keep a neutral face. "It was weird."

"The other day Tin Man got nabbed and I thought, that could be me. Wrong place, wrong time. It's not like I haven't seen that shit before, but I just want out." Skid settled on a brown parka. The fur around the hood was matted, but it was in good shape. He tossed it in the cart.

"I get it. You should get out. The longer you stay, the harder it will be." I tightened my grip on the cart. I needed a smoke. "You need any money for clothes or to clean up or anything, just let me know. Whatever you need."

"You're already getting me this stuff. I don't want to put you out."

"Don't worry about it, okay?"

Skid grinned. "Thanks E, you're the best."

After I bought him clothes, I was going to buy a bottle of Bulleit and get shitfaced for the next ten hours, and the kid thought I was the best. In addition to the panic attack I'd been fighting since pink dress, now I had a hearty dose of guilt on top of it. Great combination.

It took every bit of willpower I had to continue through the store while Skid shopped. A jacket, ski pants, and sleeping bag later, we were outside. I fished out a cigarette and lit it, sucking the thing down in a few inhales.

"I gotta go," I said. "Remember, no worries about tonight. I'll be good on my own. See you tomorrow, okay?"

"Yeah. Thanks for the new stuff. Later!"

I merged into the horde of Seattlites, my unsold inventory heavy in my pocket again, my only intention for the night to get home.

CHAPTER 5

I'm lying on my stomach on a hospital bed, head turned to the side so I can breathe. The pillow is soggy with sweat. My hands are cuffed to the railings. They dig into my wrists and make them bleed when I tug on them. A man in a lab coat is beside me. A doctor? He's dabbing rubbing alcohol into my back. It stings. How did I get hurt? Fuck. I hurt everywhere. My eyes water and the room spins.

There's another person in here. I can't see him but I feel his presence. He wears so much cologne it fills the shabby exam room. I'm gasping for air. I can taste that scent and it makes me sick.

"How did he do?" cologne man asks.

"They flogged him for two hours," the doctor answers.

"That's not what I asked," cologne man snaps. "How did he do?"

"He did exactly how you wanted him to. He didn't know anything."

"On what dosage?"

"Forty milligrams."

"Can we go thirty?"

"He developed tolerance to thirty."

Cologne man grunts. "Get him cleaned up and downstairs. We need him for the endurance trial, so don't forget the Viagra."

"I don't think you should."

"Did I ask for your fucking opinion?"

He leaves. The doctor continues cleaning my back. At one point I think he whispers 'I'm sorry' but blackness overtakes me and I'm gone.

First I heard music. Some kind of 70s rock on low volume. Then the smell; cigarette smoke, stale beer, and despite the complaints, patchouli incense. I knew where I was and opted to keep my eyes shut a moment longer before Lucya kicked me out. It was a miracle she hadn't already.

Of all my nightmares, the one I'd just woken from was the best. Or least terrible, I should say. The others jolted me back into the world in blind panic, sweaty and confused with my heart beating out of my chest. The cologne man dream was one I could deal with. It was the kind of dream I tried to get answers from after I first woke up from my lost time. Who was the doctor? Could I remember his face? Had I smelled that cologne again? Would I recognize it, or the doctor, if I saw them on the streets?

During one of my binge reading sessions I turned to philosophy. Most of it was beyond me—it was the pointless bullshit of college students—but one thing stuck. Plato's theory of anamnesis. He believed the soul was immortal. All knowledge it obtained carried on to each of its incarnations. But during the trauma of birth, it forgot everything. Learning was only recovering what we already once knew.

For a while, I was obsessed with anamnesis. During my four year blackout, there were intermittent times where I was me, where I formed those memories that now haunted me. Each of those times I surfaced from the darkness was a little traumatic birth. Each time I forgot more and more until the last birth, when I woke up on Alki beach for good.

If learning was recollection, didn't that mean I had answers buried in some deep, mystical part of my soul? I wanted to think the dreams were a cue from my soul that would help me remember. Everything I wondered, I had the answers to. The space between my memories appeared empty, but what if it was just hidden? What if it only needed the right circumstances or trigger for me to recall?

Just because anamnesis stuck with me doesn't mean it was excluded from the whole college student bullshit theory. After having the dreams enough times, I realized they were jacked up remains of memories my mind wanted me to relive for its own sadistic pleasure. That was it. My mania to discover what happened to me knew no bounds, and at the time, anamnesis seemed a legitimate concept to cling to.

According to my rough count, this was the forty-fifth time I had the doctor dream in the past year. It might seem frequent, but I was on my two hundredth replay of the ice bath nightmare. There's that for comparison.

The nightmares are the same. The feeling I have when I wake up is the same. I kept a dream journal for months, tried self-hypnosis, meditation. No matter how I try to interpret them, they give me nothing.

It was Olivia's reprint of my blog that got me to thinking of anamnesis. Maybe that sparked the rare dream to replay.

At the thought of Olivia I couldn't help but groan. Then I remembered the girl in the alley. They set me on this bender. The splitting headache, dry mouth, and nausea were their fault. It began after I left Skid at Goodwill. From there, things get fuzzy.

"He's awake." Lucya's rough voice came from across the bar. "Ethan, I let you sleep long enough. You get the fuck out of here or I'm going to have Artur toss your ass out."

I opened my eyes to get a glimpse of my surroundings then squeezed them shut. Lucya's bar was a room twice the size of my studio in the basement of a shitty apartment building in Belltown. It was a total dive the Melnikov family used as a meeting place and drug front. Windowless, it was lit by year-round multicolored Christmas lights, hanging lanterns, and a couple overhead lamps. Other than the bar, there were a couple mismatched card tables and a scattering of homeland photographs on the walls.

I dredged through the past two days and tried to figure out how I ended up at Lucya's. I remembered seeing the bottom of a bottle of Bulleit, waking up drunk and in desperate need for a meatball sub, and walking around Seattle. My jaw ached and I recalled asking someone for a cigarette and getting punched. After that, nothing. The irony of my self-inflicted memory loss didn't fall short on me.

Lucya hadn't always hated me. This was the sixth or seventh time I'd ended up at her bar after a bender. The bar was secluded and rarely had patrons. It was near two of my favorite food joints and a 24 hour Safeway. The perfect spot to crash. The first two times she was cool about it. Every time after she became increasingly hostile.

I'll admit, I'd puked in there before. On her. On the floor. Came close to burning it down when a cigarette slipped from my fingers when I drifted off. There'd been numerous hysterical rants that ended with Artur escorting me out.

"Ethan! I know you're awake. Get up."

This time I kept my eyes open. There were no patrons as usual. Lucya stood behind the bar lighting an incense. When she finished, she hauled a bag of peanuts onto the counter and sliced it open with a box cutter. She kept a fierce scowl on me the whole time.

Lucya had a huge bosom that hung over a cherry-patterned apron I'd never seen her without. Her hair was pure white, kept in a complicated braid. Lucya looked matronly. She wasn't.

"Artur!" she bellowed. "See him out!"

Lucya's husband wandered over. He was a behemoth of a man with hulking shoulders and a greying beard that went to mid-chest. Artur was much nicer than Lucya. I bet he was the one who convinced her to let me stay. He set a glass of water on the end table next to me.

I straightened up in the lounge chair and took the drink. The chair squeaked and my headache punished me for it with a deep throb from my temple to the base of my skull. The cool water felt good on my parched throat.

"Hey, guys. Long time no see."

"Long time no see?" Lucya cursed in Russian. "For fuck's sake, boy. You've been here since yesterday afternoon and—"

"Lucya." Artur patted me on the shoulder. He was a man of few words. Literally. The guy didn't know much English. "He good. He good boy. Donovan friend."

She scowled. "Fine. He can be a good boy at his own place. Go home, Ethan."

I finished my water and hauled myself out of the chair.

Artur smiled and ushered me to the front door. Peanut shells crunched underfoot as we walked. I braced myself for sunlight then stumbled out. A putrid scent from garbage cans outside the door hit me. I keeled over and puked. Lucya's patchouli incenses wafted into the mix and I vomited again. Why the fucking patchouli?

The meager contents of my stomach expelled—meatball sub for sure—I stood and stumbled a few steps before stopping for a breather. The acidic flavor of bile and tomato made me want to be sick all over again.

My phone buzzed. Trisha again. I hit ignore and noticed I had three missed calls from Skid and two texts.

U bailing again?

Come on e!! call me. worried

The last text was at 3am.

There was a single missed call from Donovan and a voicemail. "Haven't heard from you, E. Call me."

Shit. I was supposed to see Donovan days ago. He sounded calm and easygoing in the voicemail. That meant he was fucking pissed. I couldn't go to him without selling all my inventory. Looks like I had plans for the night.

I thumbed out a response to Skid. *Sorry, been out. Gotta push hard tonight. Need my best streerer. You in?*

The sky was overcast yet blinding white, typical for winter in Seattle. I squinted to keep the foul light from my eyes and made slow progress back to my apartment. There was a sharp knot in my lower back from sleeping in the lounge chair that made walking difficult.

Twenty minutes later I unlocked my front door. The apartment was trashed and smelled like piss. My mattress was halfway off its box spring. At some point I must've shoved all the garbage and library books to the walls to make space for the documents Olivia gave me. Some were scattered, others in stacks. No logical organization. I picked up a paper closest to me. My handwriting was illegible. Something about an octopus and the key to unlocking all secrets?

I navigated around the mess to the kitchen where I started a pot of coffee. The coffee maker was a godsend. The motions of preparing a pot was meditative. While the coffee brewed, I combed the kitchen and bathroom for something to relieve my throbbing headache.

Four ibuprofen and a quick shower later, I sat on my easy chair sipping a giant mug of steaming hot coffee. Still no response from Skid. I could work without him, but he made it a hell of a lot easier.

Hungover, no Skid, and a shitload of drugs to push.

It was going to be a long, long fucking day.

CHAPTER 6

I handed a tiny plastic package of Ecstasy to the leader of the bachelorette party. There were five of them. They teetered on high heels and pulled at the hems of their short dresses. Penis necklace straws hung from their necks, gross caricatures that would make their mothers blush. The bride wore a tiara that shimmered every time she moved. A decorative swirl near the top of it was broken, revealing the plastic it was really made of. At first glance they were a vibrant, lively bunch. When you looked harder, you saw too much makeup and a feral viciousness known well by a group of twenty-something women.

They were antsy, looking anywhere except at me as their friend handled the transaction.

Tolerate the drug dealer just a moment longer, honey, and we can get on our way and party. He's a necessary evil.

"We're just going to hang out in the hotel, you know? Relax," the girl said as she handed me the money, fresh from the ATM machine. People made excuses sometimes when they bought from me. It wasn't for them, of course not! It was for their friend. They didn't normally do this. It was just a special occasion.

Maybe for them it was special. What they didn't realize was that I didn't give a fuck. This was every day for me.

"Jesus, Miranda! Don't tell him that!" The bride's hand flung to her mouth as though she were shocked by what she said. She looked to her comrades for support.

I folded the money and put it in my inner jacket pocket. I grinned wide, knowing it would probably freak them out. "Maybe I'll stop by later."

They fidgeted. Some looked interested. I won't even begin to describe what I thought was going on in their minds. The deal complete, I set off down the street to return to my usual spot. It had been a busy night. I had some downers left but everything else was gone. Donovan had called every hour asking why I hadn't come to restock.

There was no explanation or excuse that would satisfy him. I could tell him about the girl in the alley or Olivia Holloway, how they shook me up. How I was trying to help Skid and it was taking up time. How I'd been drunk two days straight. Donovan's friendship—if that's what you called it—was advantageous when I first met him. I was his personal project and he helped me get some semblance of a life together. Then the micromanagement started. People like him got off on controlling others and making them feel like a charity case. Like they owed him big time, forever.

None of it mattered. If I didn't come to restock soon, he'd know I was slacking. Then it would be hell to pay. He'd say, *Maybe you aren't selling anymore? Should I take you back where I found you?*

Back where he found me. I thought of Alki Beach. The smell of saltwater. Of feeling more alone and out of control than I ever had in my life. Waking up confused, trying to dredge up a memory of where I was last and coming up with nothing.

Fuck. My hands were shaking. I reached into my pocket and took two of my remaining Valium. You're not supposed to use your own inventory, but I had to. The second I stopped self-medicating I started looking at the black voids in my memory. Sometimes they looked back. They wanted something from me. There wasn't anything I could give. It was a zero sum game.

I looked around. The Friday night crowd was still budding. Happy hour was almost over. All the businesspeople enveloped in warmth and booze, wishing that in-between moment could last a little longer. Along with the highest crime rate, Belltown had the best bars. Workerbees found the reward greater than the risk.

In about twenty minutes they'd spill from the bars and restaurants, dazed. Once they remembered where they were, they'd flag taxis or wait nervously at the bus stops. Some went back to work. Some drove home drunk to unsatisfied partners.

The rest would start a drunk rampage through the city. *It's the weekend!* They'd shout as they slammed back another round then stumble two blocks to their next destination. It was all the justification they needed to lose control of themselves. I'd be there waiting.

Downtown Seattle had a mix of people like no other. Businessmen, yuppies, homeless, druggies, college kids, hipsters, and granola hippies walking the streets with their Northface and venti Starbucks cups. They all thought they were something special. They all had somewhere important to be. Really, people were all the same. Potential customers, each and every one. I didn't care what they wanted, only how much they would pay for it. No one was immune to wanting a little upper or downer once in a while. The most saintly man would come begging if the circumstances were right.

You didn't have to put a person in my shoes to make them see things my way. Deep down, they were all like me. They just pretended they weren't. Workers thought they played a critical role at their jobs. They were just a means to an end for someone higher up than them. College kids were certain there was a bright future ahead of them if they did well in school. They were just being molded into cogs that fit perfectly into the gears of the big machine that chewed everyone up and spit them out, always greedy and always in need of more.

If I went back to my apartment I could find several self-help books that explained to me why I viewed other people, and the world, in this way. They'd point to my childhood, to ingrained behaviors resulting from it, and offer me advice on how to correct it.

I shoved my hands in my pockets and waited for the effects of the Valium to kick in. The night was still young. If I got my act together I could sell what I had left and go to Donovan for more. If Skid were here, it might speed up the process.

My brain froze. Where was Skid? I whipped out my phone and checked for any new texts or calls. He never responded to my last message. Other than the text from 3am, I hadn't had any contact with him. It was unusual. Normally he was always around and responded to my calls or texts within minutes. It was possible he'd gone to see that lady from the outreach program, but she couldn't get him in the program that fast. He wouldn't have left without saying goodbye.

I called him. The phone went straight to voicemail.

Maybe he'd gotten another burner and lost my number?

I started walking, looking for anyone who might know where he was. People were fixtures of the city as much as the buildings were, if you knew where to look. Someone had to know. The overpass he usually slept in was a twenty minute walk, so I headed in that direction. It was almost all uphill. Fucking Seattle. On the way I asked a few people. Dealers mostly, a couple of homeless. They hadn't seen him.

Panting for my life with a layer of sweat building on my back, I hit the Capitol Hill area and the overpass, filled with a sea of tents and sleeping bags. Laughter and shouting, some happy and some angry, floated above it all. The soup kitchen had been closed down. Despite the few lights they put up on the street nearby, it was still dark in the camp.

Normal people were afraid to go under here at night, sometimes even during the day. It was a short walk under the freeway, but you might see a crazy guy. Maybe a naked lady. Someone begging, someone on drugs. All things good people don't want to see.

I wasn't a good person. I didn't mind. I'd been a fixture here not that long ago.

The sweet smell of meth circulated about the camp as I navigated my way around. Then cigarettes. Hundreds of unwashed bodies under layers and layers of clothing. It was overwhelming.

A lady wearing a tattered neon green hat with dog ears waved me over. I knew her. I'd sold to her before. "You got any oil?"

"No," I said truthfully. "I don't sell that shit anymore. You seen Skid?"

"Who?"

Her eyes were glazed, flickering in a trash can fire that would undoubtedly draw the attention of the police given time. She was already rolling on something. I saw it in her slack jaw and fluttering eyelids.

"Skid. Teenage boy, hangs around here? Curly hair. Nice."

She took a gasp of air suddenly and screwed her eyes shut. Her almost toothless mouth hung open in a disbelieving O.

"Dead."

My body went cold. I sat on the empty cinder block next to her. "Are you sure?"

"Kid died. This morning."

"Are you sure it was *Skid*?"

"Janine, this guy giving you trouble?"

I looked up. Two burly men with more beard than face stood on the other side of the fire. Both were familiar. I'd seen them around.

"It's just E. One of Donovan's guys. What you doing here?" One of the newcomers asked. "You sellin' any peanut butter?"

"I'm looking for my friend Skid. Janine says a kid died this morning. Do you know anything about it?"

The man wearing a gray plaid jacket squatted next to me. "I'm sorry, buddy. It's true. One of his friends came down off something and panicked real bad. He started grabbing at Skid, asking for help, but he got rough. Like someone drowning you know, dragging the helper under—"

"We all sawd it," his friend added.

"—and before you know it, he pushes Skid. He fell and then that was it. Dead. Head cracked open."

I was going to puke. Skid couldn't be dead. He couldn't.

"What about the kid who did it?"

"Cops got him. He confessed right in front of us, said it was an accident. He didn't know where he was and got confused. Don't think he's coming back."

"Show me where it happened," I demanded as I stood. "Then I want to see his tent."

"Shi-it. Ain't his tent no more. Been hours since it happened. You know how it works 'round here."

"I don't care. Take me to it."

"Okay, come on." He stood, too, then paused. A knowing smirk spread across his lips. "Gonna cost you though."

"Fuck you," I spat. "I'll just ask someone else."

The friend's laughter was like a dog's bark. I jumped at the sound of it. "Yeah right. Teddy runs this place. No one's telling you shit unless he say so."

So the overpass had a dictator again. Great. Every once in a while someone thought they could call the shots. King of the Hobos. Even though these things never lasted long, I didn't have time to wait it out. I wanted to see where it happened with my own eyes.

"He was one of you and he's dead and you're using it to get drugs off me?" I asked, throwing in a bit of guilt just in case it hit him.

The guy shrugged, the attempted guilt trip ineffective. "Might as well. What you got?"

I pulled out a packet of two benzos. I had other pills, all downers, but he didn't know that. "This is all I have."

He took them and smiled. "Thank ye kindly. Come on, just at the other end here."

Nothing could stifle the rage massing inside my gut. In

a way, it didn't surprise me he used Skid's death as a way to get drugs. It was still a cheap move. I still wanted to punch the smile off his face.

I also wanted to believe Skid wasn't dead. They could've confused him with someone else, certainly. Maybe it was a different kid. When they took me to the steps, and I saw the crime tape, the faded spot of blood where they hadn't washed it completely, I was sure *someone* had gotten hurt.

"Where does Skid sleep, do you know?" I glared at him. "I don't have anything else to give you."

"That's fine, that's fine." He held up the drugs. "This'll get you a little further anyhow. Come on."

He led me away from the scene. His friend followed. "I seen it. The kid that did it was on that new stuff going around, fine as anything, then started screaming '*What happened? What happened?*'"

That was the third person I could, if I wanted to, link to my past. The numbers were stacking up. Pink dress, Olivia Holloway—they weren't strange coincidences. People were losing time.

We walked down a narrow, trash littered pathway between tents and rows of sleeping bags, stopping at a gray tent crammed between two others.

The man slapped the side of the tent. "Chip, get the fuck outta there!"

Someone groaned, unzipped the tent, and pulled himself out. He was thin, his face covered in sores. He reeked. I could count the number of teeth he had on one hand. "My tent now. Got it first."

"Nope, this gentlemen here needs to check it out. Now, get!"

The guy said nothing. He crawled about ten feet away from the tent and collapsed. My bearded companion grinned. "Here ya go, Skid's tent. Don't take long, once Chip there comes to he'll be pissed you's in there."

I bit my tongue and chose not to respond. A pissing match was low in my priorities. The thugs wandered off after a few moments of silence.

Skid's tent was close to the street, on the outer edges of the camp. It was lit by passing cars and the ambient light from a single streetlight twenty feet away. Beside the rank, sour smell of its new inhabitant, the tent was nearly empty. Sacks and plastic containers were tossed about, their contents long gone. I spotted the sleeping bag I bought him beneath a soiled blanket. It was the only thing in the tent that was Skid's.

I unzipped the new sleeping bag and felt around inside. I taught Skid this trick a while ago. If you didn't keep everything valuable on yourself, you had to hide it well.

My hand hit a snag in the fabric. I reached into the fluff and pulled out a tiny plastic baggie. There was one pill in it. It had no markings. A half blue, half white capsule. I didn't recognize it.

"He was going to talk to the outreach lady today."

Standing outside the tent was a teenage girl, her arms were wrapped around herself in a tight hug. Her hair was a shade darker of brown than her skin. She was dressed warmly in a clean jacket and jeans. I'd say she was out of place, but she stood unafraid like she belonged there.

"Ruby?"

She nodded. "You're E?"

I cleared my throat. "Yeah. What are you doing here?"

Ruby bent down and entered the tent, sitting cross-legged beside me. "Yesterday I snuck him into my house so he could take a shower. I trimmed his hair. He was going to talk to her this afternoon about getting straightened out. Foster parents caught him, laid into me. Don't want to be there right now. Don't want to be anywhere right now."

"Do you know what happened? These people are being assholes and—"

She pointed to the baggie still in my hands. "Last night, after they kicked him out, I met him here. His friend Cody got some of that new stuff, but wouldn't say where. He wanted Skid to take some with him and go mess around. It's supposed to make you forget everything while you're on it. He thought it would be fun. I told them it was stupid, that's not even what it's meant for."

"Did Skid take any?" I asked.

"You're holding it, so of course not," Ruby snapped. In that moment I saw her. Too mature for her age because of the life she'd been through. Too used to people thinking she was a kid. "But Cody did. He did some crank, too. Was on a binge. Skid was worried about him. He said he was going to stay with him until he came down."

I choked back an unexpected sob. "He was a good kid. He'd do something like that."

It wasn't fair. Day to day, I could numb myself to this life. I floated just above reality, and if I didn't look down it wasn't there. But when shit like this happened, I plunged back in. All the regrets, the wishes, flooded me.

Ruby reached out and squeezed my shoulder before letting her hand drop beside her. A car passed by, the headlights illuminating the tent. I noticed a wet shine on her cheeks. Her thick fringe of eyelashes were heavy with tears. "Yeah, he was. I stayed with him the whole night. I didn't want him to be alone. When Cody came down he went crazy. At first we thought he was kidding, playing up on it, but he was really confused. He got physical. Pushed Skid."

"I know," I stopped her. "I know the rest."

We sat in silence. Finally, Ruby spoke. "Skid looked up to you. You meant a lot to him. I thought you deserved to know how it went down. Been waiting for you to show up so I could tell you."

Skid wanted to get out. He could've, too. He was so close. Now he was dead. Dead because of the little pill in my hand, because of his attempt at doing something right.

"It just shows, you do the right thing and life fucks you over. Do the wrong thing and you're fucked, too." I shoved the pill in my pocket. "So why bother?"

Ruby climbed out of the tent. Before she left, she bent down and looked me in the eyes. "Everyone has to live and die for something. You can decide what that something is. Life doesn't decide for you."

CHAPTER 7

Waiting outside of my apartment was the last person I expected to see. Trisha wore neon green fishnets and shiny black boots that went up to her knees, with heels tall enough to impale a person with. She had a frumpy brown jacket on, which I guessed covered her costume. In a place like Seattle, she could pass for eccentric. I knew better.

"I called you. Twice."

"I know. I ignored you. Twice. What are you doing here?" I asked as I moved past her to unlock the door. With Skid's death fresh on my mind, I didn't want to deal with her. "We're done."

"You really don't have any balls, do you? Donnie says jump, you ask how high. Fuck, E, he didn't even know we were together."

Here we go. Trisha and I weren't a good combination. We both hated ourselves and wanted to fix each other as a means of fixing our own problems. Everything we hated about each other was just a mirror of ourselves.

It was a toxic relationship. Fucking self-help books taught me that much.

The second I got in I made my way into the kitchen and flicked on the stove light. Just enough light to operate the coffee machine. I placed a new filter in, fresh coffee grounds, and let it brew. The scent made my mouth water.

The promise of caffeine and warmth made me giddy with anticipation.

Trisha followed. She hated the way my apartment looked. Even back when we were fucking, she'd rarely do it here. I saw the look of disdain on her face even then. What was it with women and hating my living circumstances? What the hell did they want from me?

She plopped down on the easy chair and motioned to the papers I hadn't cleaned up. "What the hell is all this shit?"

"Nothing." The mere thought of explaining Olivia Holloway to Trisha exhausted me.

"Fine. Whatever."

Trisha ran her tongue over her teeth and shrugged. Her regular haughty sneer melted into something sweeter. Since I knew her, I'd call it conniving.

"I know things haven't been good between us."

I folded my arms across my chest and leaned against the kitchen counter. "They've been fine. I ended it *months* ago. I thought we were good."

Her expression faltered. She picked at her fishnets, staring at them intently.

Trisha was Donovan's girl. Sort of. Like many of the girls he claimed for himself, she didn't start off bad. Sure, she was stripping. But honest to God, that was to help pay for nursing school. She had fantastic grades and was hoping to work in oncology. Her grandmother and mother died from cancer, which is what inspired her to do it.

I knew all that because when Donovan's family took over the strip club she worked at, I talked to her. After her shift we'd get burgers at Dick's. If I was dealing around the club, we'd hang out on her breaks. One thing led to another and there was sex. Lots of it, everywhere, anytime. Sex, fucking, and even lovemaking. She was the first girl in years that took me away from myself. Sometimes I felt a glimmer of happiness. Real, pure happiness.

I loved everything about her. How she liked one scoop of raspberry sorbet and one of chocolate chip mint from Molly Moon's, how she seemed to know the words of every song we heard on the radio. The sprinkle of freckles across her nose and cheeks that got darker in the summer. The little things she noticed when we walked through Pike Place Market observing the tourists.

Then Donovan started taking an interest in her. He got her into partying, and partying with Donovan meant a lot of drinking, ecstasy, and coke. Trisha did it because she would lose her job if she refused. The money was good and she needed it. Six months later she dropped out of nursing school. The club started having girls turn tricks for extra cash, and Trisha had a habit of her own to keep up.

When Donovan started screwing her, I broke it off. Not just because Donovan would've had me trounced if I showed interest in one of his girls, but because Trisha had changed. She was hardened now. When I looked at her I saw the fried brain of someone who does too much blow and hits the bottle no matter what time of day it is. She was like me, like everyone else in my world. That's not what I wanted. I didn't deserve it, but I wanted something better. Something that gave me a taste of normal life.

"Listen, I'm here to fix us. We haven't talked in a while. I miss that," Trisha finally said. She crossed her legs, revealing a long expanse of thigh. Her skin was unseasonably dark from hours in the tanning bed.

"You can't be here. This," I pointed between her and me, "can't happen. If Donovan knew about us he'd cut me off. He'd cut you off. If he was in a bad mood, he'd kill us. You know that, right?"

Trisha unzipped and opened her coat. She wore a lime green corset that made her small chest look twice as big. A square of green satin covered her crotch. I couldn't help but stare, feeling warmth spreading in my body.

The coffee machine pinged. I forced myself to look away from her to rinse a mug and poured myself a cup. Then another and another until I felt the caffeine surging in my body. I didn't offer her one. This was my sacred liquid.

She'd been quiet the whole time, sitting on the easy chair wearing next to nothing. I didn't want her, but I wanted *someone*. Companionship. The feeling of someone's body against mine. I remembered what her skin felt like under my lips, or how devious it made me to pull her silky hair from the high ponytail she typically wore it in. That's the Trisha I wanted again.

There was a shuffling and *thud thud thud* as her heels dug into the ground when she walked. She'd dropped the coat entirely and put herself in front of me. This close I smelled cigarettes. Her pupils were dilated. I wondered what she was on.

"E, remember when things were good with us?" She reached out and ran her finger down my cheek. It dropped down my chest to the waistband of my jeans. "I want that again. Don't you?"

Fuck I did. If sleeping with her meant I had a chance of forgetting about Skid and Olivia Holloway and the pink dress girl for just a few moments, I was in.

I grabbed her and pulled her against me, my mouth against hers. Her tongue tasted ashy, her lips bubblegum flavored. The fishnet was rough underneath my fingertips as I ran my hands down her hips. She tugged at the laces in front of her corset and loosened it. I pulled it over her head and threw it on the ground. Her pale skin was indented and red where the corset dug into her flesh.

Trisha grabbed my hand and led me to my bed. The union was rough and clumsy. Nothing like what it was when we were first together. She felt stiff and cold now. All the moans and whispers were practiced.

But they worked. I let my mind go blank with her and even after we finished, naked and breathless, I had a minute of peace. She lit a cigarette for herself, then offered me one. The best part of sex was the cigarette after.

Then she was up. Trisha pulled her clothes on with lightning speed. Not that I wanted to cuddle, but it seemed abrupt.

"Leaving?"

"Gotta go to work. Bus this time of day will take a while to get north."

"Oh." I dragged on the cigarette. "Okay."

She grabbed her coat from the easy chair and zipped it to her chin, then sat next to me. "I miss you, E. You're the best thing I have in this world."

My heart fluttered. I didn't hear things like that very often. I searched for any maliciousness but found none. Trisha smiled and kissed my cheek. "See you around."

The second she left the apartment, the air got heavy and reality whooshed in. With no more distractions, that godforsaken black void was screaming at me and I couldn't ignore it any longer. It wasn't just watching from the dark recesses of my mind anymore. Whatever destroyed my life was back somehow. It was in the streets of Seattle.

I was hesitant to make the connection with pink dress. Then when Donovan all but told me about it, when Olivia Holloway walked through my door, it was hard to ignore. And I'd gotten really fucking good at ignoring it. Now it was right in front of me.

And yet it was hard to take that first step. That's why I hadn't spent hundreds of hours trying to find out who I was; I was afraid of what I'd find.

Things happened to me over the course of four years that I had no recollection of, but had scars to prove it. Burns, cuts, stitches. The topography of my body showed experimentation or torture. I didn't have any memories or pain to associate with them. Someone put them on me. Someone who didn't think of me as another human being, who thought of me as a lab rat. Part of me didn't want to know why they'd done it or what they'd found out, because there was no way their discovery gave meaning to my suffering. I wanted answers, but there wasn't an answer that would make me feel better. That would make my life whole again. This was speculation, but to find an answer would mean facing the truth of that idea one way or another.

My life was shattered into tiny pieces that would never fit back together. I couldn't do anything with myself unless I was on an upper or a downer. Even the very blog I wrote that brought Olivia to me was done on cocaine. Rantings of a person desperate for validation and comfort. Desperate to know they weren't alone. Angry that they were.

So I didn't look.

Ruby's words stuck with me. *Life doesn't decide for you.* Skid, a teenager with the world working against him, chose to stand for something. We all dreamed of a second chance, but where we went wrong was assuming it would fall in our laps. We bitched and moaned about how hard we have it but we don't actually do anything to change it.

The dredges of grainy coffee in my last mug had gone cold. I started a new pot and sat down in the easy chair to let the new feeling of resolution sink in. I wanted to find out what happened to me. I'd always wanted to deep down but never had the will to do it. I wanted to be the person Skid thought I was, who *he* was. Now that answers were closer than they'd ever been before, I couldn't look away. I wouldn't. I wasn't going to give up my second chance when Skid lost his.

My coffee finished. I poured a mug with a nip of whiskey and retrieved everything Olivia Holloway brought me, then spread it across the card table. I read her accounts. Read my own blog—poorly written bullshit, most of it, but some of it good—and let the reality sink in.

It was time to face the monster in my closet.

CHAPTER 8

Olivia Holloway hadn't left a number or an email address, but I found her office after a quick search on the shitty computers at the library. The library workers hated me. Too many overdue books. I made a mental note to get my own computer someday.

Located on the second story above a hair salon that offered services costing as much as my rent, her office boasted huge windows and had a calculated rustic appearance. Thick wood floors, brass light fixtures. The words *Holloway and Associates* was etched into glass on the door. Behind it, a pretty receptionist with aquamarine-rimmed glasses greeted me.

Greeted is the wrong word. She worked hard to keep her smile up and ask what she could do for me.

Fuck, I didn't look that bad. I had jeans and a winter jacket on. I'd showered at least two days ago. A few days of beard was an attractive look, right? According to the fashion ads I saw in Westlake mall, my almost-too-thin physique was highly desirable.

No, that wasn't it. Affluent people recognized low class from a mile away. They could smell our addictions, our ignorance. I smiled anyway. "I'm here to see Olivia Holloway."

"Do you have an appointment?"

"No, but she is expecting me."

The receptionist frowned. "She's very busy today and I don't see you on her calendar. What are you here to see her about?"

"We have a mutual interest I'd like to discuss." That sounded official, right? Was the lingo good? I threw another smile on again. "Please just tell her Ethan Knight is here to see her."

She was skeptical, but obliged. With one perfectly manicured nail, she pushed a button on her phone. "Miss Holloway? A man named Ethan Knight is here to see you."

There was a pause. No response.

"I'm sorry, sir, but she must be in a meeting."

"I'll wait."

Sometimes it was fun to be difficult.

Only two minutes later Olivia burst through the doors near the desk wearing a pea coat, hat, and scarf. "I'm leaving, Lexi. I'm going to discuss a youth outreach charity program with Mr. Knight here. I'll be back in an hour."

"But you have a conference call with the mayor in a half hour?"

Olivia frowned. "I do. Tell him Brad will talk to him about where we're at with his gala and I'll jump in after. Thank you, Lexi."

I gave Lexi a wink as we left. It felt good to be the winner.

Outside it was brisk. Eleven in the morning was blindingly early for me, but the two pots of coffee and bennie I took helped take the edge off. Olivia kept a perfect two feet between us as we walked down 5th avenue. The street looked drab with all the Christmas lights off.

"You can never, *ever* come to my office again."

I stopped. Olivia kept moving for a second before

realizing it and coming back to me. Her pale cheeks were flushed scarlet to match her hair.

"Oh yeah? Why's that?"

"What would people think if they saw a—a gentlemen of your nature in *my* office? They might think I was getting drugs or having some kind of illicit affair. In my line of work, image is very, very important. A lot of people would love to claim I was using drugs or had some promiscuous streak."

Her remarks shouldn't have surprised me, but that didn't make them hurt any less. Considering how we parted last, I was the bad guy. I gestured for her to lead the way which she did with no objection.

"We can chat at Starbucks. I don't know anyone who ever goes there."

Of course she didn't. The most popular coffee shop was obviously too low end for her. I hadn't been around Olivia Holloway more than twenty minutes in total and I disliked her. It was one thing to think you were better than someone else. It was another to say it out loud and rub it in their faces.

It took exactly one minute to find a Starbucks. This was a big one with tons of wooden tables and chairs that screeched against the tile floor when they moved. Olivia took a spot in the corner. Since I was there, I went ahead and ordered the biggest size coffee they had.

I decided to get fancy with the coffee—and force Olivia to sit by herself in a dreadful Starbucks—by adding cream, six sugars, and a dash of cinnamon. I watched her across the room as I stirred the drink. She didn't pay attention to anyone around her. At one point she checked her phone, saw me looking at her, and glared.

My passive aggressive fun over, I returned and sat down.

"What made you change your mind?" Olivia asked as she watched me gulp down the scalding liquid. "About seeing me?"

"Nothing a lady of your nature would understand."

Her face remained neutral. She pushed stray grounds of sugar on the table. "Fair enough."

"Tell me what you know, Olivia."

"Right. Did you read the notes I gave you?"

"Yeah." I dredged through the coherent times I read through them. It was hard to separate it from the drunken times. "It's good you wrote up all the dates and times. Does that help you narrow down who might be doing this to you?"

She clenched her jaw. "I suppose it does. I couldn't be certain. Many of the same people attend the kinds of events I put on. However, there are lots of people attending who I've never met or will ever see again. That wouldn't be a conclusive thing to say."

Her hesitance was understandable. It was hard for anyone to admit someone they knew had tricked them. Or in her case, something much worse. "But it seems more likely it's someone you see frequently."

Olivia nodded. I moved on.

"And you have no memory at all of anything that happened while you were out?"

"Nothing. Not a flash of an image, no smells, no voices. It's like my brain stopped recording until whatever it was they slipped me passed out of my system. But I get that metallic taste. I think it's the same one you mentioned in your blog."

"It does sound the same. From what you wrote, you're back in your apartment every time you wake up?"

"Yes. I always wake up in my bed, like I've been sleeping. I feel groggy. All but one time in the same outfit I had on the night before. At first I thought I was drugged. I woke up and was confused, but I was in my apartment in the same clothes as before, so I blamed it on too much to drink." Olivia formed a circle with the sugar granules. "Then when I started waking up with marks on my body, I began suspecting something else."

The other time she was naked. I remembered it from her notes. The franticness in her tone as she described how her body felt and other details. Scratches on her inner thighs. A bruised feeling all over.

"The other night I ran into a woman at Westlake," I said. "She was beat up and scared, asking for somewhere to hide, then she freaked out. Didn't know where she was or how she got there. Then a few days ago the same thing happened with someone under the overpass. I think where you are when you come to might make a difference. If you're somewhere familiar, or maybe if the drug wears off while you're sleeping, you don't lose it quite the same. Obviously it's just a theory. We wouldn't know for sure without talking to other people."

Now Olivia's face brightened. "That's what I wanted to talk to you about when I came to your apartment. Other people. I think we need to figure out who's making the drug to track down who could be using it on me. I'm sure you want answers to your own past and that could help us find them."

I gulped down more coffee, wishing for something stronger. I was terrified I was going down this path of discovery, but it already felt good. There were other people; I wasn't alone. What I was doing would make Skid proud. Others had suffered, maybe not as much as me or in the same way, but they had. Olivia wanted answers and she'd already found more than I had since I woke up from my lost time. But her train of thought was flawed.

"You think every guy cooking meth knows whose body it's going into?"

"No, I suppose not. But something like this seems more deliberate than meth. If people in my social circles are using it, it must be high profile."

That still didn't work for me. Some of Olivia's views of others were skewed, but short of throwing her into the drug world for a few months, I couldn't explain.

"Okay, fine. How do we find out who is making it?" she asked. Before I could offer a solution, she added, "On your blog, there were a few people who always left comments. Do you remember?"

"Sure. Some of them thought I was a nut case. Others totally agreed it was some government conspiracy drug that caused amnesia. Most said it was corrupt pharmaceutical testing, which has happened before."

"But there were a few who *always* left comments. Frequently. They believed you and said they also experienced it."

I leaned back in my chair and thought about it. There had been people who tried to reach out. Back then I didn't believe they were serious. Like with Olivia, I thought their experiences couldn't have been the same as mine. I discredited them. I was too focused on my own problem to try and make connections.

That reminded me of something. I grinned. "You know how I figured out it was four years I lost?"

Olivia's eyebrows rose up. "I think so. The Martha Stewart thing?"

"Yeah. I don't remember a lot, you know. Just random bits and pieces that didn't get messed up. For some reason, the last thing I remember was Martha Stewart being convicted of those felonies. I remember watching something about it on TV and my mom making a joke about it. The memory is so clear, like it happened yesterday."

Mom had made lavender lemonade. She saw the recipe in a cooking magazine and wanted to use the lavender she grew for it. I thought it tasted like soap. I told her so. I remembered her laugh, lofty and throaty, as she agreed. We drank it anyway while we watched the TV show on Martha.

I paused as I thought back on the blog. "All I said on my blog was that's how I knew about how long I'd been gone, because of the conviction. It was my reference point. Some person went on there and tried to get in a fight with me defending Martha Stewart even though I hadn't really said anything about her. It was ridiculous."

I laughed, but it petered out when I noted her expression. Olivia was confused. The detour wasn't amusing. I regretted bringing it up. Our relationship was business. She didn't want to hear me reminisce. Embarrassed, I shrugged and motioned for her to continue.

Olivia brushed her hair back and shifted in her seat. "I sent emails to all those people who left *legitimate* comments. Most of them came back as failures, others never responded. But then I figured, maybe these people use the same usernames all the time? There's one guy, techna1, who has been using the same username forever. I searched for him and found him on a videogame forum, then after more digging, found his real name. Then I found him on Facebook *and* where he works."

She beamed like a good dog waiting for a treat. "I don't remember this guy. What is his deal?" I asked.

"His name is Brian Stromberg. One year before you say you woke up from your blackouts, he claims he responded to a request for participants for an antidepressant drug. He did the test for three weeks. He claims he doesn't remember what happened. His posts were kind of mysterious. Like, 'Can't say too much' paranoia kind of thing." Olivia tapped her fingernails against the table. "It just seems like a solid story and I know where to find him. I think we should talk to him in person and see if he has anything else. Maybe he knows the name of the company who did the tests. He's an insurance rep. I made an appointment under a fake name to talk to him tomorrow right before their office closes. Are you in?"

Good dog. Maybe she did deserve a treat. But I wasn't convinced yet.

"It sounds like you've got a handle on this. Why do you need my help?" I sipped at my coffee. "You don't want to be seen with me and you already have all the information you need to move forward."

Her perpetual smile faltered at the corners. "I'm afraid. I have no one I can ask for help. There's no one I can tell my theories to or confide in without worry they'll tell someone.

I can't do this alone, but I have no one to turn to."

"So I'm a last resort?" I asked.

"No, you're my only option. Why do you have to spin it so negatively? Anyway, do you want to talk to this guy or what?"

"Yeah. Let me know where it is and I'll meet you there."

"Do you have a car?"

Fuck, it never ended. "I can walk. Or take the bus."

"Unfortunately it's not within walking distance. It's a thirty minute drive over 520. Listen, I can pick you up somewhere discreet and we'll go together. Meet me here."

Somewhere discreet. This little secretive thing was getting on my nerves fast. Olivia wrote down an address on my coffee sleeve. Somewhere near the science center. She went quiet and stared at the baristas, lost in thought. I shifted. I needed a smoke.

"Anything else?"

"Ethan, based on your blog it looks like you haven't done much digging into your own past." She was careful, her voice neutral. "You talked a lot about losing time, what memories you have, and your conspiracies about the government and pharma companies, but from what I can tell you made no effort to find out who you were. Are, rather."

"There isn't much I *can* do. I don't know where I went or where I lived for four years. Any memories I have are jumbled."

"But you have options. Have you searched your name on the internet?"

"Yes. Nothing."

"Done a credit check on yourself? You could find out

your living history."

"I don't have my social security number," I snapped.

Olivia didn't concede. "What about missing persons? Did you call the police to see if anyone of your age and appearance disappeared in the area?"

I hadn't thought of that. But even if I had, I'm not sure I would've done it. I quickly fell into the grasps of the drug world after waking up. Calling the police for any reason didn't seem like a good idea when your life revolved around illegal activities. I wouldn't do it now for those very reasons.

Last night I was confident in my plan to get answers. I still was. Mostly. But this was too personal, too fast. An ugly part of me reared up. It felt criticized, attacked. Before I could stop myself, I lashed back. "No, I didn't think to do that, but even if I wanted to I couldn't. The kind of world I'm in, you don't go to the cops willingly for *anything*. Where do you come up with this stuff?"

"I watch a lot of crime shows on TV. Do some digging, Ethan. If there's any way we can find someone from your past, they might know if you were part of a drug trial or who was behind it. We might be able to find your family."

It all sounded ideal. Reuniting with my family, their arms outstretched. I had memories of my mother and father. Fuzzy pictures of their faces. Birthday parties, Christmas. My first bike. Whatever happened to me ate away at my memories, leaving me with only fragments. The ones I still had were never enough to go on.

I'd spaced out. Olivia was looking at me as though she asked something. When she realized I hadn't been listening, she sighed.

"We'll talk to this guy tomorrow. We'll see what there is

to see. Maybe if we find out what company performed the tests on him, we can backtrack from there. If this is a drug, I doubt it's legal. We could blow the whistle on it."

The hour Olivia said she'd be gone hadn't come to a close, but there wasn't much else to say. Outside Starbucks, she reminded me again to never come to her work. We exchanged an awkward handshake and went separate ways.

I lit the cigarette my body desperately needed and sucked it, and two more, down before I got back to my apartment. Tomorrow I'd meet another person in my life who'd experienced what I had.

It comforted me, it scared me.

Most of all, it made me feel alive.

CHAPTER 9

Olivia drove an electric car that I imagined cost more than every item I'd ever owned in my life. The interior was a sandy colored leather with matching carpet, impeccably clean as though she'd just driven it off the lot. Maybe she had. I dubbed the vehicle the Immaculate Car.

I sat in the passenger seat like a black scuff mark on a perfectly waxed floor. Stiffly, and very aware how out of place I was.

She had a stainless steel Thermos of what smelled like floral tea that she sipped from as we drove. The car was the quietest vehicle I'd ever been in. I don't remember ever going to church, but this is what it must've felt like. Ridged and unfamiliar.

When she picked me up in a parking garage near the science center, it was more of the secretive pomp. She had on big sunglasses despite the almost dark sky and urged me to be quick as I got in. Yet there was plenty of time to scold me about not putting on a seatbelt.

"How long do you think it will take to figure this whole thing out? I asked.

She glanced at me, her mouth pursed. "I have no idea. Why?"

"Trying to keep me and what we're doing a secret might backfire eventually. Plus it bugs the hell out of me. What makes you think you can treat me like dirt?"

Yeah, I treated myself like dirt. That didn't mean other people could do it.

"Oh."

I waited for something more, but got nothing. I wasn't done yet. "You asked me why I hadn't dug into my past. I have a question for *you*; why are you keeping this so under wraps? Why not go to the police about what's happening to you?"

"Don't you remember what you thought the first second you met me? That I'd brought this on myself. That I'd been date raped."

"Okay, yes. I own up to that. And I'm sorry. But I'm a terrible guy," I said with a dose of sarcasm. "The police would take you seriously."

"Listen, Ethan, I'm going to tell you this once and I never want you to bring it up again." Olivia's voice was more harsh and aggressive than I'd ever heard. She was dead fucking serious. "Even if I told the police and they started an investigation, it would ruin my career. My life. All of this points to a certain group of people—rich, important people—who hold a lot of power. Who I work for. The second police start investigating them, word would get around. Olivia Holloway is trying to get a nice settlement. Olivia Holloway asked for it. It doesn't matter what is true or not. My life would be over."

Her jaw was tight. I noted her death grip on the steering wheel. A hazy memory of my mother came up, one I hadn't thought of in a while. She was crying while she drove the family minivan, hands clutching the steering wheel like Olivia was now. I'd done something wrong, something terrible to upset her. I could never remember what it was or how old I was when the incident occurred. The memory was nothing more than a flash of emotions and the image of my mother.

I rubbed my temples and pushed the thought aside so I could focus on the now. Olivia was almost at the edge, but I wasn't letting it go. If I was in this with her, I wanted to know exactly what her story was.

"What do you plan on doing with what we find out?" I asked. "Let's say you find out who did it. What will you do? You can't turn them in based on what you told me. Are you going to blackmail them? Ask them nicely to please stop slipping you drugs? Kill them?"

Her pause at my last suggestion was too long. I laughed in disbelief. "Really? You're going to kill them?"

"God, I don't know yet, okay? I won't kill them. The first thing I want is to know who is doing this and *how*. That would be a good start. Does that satisfy you?"

I finally leaned back in my seat, staring out the window. Olivia was as lost as I was. Stuck between what she wanted and what she was limited to. "One last thing. Think about committing to your other cover story for me, the outreach one, so we can at least be seen together. I'm tired of this cloak and dagger shit. Speaking of which, what's our back story for Brian Stromberg?"

She seemed relieved to change the topic. "I made an appointment saying we wanted to get a good life insurance plan. The appointment is just before they close so no one will be around."

"How are we going to shift the conversation from life insurance to his blackouts and my blog?"

"We'll just do it, I guess. It might be clunky and

awkward. Be ready for that."

"Fine."

Silence once again. There was something between us that put us at each other's throats from the moment we met. I suppose we, like all the other people in my life, were a bad combination. She wanted to keep me a secret and I was sick of secrets. Maybe we were both permanently pissed because someone had played God with our memories and bodies and could only let it out on each other.

Whatever the reason, the rest of our trip was spent wordless.

We crossed the bridge and entered the remnants of rush hour traffic. It took ten minutes longer than it should've to get to the square, industrial looking building the insurance company was in. The parking lot was sparsely populated. Olivia's high heels clacked loudly as we walked to the building and rode the elevator to the fourth floor. When we entered the empty reception area, a man quickly came from a room to the left.

"Are you the Smiths?"

Shit. Smiths? Could she be any more unoriginal?

Olivia put on a gracious demeanor and shook his hand. "Yes. I'm so sorry we're late. I didn't realize how bad traffic would still be. I don't leave Seattle much."

Brian ran a hand through thick, wavy black hair. He looked at me, sizing me up. "No problem. Come on back to my desk and we'll get started, okay?"

From there Olivia handled the rest of the conversation. They could've been speaking Latin for all I cared. Legal jargon and finances were two things I knew nothing about. Never bothered hitting up that section of the library. We navigated through a sea of cubicles until we reached his.

I stared out the window behind his desk. The trees were inky black silhouettes against the dying blue sky. I couldn't imagine what a miserable feeling it was to be in that place day in and day out, watching life fly by outside while you were stuck pushing papers. The smell of toner and cheap coffee was so thick it bled into your clothes. My life, as tragic and frustrating as it was, was thrilling compared to this.

Brian's desk had few personal knickknacks. Photo of an average, blond haired blond woman with two children. Wife and kids. Pinned to the corkboard to the right of the desk were work fliers and a popular newspaper comic. Sometimes I wondered what I was missing out on with the 9-5 job. Turns out it was nothing.

"So we have a lot of really great plans. But I'm thinking you might want the best one." He was hopeful. Eager.

I regretted the preface we came there on. I fidgeted in my seat and waited for Olivia to handle it. She cleared her throat and folded her hands in her lap.

"Actually, we wanted to talk about the blackouts you had some years ago."

Brian's face went slack. "What? Are you police?"

"Police?" I choked. "Fuck no."

Olivia stepped in. "No, nothing like that. We believe the same thing happened to us. We believe you."

He peered around the office. There was one remaining worker on the other side of the floor, her desk light a beacon in the darkness. She was on her phone, unaware.

Brian's voice turned into a whisper. "No one pressed charges against me. Do you have any idea how hard it was to get this job? I could lose it if someone found out I was even involved in that."

"We have absolutely nothing to do with the police," Olivia started, "We want your help. That's all."

The guy didn't trust us. Olivia wasn't giving him the right incentive. I decided to step in. "You went by technal and posted comments on my Memory Loss Experimentation blog, right? I'm Ethan."

Brian's mouth hung open as he looked at me as though I'd just appeared. "You're Ethan Knight?"

"The one and only."

"You never responded to any of my comments."

Fuck. Digital karma was biting me in the ass. I decided to go for the truth. "I'm sorry, man. I am. You gotta realize, I was coming off a four year blackout. All I wanted to do was spew about what happened to me and then I got involved in some pretty bad shit. The rest is history. I'm here now."

"So you are." Brian rubbed his face and sighed. "What do you want to know?"

"Tell us about your blackouts. You seemed to know more than you let on in your comments on Ethan's blog. Just start from the beginning," Olivia asked.

"I signed up for a human clinical trial. I needed money. I remember taking the bus there and walking in, getting settled in a room like a dorm. Three weeks later, I wake up in my bed. I have no idea where the time went. My friend came to pick me up. Asked me what was wrong. I told him I didn't remember any of the trial." His eyes bulged as he told the story. He leaned forward. "You know what he said? 'I talked to you.' He claimed we talked on the phone twice and I told him about the trials and stuff they had me do. I don't remember any of it."

"What did he say you told him?" I asked.

"The food was the same thing every day; oatmeal for breakfast and lunch, turkey sandwich for dinner. The beds were too hard, the other subjects regular people. They had us read kid books and do puzzles. Watch movies and stuff." Brian sighed. "It kind of made sense. After I woke up that day, they took me to a room. There was an exam, like something I'd do in third grade. It asked for the plot of books and movies. I didn't know the answers to any of it because I'd never seen any of them. They thanked me, gave me a check, and my friend picked me up. If that doesn't seem weird enough, there's more.

"After the exam, they brought me a bowl of oatmeal and said I had to eat it. I thought, no problem. The second I smelled it I puked everywhere. I still can't eat oatmeal or anything that smells like oats."

"Do you remember any kind of aftertaste?" I asked. "Something metallic maybe, after you woke up?"

Brian ran his tongue around his cheeks as he nodded. "Tinny, like I licked a rusty barrel. Lasted for a few days."

Olivia and I exchanged glances. This guy was the real deal. No doubt about it.

She pulled a notebook from her purse. "Do you remember the name of the company?"

"Of course. The only thing I don't remember is what happened while I was there," Brian said. "It's D.P. Pharmaceutical Industries. Don't remember what the D.P. stands for."

The name meant nothing to me. I'd never heard of D.P. Pharmaceutical Industries before. Brian's blackout, so far, didn't seem too bad. Based on his answers, I didn't doubt he was truthful. Yes, he lost the time. But he wasn't hurt. He was still a functioning adult. Same with Olivia; they were both still normal. Was it the length of time they'd been blacked out? Was the drug a different formula? I was still missing something. Then I realized Brian had omitted something, too.

"Why did you think we were police?"

Brian tapped his fingers against his desk nervously. I noticed his nails were chewed almost to the quick. "After I woke up and talked to Tony and everything, I had a breakdown. Losing three weeks is traumatic. When we go to sleep, we know we're asleep. We chose it. This was different. I was myself, but not myself. It's hard to explain. I decided I needed to get retribution."

He didn't need to explain. And he had no fucking idea what a real breakdown was.

"I went back to D.P. and caused a scene. Just pushed desks around, roughed up property. The executive assistant came down and tried to calm me. Asked what I wanted. I didn't know what I wanted. To know what they'd done to me, I suppose." Brian rubbed his face again. "They showed me the contract I signed. Long story short, I'd agreed not to press any charges against them for what occurred to me during the trial. He reminded me I had no right to the information they'd gathered and that at no point during the trial was I held against my will. I got the impression he was being clever, but he was just presenting me with the facts. Turned the whole thing around and pointed out they could press charges against me for trespassing and destruction of private property.

They sent me away and that was it. To be honest, I haven't thought about it in years."

"It must be nice to have settled down." I couldn't hide the animosity in my voice. Even I heard it.

Olivia looked down at her notebook and appeared to write, but I saw from the corner of my eye she was just tracing the lines of D.P. Pharmaceutical Industries again. "Do you remember what the drug was called you were testing? Do you have a copy of the contract or documentation?"

Thankful for the subject change, Brian said, "There was some long official name for it. They called it Whiteout, like slang for it. I remember because I always had a vision of a bottle of Wite-out and them painting my brain with it. Weird, I know. As for documents, no. I didn't think to get a copy of anything. I should've. I wanted to put it behind me. That's all I have for you. I'd appreciate it if you left now. I want to go home."

He pushed his desk chair away and stood. Our time with him was up. We followed him to the elevator. His demeanor was opposite of when we first arrived. He was forcedly happy and optimistic. Now it was obvious he was upset, his brain likely cycling through all the bad shit he wanted to 'put behind'. I'd be pissed too if someone came out of nowhere to dredge up something nasty. I was when Olivia came.

Brian smacked the 'down' button highlighting it orange. "Whatever you two are getting into, I'd be careful. When I walked into D.P., I was confident I'd get answers and have things my way. Not only did they turn me around, but they made me feel like a complete idiot who'd lose everything if I tried to put up a fight."

A chime, and the doors slid open. Brian left without a goodbye.

CHAPTER 10

"**W**ell, I think that went well!" Olivia was beaming. She flicked through her smartphone at what looked like a calendar and spoke to me in a distracted tone. "We got the name of the pharmaceutical company and at least we have a name for the drug. Whiteout sounds like a working name though, but it's something. Too bad he didn't remember the actual name."

"It does sound kind of blatant," I admitted. "Fits the product."

By the time we hit the first floor she had a search open on D.P. Pharmaceutical Industries. We stepped out of the elevator and she hovered beside it, scrolling through the search results. I leaned over to see and caught a whiff of her perfume. It was like her tea; too floral and sweet for my taste.

"No official website. No drugs on the market." She thumbed quickly through results, clicking on a page here and there. My phone was a clamshell piece of shit that made texting look high tech.

"They could've gone under at some point."

"It seems like it. Let me search for that specifically."

I looked around the first floor, uneasy. It might've been because half the lights were turned off for the evening, making the place big and shadowy. It also could've been my mind turning Brian's last words into something more foreboding than he probably intended. Or that I hadn't had a smoke in over an hour.

The people making Whiteout were bad people. The kind of people who wouldn't want their secrets found out, or their work put to a stop. Like any drug cartel, they'd be powerful and ready for a fight. How much could a goody campaign manager and jacked up drug dealer do against them?

My brain drifted even farther. This would be the perfect place for someone to kill us. No one around. After hours. Maybe Brian or the lady upstairs would find us when they left work for the night. Or more likely, our bodies would be melted in acid or thrown into the Puget Sound.

"Ah! Found something."

I jumped, jammed my elbow against the wall behind me. Olivia furrowed her brow then rolled her eyes. "They went under a little over seven years ago."

"That's about when I woke up," I said. "Why did they go under?"

"This article in the Seattle Times isn't clear. It just says, 'Up and coming Seattle pharmaceutical company has announced its closure after experiencing funding issues credited to the recession and economic hardship.' Looks like the bank seized the building."

D.P. dissolving seven years ago did not help us. If they created Whiteout, someone saved the recipe and was making it under their own terms. This brought up more questions and no answers. I'd hoped by at least knowing who originated the drug, we could go from there.

The air was too hot in the building. I was stifled and headed for the doors, leaving Olivia flicking through her phone. I made it five feet before she looked up and shouted for me.

"I need a smoke," I said as I burst through the doors.

The frigid air and open space felt much better. I retrieved a cigarette, noting I had only two left, and lit it. The nicotine soothed my nerves instantly. I inhaled the thing in two long pulls and finished it before Olivia met up with me, still pulling on white leather gloves. I dropped the ashen husk of the smoke on the ground and lit another.

"Do you have to smoke so much?"

"Do you have to be so controlling?"

She made a small *hmph* noise and put more distance between us, then made a point of holding her hand over her nose and mouth. "This isn't a complete setback. I can do more research on D.P. I'm sure I'll find something."

"Good."

"I was thinking you could maybe, I don't know, see if you can find out anything on the streets?"

My laugh came out in a hoarse bark. I imagined what Olivia thought the 'streets' were like. Set aside the humor, it was a valid option. Donovan already knew a little. I bet he, or one of his contacts, knew more. I was generally well liked, even outside of my own circles. "I will. It's the best chance we have at finding who's dealing it now. I can try to work my way up the ladder to see who's supplying."

I saw a beaming smile peeping out from beneath her hand. It reminded me of something I noticed before. Olivia seemed to smile a lot. Not always in a good way, but reflexively. Her attitude was too upbeat to be realistic for someone who'd been drugged and abused multiple times. It made me realize there could be more layers to her than expensive cars and flowery teas.

"We need to head back. I have a meeting with a client tonight. After that I'll see what I can find out about D.P."

"This late? Must be important."

Olivia nodded. "The mayor running for a seat in the Senate? It's my biggest project yet. I'm in charge of his entire announcement gala. It's more work than I've ever had."

Second cigarette finished, we went to her car and headed back to Seattle. I didn't harass her once on the way back, though she provided good opportunities for a fight when she made comments on how her car now smelled like cigarettes and perhaps I should consider quitting.

This time she drove me all the way to Belltown instead of a shady drop off in a parking garage. She pulled into the loading zone out front.

"Ethan, please consider looking at missing persons reports for yourself. If my research on D.P. and your efforts on the streets don't pay off, we're going to have to turn to ourselves for more." There was no smile this time. "It's your decision of course, but if it comes down to it I will do it for you. Whether you want me to or not."

Fuck me. The next layer of Olivia revealed. "I'll do it."

After I drank myself into oblivion and was just numb enough to keep going.

"Goodnight, Ethan."

Inside my apartment, after I collapsed in my easy chair, I checked my phone. There was a voicemail from Donovan.

"Hey, E." It was quiet in the background. I wondered where he was. "Haven't seen you in a while. No one's seen you around much actually. Hope you're selling my inventory and not getting loaded off it. You know what I'll do. Got that bench ready for you."

It amazed me how Donovan could keep a light, joking tone while he threatened my life. And it wasn't an idle threat.

Seven years ago, I woke up and was missing four years of my life. It was as though someone put me in hyper sleep in a sci-fi flick and forgot about me. When I came to I was on a bench at Alki Beach. Confusion took over and I went ballistic. Where the fuck had I been? What was I doing there? I knew my name, had fragmented memories of my life before, but big chunks were gone.

More than chunks. That word doesn't describe the feeling of having *years* missing from your life. There were flashes of memories, no more than a still frame, from the missing years. I couldn't put them in order. I didn't know what they meant. There were images from my childhood and teenage years, none of them meaningful.

What I did know was that I was in pain, agony like I'd never experienced before. My body was alien to me, almost as though I'd just teleported back in and forgot how to use it. My brain couldn't reconcile what was happening. I was sweating and my heart raced as I stumbled around the beach.

Donovan was a dealer then. Still small time. His uncle and father gave him a chance to work his way up like everyone else did. He'd been working the beach when he spotted me. He thought I was coming off a bender or something and gave me a few Xanax out of pity and a swig of vodka from his flask. Back then he was nicer.

Ethan, meet benzodiazepines. Meet booze. Meet your new friends that will help you exist.

That soothed me and lessened my panic. We got to talking. Donovan figured I was experiencing withdrawal, but I told him I didn't remember being addicted to anything. When he found out I had nowhere to go, he let me tag along with him. Sometimes I slept over at his place as long as I wasn't intrusive. He gave me work here and there.

Donovan had a way of making you think he was your friend. You'd be totally convinced he had your back until you did something wrong and suffered the consequences. Donovan was no one's friend. He made it easy to overlook that with his humor and seemingly light attitude.

I wasn't serious or committed to dealing at first. I did some panhandling. There was an art to making the perfect cardboard sign. In some places you looked right at the people walking by. In others, you stared at the ground. I learned a lot about people during those times. I dealt a bit on the side with Donovan as my supplier. I needed just enough money to keep my bloodstream toxic enough to get me through the day.

To my credit, there was one decent thing I did for myself. When I wasn't working, to fill my time I went to the library and read. To leave my own world for hours at a time was heaven. I checked out self-help books en masse. Meditation, cognitive behavioral therapy, dream analysis. Everything. I drank them up. It was an addiction. Eventually I started that fucking blog. Since shouting into the internet gave little back, I soon gave up.

Donovan climbed the ranks and brought me along. That micromanaging bastard got a thrill out of it. Eventually he owned me. He was my only source of income. I didn't know who I was, was afraid to go to the police now that I was a criminal. They had my prints from shootings and I was a known associate of Donovan's family.

I had my books and my apartment, but it all came back to getting more money from Donovan to keep it up. Normally a person in my position had to be ready to bounce at any moment. I hated that feeling. I liked my apartment, as shitty as it was. Donovan knew that.

Since the day he found me, whenever I tried to go clean and break out, he reminded me they could always take me back.

What that meant now was, we'll kill you. We'll kill you and leave you on that bench at Alki.

I checked the time on my phone. Plenty of time for a trip to the liquor store.

CHAPTER 11

After waking up at 10:00am I was confident anyone who thought themselves a morning person was mentally disturbed. I gripped blankets tighter around my body, halfway up my face, and tried to figure out what woke me up. It hadn't been another nightmare. That, I would've remembered.

Outside, the city grumbled as it, too, went about its morning routine. The echoing screech of garbage trucks in alleyways penetrated the thin apartment walls and did nothing to help my headache. From my bed I saw Seattle's typical overcast grayish white sky peeking from behind skyscrapers. Not raining. It didn't rain here as much as people everywhere else thought. The light made the concrete and metal city look even more industrial. Charmless. I definitely liked it better at night.

I closed my eyes and tried to will myself back to sleep. I was warm and comfortable. I had nowhere to be. Just a few more hours of sleep then…

Bzzbzzbzz. Bzzbzzbzz.

I sat up just in time to see my vibrating phone clatter and fall off the kitchen counter. Cursing the phone, I tossed the covers aside and made six large strides to retrieve it before dashing back to my bed. I tripped over a poorly stacked pile of books on hypnosis and cursed louder as I stumbled and hit my toe on the easy chair. Only when I was safely back in bed did I look at the missed call.

Two from Donovan. The first one must've been what woke me up.

I had a vague memory of curling up in bed and reading a book on bodily awareness. I did a body scan on myself, putting mental awareness on each body part. I couldn't get past my right chest where the acid burns were. I panicked and started drinking. Apparently I passed out early.

I hit the call button. Donovan picked up on the first ring. "Surprised you don't sound too shitfaced this early."

"I'm full of surprises. What do you want?"

"You never came to resupply. *And* I have something you might be interested in."

I yawned and flung an arm over my eyes to stop what little light my apartment offered from bombarding me further. "I'll come over today. Where are you?"

"Sands. Trisha is dancing today. You know I hate it when guys get handsy with her."

Donovan's love for his numerous stripper or junkie girlfriends was a mystery to me. In the years I'd known him, he always gravitated to women who were used up. Emotionally and mentally spent. I don't think he wanted to fix them, because whenever one wanted to get out of the scene he'd make sure they couldn't. He liked having them in a position of little power, but didn't like it when other men liked it too. Trisha hadn't started out that way, but I think Donovan liked the challenge of ruining a good person. Now Trisha fit his type perfectly.

I hated going to the strip club. It was nestled in an old industrial area in north Seattle that required two buses to get to from Belltown. The place smelled salty and damp.

I found the girls a sad reminder of the world we lived in, even the ones who Donovan told me loved being strippers. Going there also made me notice the callous barrier I built up between Trisha and me. Maybe the sex earlier that week would change things. I hoped it wouldn't because Donovan would kill me if he suspected anything.

"You'll be there all day?"

"She gets off at eight, then I'll get her off right after. Right baby?" I heard a squeal and giggle. Donovan's muffled grunt.

"I'll be there in a few hours. What else do you have for me?"

"That shit you were asking about a few days ago? We got some. Not much, but enough to maybe get us in on it. You're one of my best dealers. Maybe not lately, but usually. If you want in..."

I imagined Donovan doing his trademark shrug and side smile on the other line. Even though my insides shook and my mouth was dry, I said, "Sure. I can take a few."

"Cool. That's it, peace."

I snapped the phone shut and set it on my milk crate nightstand. This could be good. Donovan might know names or the hierarchy of who was supplying it. The more we knew, the better.

Two hours, thirty ounces of coffee, six cigarettes, and a shot of bourbon later, I stepped off the bus a block away from the strip club. This part of Seattle was depressing. All the buildings looked bad, with worn paint and overgrown lawns. It might've been nice once, but not in my lifetime.

The houses that lined the streets were generally in equal disrepair. That was another reason why I didn't like coming down here. Downtown, you didn't see anything close to a traditional home. There were skyscrapers, malls, apartment complexes. There was a sore throbbing in my chest when I thought about my parents. An inexplicable longing. Houses triggered that feeling, so I avoided them. I kept my head down and made quick work of the block between me and the club.

Sands Showgirls was a squat, army green building that had no windows and ample parking all around. It opened a half hour earlier but there were no customers in the lot yet. I went to the entrance. The bouncer knew me. I sold him weed once or twice, whenever I happened to have some.

The club was all soft pink and purple lights bathing the metal dancing platforms. Anywhere a patron would sit was kept darker. Private. Behind the bar a single bartender was taking inventory of their liquor. On stage was Trisha, dancing in a white sequined outfit that glowed under the lights. Her white glittery cowboy hat acted like a disco ball, reflecting light onto the walls as she moved.

Donovan leaned against the platform, his elbows jutting outward as he rested his head on his hands and watched her. All the ladies thought he was a handsome man. Even I could admit that. He looked like an extra who walked off the set of a Russian mob movie. Black slicked hair, icy eyes, a chiseled face with a bit of a hawkish nose.

He didn't notice me until I sat down right next to him. "E, fuck! I didn't know it was possible for you to walk during daylight."

I made myself grin. Donovan liked to keep things

casual. When things got serious, he shut down. I needed him open and willing to talk.

Trisha was suddenly on her knees, crawling over to him. She knew all eyes had to be for him, so I was a ghost. I let them have their moment before speaking.

"Found a new bean at Pike Place. So much caffeine I can stay up for a whole night."

"Ah, yeah. You always liked coffee." He sat back in his chair, knees splayed wide. "I think it tastes like shit. You want something to drink?"

"Of course."

"Jim! Two!"

Ever patient, I waited until our drinks came and we'd knocked back the first round. Another patron showed up. I watched him take a seat in the far corner of the club. He was exactly what you'd expect; middle-aged, kind of chubby. I bet he had a wedding ring and a very good story about why he was there.

When Trisha's second dance finally ended and she went to take a break, Donovan broke from his trance. "Sorry to hear about the kid. Heard about it from the grapevine, you know?"

Surprised he mentioned it, all I could manage was a shrug. Then, "Thanks."

"So, how you been? Besides that? What's your inventory like?"

"Sold everything," I said. "Been feeling under the weather so haven't had a chance to stop by and resupply."

"You doing smack again?" Donovan clucked his tongue. "You know how you get on it."

"I'm not. Just tired."

"Okay. Well, I got the usual for you. And something extra."

His tone became conspiratorial. "This stuff is called Whiteout, and it is seriously fucked up."

There was that slang again. It was called Whiteout when Brian was on it. The name stuck. "What does it do?"

"What we're telling people, is that you give it to someone—or yourself—about ten minutes before you need it to start working. Once it does, they won't remember a damn thing you do to them. Nothing. But they won't be unconscious or loopy or anything. It's just like their brain stops remembering. Lasts eight to ten hours."

Nothing new there. I thought for a moment, then asked, "Anything else you tell them? Tips since it's new?"

Donovan appeared to think hard. I noticed the sweat on his temples and the flickering of his eyes. He was drunk. Must've been when I first got here, too. That was good for me. Happy, drunk Donovan had loose lips.

"Yeah, actually. They said you gotta drug your mark again near the end, put them to sleep. It makes it easier for them to come off it. Otherwise you at least have to make sure they're somewhere familiar when they wake up or they'll freak out. I thought they were bullshitting. That seems kind of stupid. But last night, Trisha wanted to try it." Donovan frowned and slammed back the rest of his drink. "She said, if it actually worked then she could take it before a shift and wouldn't have to remember any of it. I guess she…well, whatever."

I finished my drink and told Donovan I was getting another. I needed a moment away from him to think. This felt too real. Whiteout—fuck, I didn't even have a name for it before—had been an intangible concept in my life until now. I figured something like it existed, but now it truly was here in front of me.

And for the first time, I thought about another use for Whiteout. People like Trisha who worked jobs they hated, wished they could just put themselves on autopilot, would pay big bucks for it. You were still you, still did the work, but another part of yourself wouldn't have to deal with the memories of it. Or even a stay at home parent who needed a mental break. Someone who worked in hospice. I could think of dozens of honest people who'd want it.

But I also thought of the dozens of terrible uses for it. Rape. Torture. Kidnapping, abuse of any kind. Experimentation. There was no mind or body altering substance that wouldn't be used in the wrong way. Whatever good Whiteout offered could never outweigh the bad.

I threw back a vodka and asked for two more, one to take back to Donovan. A new girl was on stage. Admittedly, she wasn't as good or pretty as Trisha. Donovan's gaze hovered on the girl's giant chest.

"This Whiteout stuff sounds intense." I thought carefully about the questions that I'd ask for any other drug first. "How much are we selling it for?"

"I was right before when I said they were getting a feel for it. Now that people have a taste, we're supposed to push it for as high as we can. Starting at $200 a pop. You ask me, we could sell it for $500 no problem to the right people."

"Fuck. How much is your cut?"

"30%."

I was still reeling. "Not bad. Where's this stuff coming from?"

Now Donovan's mood shifted. He picked up his shot glass, and finding it empty, set it on the table with enough force to slide it across the surface and almost off the edge. "Don't know."

"You don't know or you can't say?"

"What difference does it make? I'm in. If we can sell enough of this shit for the best price, we'll be in on it forever. Whiteout is going to attract a better clientele for me. No more roofies and weed. I want to go big time. I'm better than this." He sat straighter and tried to get the bartender's attention. He waved his hand and showed two fingers. "I'm going to prove it, E."

I knew that tone. I'm sure he planned to use those same words on someone else. Donovan was a few rungs down the ladder from his dad and uncle who called the shots. No one thought little Donnie was good enough to handle big projects or hard stuff. Just pills, maybe some smack here and there. I imagined he got a connection to sell Whiteout from a friend-of-a-friend without the permission of his family.

Who would be willing to sell to him knowing they weren't talking to the boss? Someone who didn't know how things worked. Someone who thought we were all the same. I wanted to whip out a notebook like Olivia and start writing down all the clues.

"I know you'll prove it. You're a smart guy," I said.

Donovan smiled. "Thanks. I trust you, Ethan. All the Whiteout I got, I split with you. Only you and me are dealing it. Keeping it tight, okay? My dad and uncle don't know shit about this to tell you the truth."

That was a small bit of relief. The less Whiteout on the

streets, the better.

By the time the bartender brought Donovan two more vodkas, Trisha was back on stage and I'd lost the guy to drunkenness and a hard-on. It took another ten minutes to get him to give me my next supply, which included four half blue, half white, unmarked capsules. Whiteout. I didn't have to check to know if I compared them to the pill I found with Skid, they'd be the same. Donovan barely acknowledged me when I said goodbye and that I'd let him know how the sales went.

The moment I stepped outside the brisk air made my lungs seize up, the low winter sun blinding me. I went to fish out a cigarette and remembered I was out. After I tried unsuccessfully to bum one off the bouncer, I walked down the street to the AM/PM to buy as many boxes as I had cash for. That turned out to be four. Just enough to get me through the rest of today and tomorrow night.

I settled at the bus stop bench and waited. The bus wouldn't be here for an hour. It was a good moment to call my partner in crime.

Olivia picked up almost instantly. "Olivia Holloway."

"It's Ethan," I said. I glanced around me to make sure no one could overhear. "I talked to my supplier about Whiteout. He gave me some."

"*What?* Did you ask where he got it?"

"He wouldn't say." I explained my theory on the supplier not knowing the chain of command. "It points to someone outside of the game. They just want Whiteout on the streets. They're probably giving it to anyone they think can push it."

There was chatter on the other line. Olivia rattled off

the names of caterers to her assistant, stressing they could only use local or fair-trade ingredients. Then she was back. "So eventually he has to get more of it. Or at least report to someone. Can we ask him who that is?"

I sighed and stared at the ground. A glob of chewed gum with a dead ant atop looked back up at me. If only it was as easy as asking. Most buyers and other dealers liked me, but no one who mattered liked me. I was too into using what I sold for them to take me seriously.

"If I try to squeeze him, he might cut me off. He's my sole source of income, Olivia. I'll pick up what I can, but I can't *interrogate* him."

"Oh. Okay." I tried to imagine the expression on her face. What did Olivia think of the squalor I lived in? What had she thought when she entered my smoke-addled apartment and saw the bottles everywhere? The overdue stacks of library books? Did she feel bad about how I lived?

For her sake, I changed the subject. I can be kind every once in a while. "Have you found out anything new on D.P.?"

"I haven't had a chance. The mayor gala and all. It's an extremely demanding project. But I will tonight. I'll call you as soon as I know."

Everyone had to work. I needed to get rid of the inventory Donovan gave me. As for the Whiteout, I wasn't sure. I had almost a grand worth of it and if I didn't sell it, Donovan would be pissed. Morally, I couldn't do it. I wouldn't. I could always lie and say no one wanted it. That would only work for so long. It might not work at all if Donovan sold his quickly.

Yes, morals. I had them in my own fucked up way.

"Fine." I hung up and secured the phone in my pocket.

Only a moment later I heard the clopping of high heels approach. I tilted my head and saw a woman in a bulky winter coat coming towards me. Her legs were clad in hot pink fishnet that stood out against the plainness of her brown coat. She had the hood up. A brown fringe of fake fur curled around her face.

"What are you doing here, Trisha?"

She sat down next to me and glanced to her side in the direction of the club. Outside in the unforgiving sunlight I could see the damage on her face from too much tanning and smoking. In the club she looked young, the shadows and colored lights smoothing what was really there. It amazed me how fast dancers could turn off their acts.

"Donnie's doing blow off Chastity's tits."

I wasn't sure what my reaction was supposed to be, so I didn't say anything. She came to me for a reason. The ball was in her court.

"Before Donnie called for her, Chastity told me you'd been asking him about that Whiteout shit."

"She heard all that?"

Trisha shrugged. "We see and hear everything. Anyone with a dick forgets that."

"Fair enough," I agreed. "You have something you want to say about it?"

She pulled her lower lip between her teeth and chewed on it for a second. Sparkling pink lip gloss rubbed away, showing the chapped lips underneath. I was curious now, if not a bit nervous. Donovan would be enraged if he knew Trisha was talking to me, especially about something so sensitive.

"It seems like you have questions that need answers."
She paused, her voice even lower now. "I need something,
too."

What could I possibly give her she couldn't get from
Donovan? "And what's that?"

Trisha looked back towards the strip club, then all
around. I don't think she could've looked any more
suspicious than she already did.

"I want out of the scene."

"Fuck, Trisha. You know how many girls say that?" I
laughed. "Whatever you think you have waiting for you out
there, it doesn't matter. Take it from me, you can't escape
this life. Maybe a couple years ago when you still had a
chance, but not now. You'll be back and begging for scraps
before you know it, only you'll be at the bottom of the food
chain."

The moment I said it, I regretted it. Here I was, trying
to get out, and I put Trisha down. I needed to learn to keep
my mouth shut.

"You're a real asshole, E, you know that? You have no
idea what it's like shaking your tits and ass up there every
fucking day while sticky men grab at you and screw you
with their eyes."

I didn't know. I would never understand what it was
like, but I could look at all the evidence from strippers
before her to know there was little she could do. Then I
remembered I needed to play nice. She implied she knew
something about Whiteout. That's what I needed.

"I'm sorry. I am. Where do you want to go? Why can't
Donovan help you?"

"He's part of the problem. You know what he does to

me. He wants me to be a slut on stage just for him and no one else. Then when I pull some tricks on the side—because God only knows I can't make enough money dancing—he goes ballistic. I want to get so far away from him, he has no choice but to give up." Trisha wrung her hands together. "That means I need money."

Trisha was getting ahead of herself. She was already outlining her terms like I'd agreed. But I didn't have a clue what kind of information she had to offer me.

A thought dawned on me and I felt rage boiling up inside. "When you were over the other night, what was that? Just priming me up? Did you really think a quick fuck would make me risk anything for you?"

By the frown and displeasure on her face, I knew I was right. She sighed. "Sure. You're a lonely guy, E. Everyone knows you don't have much. I thought showing you a little kindness might make a difference when I asked for some."

I hated being manipulated, but I had to be honest with myself. Trisha showing up like that was weird. If I'd been thinking with my brain instead of my dick, I would've known it was too good to be true. I hadn't spent a minute alone with her in almost a year, then she shows up? I had to let it go. Especially since she might have something I wanted.

"I don't have stacks of cash laying around to give to you. Shit, I'm broke almost every day of the week. Before we even talk your terms, I want to know what information you have."

"I know a guy who's supplying Whiteout. One of the guys I do on the side. I don't want money from *you*, I want it from *him*. You help me, you get his name and whatever else you want out of him."

Her phone buzzed. She pulled it from the depths of her jacket and looked at the screen. She stood up a second later. "I'm on in ten. I'll call you soon with details, okay? If we work together, E, we can both get something we want."

I watched her teeter away on her five inch heels and wondered what I'd gotten myself into.

CHAPTER 12

"I come bearing gifts."

Gifts meant white plastic takeout bags that hung in both of Olivia's hands. One shoulder was hiked up as she attempted to stop her large shoulder bag from slipping off. Today she wore a different jacket than I'd seen before, different boots, and had her auburn hair in a round bun on the top of her head. I think she owned more clothes than all the people I knew combined.

I was still a little loopy from the Valium I took earlier, forgetting Olivia was punctual. When she said she'd be at my apartment at eight, that meant she'd be knocking on the door precisely then. I intended to clean up a bit, but once I was lying on my bed feeling good, cleaning didn't seem important.

"I hope you like Chinese food." She looked past me into the apartment. "Can I come in?"

"Right. Yeah." I stepped aside and let her pick her way around the scatter of clothing and shoes on the ground to the folding table. It, too, was full of junk.

She set her bags on the chair and cleared away the items on the table. Empty bottles, both glass and the plastic orange of unlabeled prescription drugs. Makeshift ashtrays. It was strange seeing her in my apartment again. The first time she was uncomfortable and out of place. This time she was still out of place, but was making an effort not to stare at any one thing too long.

"Quite the collection of books you have," she said. She stared at a stack of dream analysis books beside the folding table. "Are you into psychology?"

"A little. Mostly I keep reading through them because I hope they'll fix me, or I'll find answers in them."

"Get anything yet?"

I laughed. "No. Never do. For all the books I've read, I don't think I'm better off. I read them, but don't apply them. Just criticize myself more effectively through them."

I sat in my easy chair near the folding table and continued to watch as she opened and arranged each takeout container. She'd brought paper plates which she unwrapped and set down, too. The food meant something. Maybe she thought of it as a handout. A peace offering.

Or maybe it was just fucking food.

"Thanks for the food," I finally said, having mulled over the symbolism of it long enough. I leaned over and dished myself some of everything she'd brought. I caught her staring at the scars across my hands as I went.

Thin and wire-like, they wrapped around the tops and undersides of my hands, just under the knuckles. Some were deep and ragged, others nothing more than shiny white skin. The thin flap between my thumb and pointer finger was clipped into and misshapen.

"I don't know how I got them," I said. Olivia quickly looked away, suddenly finding her fried rice very interesting. "Sometimes I have dreams that show me where I got the other scars. Acid burns alongside my body. Cuts. Never these."

She gave me a consoling half-smile. "I'm sorry. It must

be very disturbing to see them and not know."

I accepted the remark and settled back to eat my food. We were quiet for a moment before I spoke. "I'd offer you something to drink, but your options are tap water or whatever dredges of hard alcohol I have left."

"That's okay," she said and reached into her endless purse again. "I have my water bottle."

"Of course you do."

She swallowed a bite of noodle and frowned. "Why do you have to do that, Ethan?"

"What?"

"It's like you can only be nice for a split second, then you have to do something to cancel it out."

Olivia had a point. There was a split moment right as I said something and immediately after where I thought, Ethan, what the fuck did you say that for? Like with Trisha. That's how my brain worked. It was going to take years to reverse the habit, which required a profound desire to fix it to begin with.

I decided to try being honest with Olivia. After another few bites of sweet and sour pork, I set my plate on my lap and looked her in the eyes. "This is the way I am because it protects me. If I'm mean and never let anyone get to me, I'm safe."

There was something in her perfect facade that shifted. Her eyes seemed less wide open and her mouth, for once, completely lost its perpetual uplifted corners. I felt like I was looking at a different person. A mirage, and if I looked away and back, it wouldn't be there any longer. So I kept staring. Waiting.

"You won't believe me, but I know what you mean."

Don't say something stupid. Don't be a jackass.

"How's that?"

She pushed food around her plate with a flimsy plastic fork, lost in thought. "You know commercials for anti-depressants?"

I didn't watch much TV, but I'd seen enough to truthfully nod.

"When you're watching them, your brain is happy. It sees these images of people enjoying their lives, taking control of their emotions. They're being creative, laughing, and playing around. Your brain likes it so much, it basically ignores the dialog over the commercial listing all the terrible side effects of the drug. If you stop for one second, close your eyes, and just listen, you realize that drug isn't the best thing in the world."

Olivia leaned back in her chair, shoving her plate of food forward. She glanced to the windowsill where a box of cigarettes rested on its side. She picked it up and turned it over in her hands. "I know it's cheesy, but my life feels like the images on those commercials. Yeah, it all looks good. Then when I stop looking and listen, it's a sham. You use substances and that asshole attitude to protect yourself. I protect myself by looking perfect when I'm anything but. This world loves a perfect girl. It overlooks and forgives a perfect girl. It doesn't care what it takes to maintain the facade, as long as it's there."

She smiled wide and put her sweetest expression on. It was a flawless mask.

"What's your story, then?" I tried to keep my voice level. Not accusatory. Just mild curiosity. I found that I really did want to know.

To my surprise and wayward pleasure, Olivia withdrew a cigarette from the box and put it to her lips. There were a dozen colored plastic lighters for her to choose from within arm's reach. She picked one with a dragon on it and lit the smoke with expert hands. She inhaled and blew it out through her nose.

I grinned at her before I could stop myself. This time, she smiled back. A real smile. A conspiratorial smile. This was our little secret.

"My mom and dad both come from money and power. Those two things destroy people. Dad never beat me, or my sister or mother. He did it to his employees instead; the live-in housekeepers, gardeners, nannies. He paid them huge sums of money to keep quiet and let him do it. Most of them were illegal immigrants and he threatened them with deportation if they talked."

My food was growing cold, but I'd lost interest in it. Learning about Olivia's past was like seeing the dark side of the moon. "Why didn't you or anyone say anything?"

She took a slow drag off the cigarette. "I didn't know until I was older. About sixteen. I knew *something* was wrong. There was a lot of tension in the house. Verbal fights. My mother had become addicted to anti-anxiety meds at that point. In a drug induced haze, after my sister left, she confided in me. Told me about the beatings, the rape. I suspected he might've killed some of them based on their sudden 'termination' but didn't know for sure. I was going to graduate early from high school and go to college. Escape all of it. I didn't have proof he was doing anything wrong. I was never hurt. Like my mom, I just let sleeping monsters lie."

"Fuck, that's heavy."

Startled by my remark, she laughed before getting serious again. "Yeah. Yeah, it is. All these years I've lived with this guilt that I kept my mouth shut. Much of my success in life is because of his money, his title. But it's dirty. Between you and me, what's been happening to me, I…It seems like karma. I'm in the same position now that those people were in. Trapped. I can't say anything or I'll lose everything. I feel like I deserve it."

There were tears in her eyes. I saw them now, shining in the dim light of the lamp by the folding table. Just enough to start smudging her eye makeup. I set my plate on the table and went into the kitchen where I found a glass, rinsed it with hot water, and poured her a bourbon. I brought the bottle back for myself and set the glass in front of her. It was the best I could do. The only thing I *knew* how to do. The amber liquid was comfort.

"Don't ever say that, Olivia. Never. You were wrong not to do something about it, but that in no way means you deserve what's happening to you. Life isn't an eye for an eye, no matter how badly we want it to be."

She took the bourbon and tossed it back. Between that and the cigarettes, I could only guess she had darker parts of her life that she kept well hidden.

After her drink settled, her words became bolder. "I want it to be an eye for an eye. I want to destroy whoever is doing this to me. It goes against my pacifist beliefs, so obviously I'm conflicted." She smiled at me. "Thank you for saying that. I've never told anyone this, but you already know my other darkest secret. What's one more to add?"

"Your dad seems like a monster. I'll add that."

The spurn pleased her. "He's terrible. I hate it, but I'm sure my preoccupation with image comes from him. I learned to look prepped and pretty on the outside while everything was rotten inside. Just like him. That's also why this gala for the mayor is so important to me. I landed this job all on my own. A lot of my work comes from referrals from my dad. He holds it over me, like somehow I owe him my life for it. But the mayor? That's all me."

"If you know you get it from your dad, that it isn't your choice, why do you stay that way?"

"The idea of changing is easy." Olivia sighed. "Doing it is another story. It's a defense mechanism I had to create to survive my family. Only, my brain decided to keep it up once things were safe again and I didn't need it. It's so ingrained it's a part of me now. There's nothing I can do to change at this point."

Straight from the fucking self-help books. I wondered if she'd read the same ones I had or if she simply had a higher level of human understanding than me. I hoped it was the former.

"Take happiness where you can get it, I guess. Good for you on the mayor," I said honestly. "I don't know shit about galas, but I'm sure you'll do great."

Our conversation naturally died as we returned to the food. I ate everything on my plate and took more after Olivia said she was finished. Between the couple shots of booze and food, and the remnants of the downer, I was feeling good. Olivia described the place she got the food from. I told her a bit about Donovan and his stripper girlfriend. How Trisha offered me a deal.

"Can you trust her?" she asked.

"I don't know. If 'never trust a stripper' isn't a common saying, it should be. I've never met one that did right by me. They're in it for themselves. Trisha used to be my... well, she was amazing. Trustworthy. Not anymore."

"Way to stereotype. I would still pursue it. When she calls, see where it goes. If she really is sleeping with a man who is supplying Whiteout, that could end our hunt."

I still had a bad feeling about it, but I promised Olivia I'd follow up. The problem was, I was waiting on Trisha. She might call tonight, but she might not for weeks. We could have our answers before she ever even made a move.

Once the food was gone and we'd settled, eventually we turned to D.P.

"What else did you find out?" I asked her.

"D.P., which stands for Draper-Paulinsky by the way, owned a building in south Seattle. I did a search on it and it's been condemned. Looks like after the bank seized it, they couldn't sell it. The recession was in full swing at that point."

She told me the exact address of the building. "I used to deal in that area. It's a shithole. Tons of addicts live around there. Big abandoned industrial areas are the perfect place for people to squat."

"We have to go," Olivia said. "There could be old paperwork or files on where the drug was manufactured. There must be something. It could really move us forward on this."

I'd spent enough time trying to convince myself. I knew what she was doing. Getting herself pumped up in the face of something scary. People used words as a way of building armor around them and numbing their brain. I'd seen teenagers do it more times than I could count.

It usually plays out the same way. One of the teenagers starts to approach, but aborts and returns to the flock. They huddle together for a bit. I wait. I know they will find the courage soon enough. They talk, and finally one of them makes it all the way to me. Once it took over an hour before one of the kids in a group grew the balls to make the deal. For a tiny amount of weed. How silly.

"I never said we weren't going. I'll bring my gun. As long as we don't hassle anyone and make ourselves look small, we'll be okay."

"You have a gun?"

I diverted my attention from the mold pattern on the wall directly across from me to give her an amused look.

"What? Does it really surprise you?"

She paused before laughing. "No. I guess it doesn't."

"So back to D.P. We go to the building, rummage around and see what we can find. The building has been condemned for some time, so don't get your hopes up," I said. "People tend to burn, vandalize, or destroy the stuff in those places."

"Okay. We—"

Olivia's phone rang. Instead of a hip song, it was a regular beeping noise. She seemed so young to me—even though she was likely my own age—that I expected things like that from her. Every time I was proved wrong, I felt a tiny flush of embarrassment. I was good at knowing people. Their weaknesses, their type. I had some of Olivia pegged, but there was another part I'd only skimmed the surface of.

"I've gotta take this, Ethan. Hold on." She swiped the phone and stood, walking ten feet into the kitchen. Her voice was hushed, but there was nowhere in the studio apartment that offered privacy.

The conversation was urgent. Olivia kept asking questions like who? Where? How? In the space of the five minute call, she must've asked 'are you gonna be okay' ten times. She hung up and returned to the table, but something had changed.

"That was my friend Kaylee's mother. Kaylee had a nervous breakdown a few days ago while shopping. I wondered why I hadn't heard from her recently."

I shifted in my easy chair, letting my body sink further into its soft embrace. The moment Olivia left, I planned to polish off the bottle I brought and doze until morning. "That sucks. What time are you picking me up to check out D.P. then?"

Her lips pressed tightly together. "I think someone is using Whiteout on Kaylee."

Damn. Never a dull moment. I'd need a vacation once this was over. "How long have you thought that? Why are you telling me now?"

"She's confided in me about losing bouts of time over the past two month. But it happens a lot. At least once a week. Kaylee has some drinking issues and likes to party, so I credited it to that. I didn't make a connection until now. Her mother said she was getting supplies at Staples for work when she smelled something and then just lost it. She said Kaylee became hysterical, then passed out. She was at the hospital two days ago. They haven't heard from her since she got home and called them to tell them what happened."

It *was* suspicious. "You think she might've remembered

something? Or was coming off the drug?"

"Maybe something like that. Her mother wants me to go check on her. They're in Hawaii right now."

My evening plans came to an end before they even began. If Olivia's friend really had been suffering from a Whiteout-induced breakdown, she could be violent. She might hurt Olivia or herself. I took a deep breath and heaved myself out of the chair, scanning the apartment for my shoes and jacket.

"Ethan, you don't need to come. I'm just going to swing by her house. I'll see how she is and call you."

I found my jacket slung over the edge of the bed. I pulled the thing on before starting the search for my shoes. "There was a street kid who panicked after coming off it and accidentally killed someone. If she's been drugged as many times as you suspect, she could be dangerous."

Still, Olivia wasn't convinced. She had the tips of her fingers against her temple, her stare vacant in front of her. It seemed like she was running through the options. The sooner she realized there weren't any, the better.

"She can't see me with you," Olivia finally said. "Let me go inside and you can wait just outside the door. I have a key. If you hear anything odd you can come in, okay?"

That was as close as I was going to get. "Deal. Come on, let's go."

Olivia grabbed her purse and headed out of the apartment. As I turned to lock the door, I stopped. "I forgot a lighter."

She gave an exasperated sigh. "I'll go get the car. Meet me out front."

I waited until she'd cleared the stairs by the elevator

before I got my gun. I always carried a pocket knife, but we had no idea what we were facing. I wasn't going to get caught without some firepower.

CHAPTER 13

The condo was in a nice part of Queen Anne. Unlike most places, it looked as good in full daylight as it did in the pretty dying sunlight. Orange faded into dark purple and blue above as the sun set. Streetlights were just flickering on as we drove in the Immaculate Car to Kaylee's. Traffic from a Sounders game reached in every direction from Seattle proper.

Using her voice command, Olivia kept telling the car to call Kaylee. It went to voice mail four times before she gave up.

I hated the feeling of urgency welling up inside of me, only to be mocked by the sluggish traffic. I tried to occupy myself by studying the myriad of gadgets and touch screens Olivia's car had to offer. I watched the alleged gas mileage estimate. Eventually that tired me. I stared at the faded denim on the tops of my thighs, the tear in the right knee of my jeans. My fingernails were dirty, the tips tobacco stained. In the Immaculate Car, I was aware of how I smelled and the semi-permanent scent I'd leave behind. Despite that, I still wanted a cigarette but knew there was no way Olivia would let that fly. Just like I doubted she'd approve of me bringing my gun.

The Glock resting in its holster on my side made me self-conscious. I never got used to it. Did she notice it right away when I slipped into the car? Would I need to use it?

Not that I was shy about using it. I had a few times before. While I wasn't sure if the men I shot died from their wounds, I'd fired knowing they might. Whether my own life was at risk or because I had no choice, I knew I could open fire when I needed to. I hoped I wouldn't have to around Olivia; if she got caught in the crossfire, I'd blame myself.

The thought hit me hard. My concern for Olivia's wellbeing crept up on me. She was the first person I'd met who had been drugged with Whiteout. I couldn't count Stromberg or the woman Skid brought me. I didn't know them. Olivia was the only one who knew even slightly what it was like to be me. On some level, she was interested in my wellbeing. She'd confided in me and depended on me. Yeah, she was high handed and got on my nerves. Who didn't?

"Earth to Ethan, we're here."

She parked the car in front of a modest condo. There was a small patch of grass for the yard, perfectly manicured. Big terracotta pots boasted Asiatic looking plants. I looked up and down the street; the whole block was made up of buildings just like it. Slightly different colors and trim, but the same.

Behind large double paned windows was blackness. There was a white Jetta in the driveway. A knot began to form inside my gut. There was something wrong. That primitive, superstitious part of me growled at the building. "I'm going in with you."

My voice sounded loud in the car. I turned to face Olivia, whose gaze was fixed on the condo. Her face was bathed in the soft white glow of the touch pads and gauges on her dashboard. She said nothing, but nodded then exited the car.

As we walked, Olivia searched her purse for the key. She took her time and I wondered if she was more frightened than I thought. Even as we stood on the doorstep—tall frosted windows making the inside a foreboding mass—she moved slowly.

"Should I ring first?"

"If you want to," I answered.

She pressed the buzzer. I heard it playing inside, a muted jingle. I thought I heard shuffling, but it lasted only a second. No lights turned on. Olivia hit the buzzer again and waited. As her hand went up a third time, I stopped her. Her breath was ragged. She moved to unlock the door.

"There's an alarm system. I need to disarm it before you come in." She paused. Anxiety flashed in her eyes. "Assuming it's even on."

It was. The second Olivia unlocked and opened the door, it omitted even beeps as it waited for the code to be entered. It was loud and conspicuous, doing nothing to dispel the sense of unease that kept building inside me. Olivia's fingers flew across the console just inside the doorway. When the beeping stopped, it was still pounding in my ears.

Olivia was quick to turn on the light to the entryway, revealing hardwood floors that looked almost scrubbed white, and medium gray walls. The condo was surprisingly modern. To our right was a flight of steps with a metal railing leading upwards. What I guessed was a coat closet across from the front door. The living room, kitchen, and dining room were one space joined by large arched doorways. I followed Olivia as she systematically walked through the first story flicking on each lamp and light switch available.

"Kaylee?" Her voice cracked. She coughed and said again, louder, "Kaylee, are you home?"

No response. She tried a third time.

The only sign of human interference was in the kitchen. Two mugs of tea on the counter. I pressed the back of my hand on one of the mugs. It was cold. An opened package of Fig Newton cookies sat beside it. There were two barstools pushed away from the counter. Someone other than Kaylee had been here.

Since the alarm was on, and the door locked, they probably still were.

"Does she have a roommate?" I asked.

Olivia shook her head. "Not that I know of. She never mentio—Ethan, what's wrong?"

If my nerves were buzzing before, they were on overdrive now. When I turned to face the living room, from where I stood, I noticed the front door was open. We shut it. I knew we did.

I withdrew the Glock and chambered a round. Olivia stared at me, her mouth agape. I moved around her to check the front door. The door across from it was indeed a coat closet and it was open, too. The jackets were pushed to one side.

Fuck. Someone had been hiding.

I lowered the Glock to my side and ran outside, scanning the street for movement. Nothing. Not a single person in sight. I couldn't tell if a car had left since we came in, although I figured I would've heard someone peel out.

"Ethan?" Olivia stood in the doorway, her arms

wrapped around herself.

"Check up the street," I told her. "Don't go far."

If anyone saw me with the gun out, they'd call the cops. I shoved the gun in my waistband and jogged down the street opposite of Olivia. For a moment I considered telling her to stay put, but we needed to cover ground and there was no reason why she couldn't help. Whoever had been in the house, they couldn't have made it far.

I checked behind cars and looked down the narrow space between condos. After a block, I called Olivia's cell. She picked up on the first ring.

"See anyone?"

"No." She sounded flustered. "I'm going back to Kaylee's."

"Okay. Meet you there."

I walked back to the house, eyes still open for anyone suspicious. It was strange being the one looking for someone out of place. Normally I was the one trying to blend in.

Olivia stood on the steps to Kaylee's. She hadn't gone far from the condo. Now *there* was a suspicious character. Olivia's head snapped back and forth as she watched the street. Her right foot tapped on the ground and she couldn't find anywhere to put her hands.

"Get in. You look like a criminal," I said.

She didn't move. "Should we…Are you sure we should go back in?"

The condo was less ominous now that the lights were on in the first story. I had my gun. And I was a hell of a lot more interested in checking out the place. "People don't bolt like that for nothing. Come on."

She stepped aside and gestured for me to lead the way.

Upstairs was the only place unsearched. I closed and locked the front door behind me and pulled out the Glock. I went to the staircase and began my ascent. The railing shuddered with every step I took. Then, halfway up, I smelled it. You only needed to smell a dead body once and it was cataloged in your memory forever. It was earthy, putrid, and metallic all in one.

My grip tightened as I reached the top. The light from downstairs stretched to the top hallway which extended right into a bathroom, and left where there were two shut doors. I scanned the walls and spotted a light switch directly across from me. My hand snapped out and I turned it on.

The first thing I noticed was the smudges of blood on the light wood floor. They came towards me and stopped at a rug where someone must've wiped their feet before continuing.

While Olivia stood back, I searched the bathroom. No killers hiding behind shower curtains. I opened the next door and found an office. Also empty.

That left what must be a bedroom. The smell was stronger as I neared. I prepared myself for whoever—whatever—was behind the closed door.

There could've been a man waiting with an Uzi somewhere in the room, and I wouldn't have noticed. The first thing I saw was the woman's body on the bed, lit by the blue light of a TV mounted in the upper corner of the room.

She was naked, her left cheek pressed against the mattress. Her arms were yanked up at an awkward angle with each wrist tied to a bedpost. The bindings were so tight they'd drawn blood which dripped down her arms.

Every inch of her body was covered in words scrawled in marker.

Bitch. Slut. Tease.

Blood had poured from dozens of stab wounds from her shoulders down her legs, obscuring some of the writing. Her legs gaped open, everything between gored in a mess of slashes and stabs. The bedding had been stripped from the mattress, which was now soaked in blood around her body.

Some of the blood was brown and matte compared to the red closest to her, still wet and dark. Whatever happened to her, it took a while. Long enough for blood to dry.

I tore my gaze away, sickened, to finally check the room. Not that there was anyone there; they would've attacked me the moment I walked in. At the same time I chose to look away, Olivia came up behind me. I heard her gagging as she dashed into the bathroom and vomited.

It took everything I had not to do the same.

I squeezed my eyes shut. The question was stupid and I realized that even as I asked. "Are you okay?"

She didn't respond. I clenched my fists and took a deep breath, opened my eyes.

Next to the TV was a video camera on a tripod, a cord connecting the two together. I walked past it into the master bathroom where there was red smeared on the sink and counter. It looked as though someone had washed up. The blood was fresh. Had we interrupted our runner when we rang the doorbell? Obviously they hadn't expected company. They would've snuck downstairs and waited for the right moment to bolt.

When I turned to go back into the bed room, I had a

perfect view of Kaylee's face. The left side pressed into the mattress was blue and swollen. Then it hit me. I'd seen her before.

"Ethan?" Her voice was shaking. "I'm going to call 911."

I dashed from the bathroom, holstering my gun as I went. "No, Olivia. If they find me here, I'm going to jail. They have my prints from other crimes. I'm a known associate of Donovan's family."

Tears streamed down her ruddy face. Her lips were wet with saliva, her gaze was locked onto the massacred body of Kaylee. "I can't *not* call the police," she wailed. "Look at her! For God's sake, look at her! I can't do this. I can't—"

I walked in front of her, blocking her view of the body. "You don't have to do anything. Give me ten minutes to look around. I'll leave, you call the police."

"No! Whoever did this was just *here*. If we call the police now, they can canvas the streets."

"Olivia, they're long gone. Please. Please let me look around."

After a moment, she blinked slowly and nodded.

"There's something else."

"What?"

"I've seen Kaylee before."

"*What?*" Olivia's eyes focused on the room behind me. "When?"

Kaylee was the girl in the pink dress, the one who wanted the roofie. I explained what happened with as much detail as I could remember. "I don't remember what the guys who took her away looked like. It was dark and I split as soon as she freaked."

"Why didn't you call the police? That's abduction."

"Olivia, you know why I didn't. It's the same fucking reason I'm telling you not to call them now. Also, it wasn't my problem."

"Yeah? It is now." Without another word she left the room. I heard her going down the stairs, then quiet.

I could've handled that better, but Olivia stonewalling me wasn't productive either. My back to the scene, I let my mind race. When I met Kaylee, she came off Whiteout and flipped. The men dragged her away. Two days later she had another breakdown—which, I bet my life, was Whiteout related—and some point after that was murdered.

It was a silencing. The Melnikov family did it all the time; when someone put the family at risk, they were put down.

I had to deal with the task at hand and refocused. I tried to remember what I'd touched outside of the room. I found disinfectant wipes in the bathroom and systematically cleaned every surface and door knob I might've touched.

Then I turned my attention to the room. I turned the light on which worsened the horror of the scene. Now every detail was revealed in bright overhead light. I gave the mattress a wide berth, avoiding the blood saturated carpet, and went to the night stands. There was a spool of paracord and scissors. The scissors were bloodied. Closer to her now, I saw her side. Her breasts hung strangely off her chest. I looked at the scissors again and realized they'd been used to cut her up. I wondered if they'd been used to stab her everywhere else, too.

I wasn't sure what I was looking for. The police would collect evidence. They'd find prints I hadn't destroyed and might be able to find the killer. What good would that do me? Kaylee's killer getting justice was fine, but who knew how long it would take or if it would ever happen. I'd taken things into my own hands thus far. There was no point in giving up now.

When I surveyed the room again, my gaze fell on the video recorder. The most horrifying thing in the room. Someone murdered and violated Kaylee with vicious purpose, and had the forethought to bring a camera. I studied it. The camera was connected to the TV. The same blue screen on the TV showed on the LCD screen on the camera. Someone was either playing a video from the camera onto the TV, or displaying the footage they were recording.

A shudder ran through my body. What if the killer did it so Kaylee could see, in full, what he was doing to her?

I found the memory card compartment on the camera. It was open. The two spaces for cards were empty. I pulled open Kaylee's drawers and searched anywhere the killer might've stored them. Of course, I found nothing. He took the cards with him. But why not the camera? Was it an accident?

If there was anything to find, any clue, I wasn't going to find it. This was beyond my abilities. And I couldn't look away from Kaylee's body enough to really focus.

I retrieved another wipe and cleaned everything in the room I touched. Afterwards, I was confident there was no trace of me anywhere in the house. At least, nothing that would incriminate me.

The bathroom was still covered in blood. I saw handprints on the faucet and counter. I hadn't touched Kaylee or the mattress. The cops would surely get prints somewhere, despite what I'd cleaned up. I went back downstairs to find Olivia sitting ramrod straight on the couch, staring at everything and nothing all at once. She held a wireless home phone in her hand.

"I'm done. You can call now."

She had the phone up and to her ear in a split second. "I want to report a murder. 914 29th Street in Queen Anne. I can't give you my name. No. No, I'm not. I'll wait outside." Olivia placed the phone in its cradle on the end table beside the couch. "They're on their way. They said ten minutes. I said I'd wait in the car until they got here."

"Why didn't you give them your name?"

Her head hung low. She spit back the same reason I'd given her. "You know why. No one can know I've seen this. No one can put me back here, and not just because I don't want my name tied with it. What if whoever did this is the same one hurting me?"

"You're right," I agreed. Now that the cops had been called, I didn't have much time to clear the area. "Do you want me to wait somewhere nearby?"

"Wait. Please." She rubbed her neck and stood. "I don't know how I'll be after I talk to them, you know?"

I nodded. I understood. "I'll wait."

An hour later Olivia still hadn't called me. I hadn't heard any sirens. The night got cold and I sat huddled on a bench in a nice park about half a mile away from the condo. Christmas lights twinkled on most of the homes around me.

I was likely to get picked up for loitering if someone decided to report me. Thirty-something questionable male, chain smoking, alone in a park at night? Especially once they heard sirens in the neighborhood. That was grounds for calling the police as far as the population around here was concerned.

Olivia finally called me. I flipped open my phone. "What's up?"

"The police never came."

The knot that formed when we first arrived at Kaylee's had loosened. Now it got impossibly tighter, extending up into my heart, my throat. The police never came.

"Did you call again?"

"Yes," she said, her voice meek. "Twice. Both times they said someone was on their way. They kept asking me who I was but I didn't tell them. I don't think anyone is coming, Ethan."

"Fuck. That's impossible. They have to come."

"I know."

We were quiet. I spotted two dog walkers nearing me. Both wore expensive rain gear. Lo and behold, one sported trekking poles. Welcome to Seattle. I waited until they passed to continue talking, but realized I didn't have anything to say. Olivia was still on the other end, breathing softly.

"I'll come pick you up. Where are you?"

I described my route. She hung up after repeating the directions and I was alone again. It only took her minutes to drive over. I crossed the damp grass and quickly got in her car, tossing the remainder of my cigarette onto the sidewalk before closing the door. Olivia's face had dried, but her eyes looked puffy and her hair rumpled. The second the door closed she was driving.

"I'm going back. We'll park down the street so they won't see you," she assured me. "But I just need to wait a little longer. What if they show up and I'm not there?"

"They'll go in. After you calling them that many times and what you said happened, there's no way they won't investigate."

"I know. I just need to..."

"I get it," I cut her off, thinking of Skid's tent. "You have to see it for yourself."

When the squatters told me Skid was dead, I had to see his tent to know for certain he was gone. As much as you wanted to, it was hard to draw yourself away from something that causes you pain. Like picking at a scab, Olivia would mull over what she'd seen for years. I knew I would. Going back probably made her feel like she wasn't giving up.

She took a long route back to the condo, taking ten minutes to get back to the block by the building. She found a free spot on the side of the road and parked. Kaylee's house was six condos away from us, still dark with not a single car besides the Jetta in front of it.

We waited another hour. Neither of us spoke. I tried to breathe evenly to get my heart rate down and calm myself. Nothing worked. All I could think of was the body. The blood. The mess of flesh destroyed between her legs, the stabs and writing that marred her figure. Each time I brought the memory up it became more vivid.

I had a chance to help her back in the alley. I knew something was wrong. I did nothing.

"Ethan, look."

Her voice jolted me from the daze. A van had backed

into Kaylee's driveway. The logo for a local plumbing company was plastered on its side. One man got out of the passenger side and went to the front door. He rang the doorbell. Knocked.

Then walked right in. Minutes passed and he returned to the van. Four men got out and went into the condo, walking confidently with toolboxes and some duffel bags. They wore uniforms. They looked normal.

I knew about people like this, though I'd never seen them myself. I'd heard enough stories from Donovan to know they were a cleanup crew. Look like you belong, walk in, get the job done and leave. Later, if something went wrong and cops started asking questions, people might remember the plumbing van. It would lead to nothing.

"What are they doing?"

"They're cleaning up the scene."

"Where are the police?" She was exasperated. "How are these men here and not the police?"

The question hung in the air as the answer dawned on us both. Somewhere, someone with authority was involved in this. Olivia's call had been intercepted somehow, the call for help ignored. They must've been waiting for her to give up and leave before they came to clean up the mess. Someone's mess that they were protecting.

Olivia started the car and pulled out of her spot. The road was too narrow to turn and go the opposite direction, forcing us to drive past the condo. As we neared, I watched as the group of men brought unassuming equipment into the house. I wondered how they were going to break down the body. How they'd get all that blood out of the carpet, the mattress. If the killer would ever receive justice for what they'd done.

The killer.

I'd been searching for answers in the murder room. Then I realized we'd found the most important clue the moment we walked into the house.

CHAPTER 14

In mulling silence, Olivia drove back to my apartment. She circled the block twice for a parking spot, but was forced to go into a garage two blocks away. The greenish blue light overhead made her runny mascara and puffy eyes look even worse. She was on the edge of a breakdown. I knew it when I saw it because I rode that edge almost every day. I wanted to tell her she should just go home until she was feeling more stable. It didn't matter what I said; she was hell bent on talking about what we'd just seen before she left.

I was on the edge myself in that moment, though for once I was trying to be strong for another person. I wanted a benzo so bad I was feeling dizzy, my heart fluttering. It was in the front of my mind before anything else, even the memories of Kaylee now. I had some in the apartment in the new inventory Donovan gave me. Just two blocks over was a blissful knockout waiting to happen. Olivia didn't realize what I'd seen had hit me hard too. When I closed my eyes, I saw Kaylee's mutilated corpse right behind them, plastered to my eyelids. It would take a lot to put me under tonight.

"I know you're exhausted," I said, trying my hardest to keep any accusatory tone out of it. "I know it's hard, but we need to keep going. We're on to something."

"You know it's hard? How can you say that? My friend was just murdered. No, not murdered. Slaughtered. Abused.

And her remains are being ferried off to God knows where. The killer is never going to be brought to justice, just like I'll never find out who is hurting me."

"Calm down, Oli—"

"No! Don't tell me to calm down. This isn't a time to be calm."

Her tight grip on the steering wheel made her knuckles white. Her shoulders were lifted high towards her ears. Even though we were parked, the engine off, she was ready to peel out at any moment. Olivia wasn't going anywhere until we reached some kind of resolve. Fortunately, I did have one insight.

"I noticed something at the condo. It didn't seem like anything at the time, but now it does," I started. She relaxed her grip and faced me. There was too much hope in her eyes. Too much opportunity for disappointment. "When we walked in, the alarm was engaged."

"So? Whoever was in there could've forced her to engage the alarm before they killed her."

"Maybe. Or maybe they knew it already, like you. There were two mugs of tea on the counter. I'm not an expert host, but I'd imagine when someone visits you, you turn off the alarm and let them in. You don't reengage it when you have company. Not until they leave."

"I see what you're getting at," she said, dismayed.

"Someone she knew killed her," I finished. "She knew them, invited them in. Had tea. There was no sign of a struggle downstairs. Either they drugged her downstairs and took her up, or she went willingly."

"What about the police?"

"What about them?"

"Shouldn't we report the murder?"

"You're fucking kidding me. After what just happened, you still think the police will help?"

I needed a cigarette and wasn't going to hold off any longer. I opened the car door and squeezed between the narrow space separating the Immaculate Car and a giant SUV. I leaned on the back of the Immaculate Car. A moment later Olivia was beside me. Her energy had changed and she'd become more agitated than shocked.

"It would be a miracle if we could carry on a conversation without you having to smoke or drink or do whatever it is you do."

I tapped the cigarette box against my wrist, then pulled one out to light. The nicotine soothed my lungs. My shaking hands calmed down a little. I blew smoke upward towards the ceiling and didn't speak until it dissolved.

"The police are in on this, Olivia. That should be pretty damn obvious. Whoever is behind it, their reach goes far and wide. You called 911 over and over, and did anyone ever come? No. When you called 911, they didn't inform the police. And when someone *did* come it was to clean up the evidence. The killer could've called the cleanup crew, but no matter what, this proves whatever is happening goes beyond any normal gang around here. This is bigger."

"So you're saying some kingpin intercepted my 911 call, and just didn't pass my message onto the police?" She threw her hands up in the air and laughed. "That's ridiculous!"

"Do you have any other way of explaining it? It's simple. The operators are dirty. They're told to flag any calls from you, or to do with Kaylee, or that address. They tell you help is coming, but it isn't because they never passed it on."

"There has to be a reason. How could someone pay off *every* operator? What about this: I left, and maybe the cops came right after."

My skin broke into a cold sweat. An acidic taste bubbled in my throat as my stomach threatened to seize. I'd been telling Olivia to calm down when I was pretty fucked up myself. My 911 theory was a little insane. Now that I'd sat on it, I saw that. In the heat of the moment I got ahead of myself.

"The police didn't come. We waited long enough and they were no-shows. I will admit it would require a lot for all the operators to be bought," I said. "There's other possibilities. You called from Kaylee's home phone. It could've been tapped. Taps are easy, Donovan's family does them all the time. You might not have called 911 at all."

She picked at the hem of her jacket. Finally, she nodded. "That seems possible."

Satisfied with myself, I tapped ash onto the ground and took another long drag to finish the smoke off. "And the known person thing, too. The person that used Whiteout on Kaylee killed her, too."

"Possibly."

I groaned. The tension between us doubled.

"Why are you denying this? You're smarter than this. You know the people who are slipping you Whiteout must be people you know. People who know girls like Kaylee enough to know their alarm codes and have tea with them before killing them."

"We don't know for certain who is drugging me. Besides, that isn't the issue right now. The issue is that my friend was murdered and we're not doing anything about it."

"If you care so much, call from your phone right now. See if you get the actual police. That cleanup will take hours. Plenty of time."

"I can't."

"Call from a fucking payphone then. You have no excuse right now."

I was at wits' end with her. Thus far Olivia had been rational and eager to find out who was behind the Whiteout. Now she was slipping away, denying what was right in front of her. Knowing it was likely someone who knew Kaylee put me one step closer to finding out who was supplying Whiteout. I needed to work my way up the ladder, from users to dealers to suppliers to creators, and eventually I'd get my answers. Olivia was between me and the best way up.

"Why are you doing this? We're finally onto something useful and you're trying to backtrack. Don't you want to find out who's been drugging you? Don't you want all this to end?"

Olivia wrapped her arms around herself and hugged tightly. Her chin was tilted downward, her gaze focused on the filthy concrete ground. "Not if it means I could get killed."

"You could get killed anyway. You have no idea what they do to you while you're on Whiteout. You could be next. Wouldn't you rather know the complete truth than live every day knowing it will happen again? That you're in danger?"

"It isn't that easy, Ethan! To admit that people I trusted,

that I've worked with and am friends with, could be violating me. My career is at stake. My life, *everything*. I did want to know who's doing this, but after I saw Kaylee lying there I realized how dangerous this is. I'm a fucking fundraiser coordinator! I'm not a detective. I'm not Rambo. This is too dangerous." She ran her hands through her hair, tugged the ends and sighed. "I can just see myself now. Everyone would feel sorry for me, tsk-tsk me. They'd talk to me but never work with me. I can escape this. I'll just move. I'll move and start somewhere far away from Seattle."

"Fine. If you're out, at least tell me people who'd know Kaylee's alarm code."

Olivia shook her head. She turned to get back into the car. I grabbed her shoulder and jerked her backwards. She inhaled sharply, turned, then pushed my chest hard enough to make me stumble back. "What are you going to do, Ethan? Beat it out of me? I should've figured that's what someone like you would do."

"Yeah? I should've figured *this* is what *you'd* do. I had you pegged from the moment I saw you at my doorstep. Privileged girl who thinks it's fun to take a break from her happy, rich life to try and solve a mystery. Then when things get serious, she runs." I closed the space between us, using the extra inches I had on her to try and intimidate. "I can't run, Olivia. This is my fucking life. You barge in here bringing up something I've worked for years to ignore and now want to drop it like it's nothing?"

"You can run. You *have* been running you hypocrite! Did you ever do what I told you to? Did you ever search the missing persons database for yourself? Why is it that my life is the one we put in the most danger to find out what's happening. Why can't you look at *your* life to help us figure this out?"

"Don't try that. You know I'm not doing anything that involves putting me near the police. In fact, I'm still kind of hazy on how you found out where I lived or found my blog. That blog was from seven years ago and you magically stumble upon it?"

Olivia fidgeted. I hit something. I wasn't sure what, but I was getting warmer. "You're not telling me something. I don't know what it is, but you're not being honest with me. You're all over the place with me. You could be doing all of this on your own. That whole 'I'm too afraid to do it on my own' story is bullshit. You're perfectly capable of doing all this on your own. Why me, Olivia?"

She turned her back on me and opened the trunk of her car. It was almost empty, save for an emergency bag and a small file carrier. Olivia opened it and pulled out a thin manila envelope. She tossed it on the ground at my feet, not unlike the first time we met. I crouched down and snatched it up, tearing open the top. Inside were two photocopied pages. On the top was a photo of a young man. The name on the right said William Grigg.

"You looked a lot better when you were young. How old were you then? Probably just about nineteen. Do you have any idea how easy it was to get these? I went to the police station and asked to see old missing persons files from the years you were gone. They didn't care once I told them who I was and how I was working on an outreach program. Advantages to being a privileged girl. I spent hours poring over them. Then I found you. It was so easy. There's your social security number, your parents' names, every-fucking-thing." Olivia slammed the trunk closed, her gaze locked on me. "I wanted you to do it yourself. I figured it would be good for you to get to a point where you were ready for it. But since we're trying to force each other to do things we don't want to, there you go Ethan. Sorry; *William*."

Olivia walked to the driver's side. This time I didn't stop her. I was still in shock by the slips of paper telling me who I was, resting in my hands so casually. I couldn't believe she'd had them all this time. That she knew who I really was. She flung open the door, grazing the car next to her. She didn't care.

Whatever suspicions I had retreated to the back of my mind. Olivia wasn't telling me something, but with my true identity staring back at me, I didn't give a fuck about her motives anymore.

"Don't think I didn't see what our relationship was. From the very beginning I knew you didn't care about me or what's happening to me." Olivia said. "You're in this for yourself. I was okay with it because I'm in this for myself, too. But I'm more afraid than I've ever been and I need a break. I need time to figure this out. Like you said, we both need to take a break then come back to this."

"Oh, so now that's a good idea? You were fucking pissed when I suggested it before."

"I know," she said. "Now I've thought about it and I believe you're right."

For a moment, we looked at each other, neither saying a word. If Olivia was waiting for me to say something, to stop her, to keep badgering her, she was out of luck. I was angry she'd done this without my permission. That she'd thrown the secret at me just now, to make me feel bad.

I slid the papers back into the envelope and folded it, neatly tucking it in my jacket pocket. Olivia shook her head, still quiet, and got into the Immaculate Car. It barely made a noise as the engine turned over and she pulled out. She didn't look behind once as she left the parking garage.

My mouth was dry. I was more aware than usual of the ashy taste in my mouth from the cigarettes. A headache was brewing, induced from the argument, the terrible parking garage lights, and every other little fucking detail. I felt alone in the garage, not just physically. Olivia was gone. Skid was gone. All I had now was the darkness staring back at me, and now it had a name.

CHAPTER 15

There she is again, the redhead. We're friends, in this hell together. Today she has bandages on both crooks of her elbows. They were taking blood. Or putting something back in.

We sit in the cafeteria. The windows are barred with wire mesh outside. There aren't many of us now, but there's still her. The girl is pretty and smiles at me, tells me it was just the usual. She sits stiffly in the metal chair. We will be out of here soon, she says. We'll be better. We can restart.

I don't tell her we've been here much longer than she thinks, though I'm not sure how long. We're not going to get the money they promised us. We're not feeling any better. They're hurting us. We didn't sign up for this.

The shadowy tendrils of dread spread throughout my body as I realize we have been here for a very long time. Lights dim around me and I can't breathe. There's something in the air, it's making me tired. The girl's head is rolling around as though she is stunned, until finally she slumps forward and hits her head on the table. When I lift her up by the hair, she is a blond with a different face. I know this woman. I know her.

A man in a yellow hazmat suit with a plastic shield instead of a face is painting acid onto my body. It is burning. I picture it eating through my muscles, my organs, my bones. The acid will melt me. He tells me to focus on the pain. Is it *familiar? How badly do I hurt? On a scale of 1-10, 10 being you want to kill yourself.*

Yes, I'd like to kill myself. I want to die.

When he's done, he gives me an orange bottle of pills. They will make me feel better when I wake up. Take them whenever I hurt. When I wake up.

But I am *awake? Aren't I?*

I lie on my stomach, head turned to face the wall, remembering the dream. The sheets were damp from my breath, my drool. My body warm and tingly from the benzo and bourbon. I didn't want to move. It was easier to stay there than do anything. Anything at all.

Since I woke up on Alki beach, I'd had the dreams. It didn't take long before I realized they were fragments of memories from whatever happened to me. None of them ever made much sense. I used to think there were clues in them. That I'd see the face of a doctor and find him in real life, get answers. That the redhead was my lover, or at least some hallucination I made up to keep me happy. The only thing truly real in the dreams was the memory of the pain and suffering I underwent. For seven years I thought the dreams were the worst part of my life. Now I had something new competing for the title. The agony I felt that I'd pushed the only person away who wanted to help me. Sure, I didn't know *why* she was hell-bent on helping me. But she was.

It had been two days since Olivia gave me the folder with my alleged true identity. I had the content of the two pages memorized. My name was William Grigg, age twenty-nine. I was reported missing by my parents seven months after I would've gone into the Whiteout trials. They said I voluntarily admitted myself into a trial for a new drug that helps addiction rehabilitation that was to last six months during which they could have no contact with me. Seven months later when I didn't return, my parents started asking the pharmaceutical company what happened. They were informed that I voluntarily and suddenly removed myself from the program. My parents tried to initiate a lawsuit against the company, but I was an adult when I admitted myself. All participants retained the right to leave the trial. They didn't break their end of the agreement.

The second page had a log of each time my parents inquired about the case. They did so twice a month for two years after their initial report. Then they stopped. I wanted to be angry at them; why did they stop looking? Why couldn't they find me? A tiny voice kept reminding me that they *did* look. They *did* try. God only knows where I was while they were looking. Probably somewhere they'd never find me.

Much to my surprise, reading about William Grigg, my old self, wasn't as hard as I thought it would be. William wasn't me; not anymore. It felt like I was reading about a different person all together. I mostly took the information objectively. Now I knew my real name. I knew where I was born, my birthday.

Olivia was right. I knew she was. I'd been running from this. While I still believed her path would lead us to answers faster, investigating myself was for my own good. It's what I promised myself I'd do after Skid died. It would've made him proud. Plus I had a feeling I'd be on Olivia's bad side for a long time—fuck, maybe forever—and decided I'd use the time to discover my old self.

But first, that meant getting out of bed. Not an easy feat. I'd been lying there for four or five hours since I woke up. I heard the familiar noises of the workday ending. Traffic, honking, the buses' brakes squealing. People walking the streets. The library was going to close in a few hours. If I was going to go do the credit check Olivia carried on about, it had to be soon.

I took a deep breath and pushed myself up into a cross legged position. My head swam, and my vision dimmed. After a second, I reoriented. The mess from the Chinese takeout was still on the table. The studio smelled like soy sauce. With every ounce of energy I had, I swung my legs off the bed and walked to the bathroom to relieve myself, grab a shower, and swallow an Adderall.

My hope of the shower waking me up was futile. Instead I felt more relaxed. Hot water beat down on my skin, massaging and soothing me. I kept at it until the hot water ran out. To combat the malaise, I went to my coffee maker and got it brewing while I found clothes and shoes.

I drank the pot of coffee by the window facing the street so I could watch the people go by. Dinner consisted of a handful of stale fortune cookies to keep my energy up. They tasted like cardboard but were sweet and went well with the coffee. The stimulants started to kick in and I finally felt like I could be awake long enough to get the library work done and maybe sell some of Donovan's inventory.

Shit. Donovan. He'd been calling on the hour again. The man liked to micromanage, even worse now since I had the Whiteout to push. I gulped down the remaining coffee and set out on the short walk to the library.

It was cold outside with icy rain that wanted to be snow

but was thwarted by the nearby sea. The hem of my jeans was soaked by the time I got to the giant Seattle public library. I wasn't the worst off in the area. Homeless congregated inside and out of the library. I recognized some of them. They gave me knowing looks and nods.

I waited twenty minutes before a computer freed up and typed in my password and library card number by memory. After searching a few options, I found a credit check website that seemed adequate. I typed William Grigg's social security number and other information in and hit enter.

Olivia was right. Before me was my living history. There were two locations. The first was my parents' house which I learned was in SeaTac. There was a huge gap of time between then and an apartment in Ballard. After that, there was nothing.

For what it's worth, my credit score was terrible.

I found a piece of scrap paper by the printers and wrote down the address, then searched for it in Google maps. Nothing stuck out. The location meant nothing to me. I dug further and found the name of the apartment complex and searched that specifically.

There was an official website, some bad reviews. Management never addressed an ant problem in building C, lights were never replaced in the parking lots. A sister apartment building farther north popped up in the search.

And an article. It was archived on a local news website. I opened the link. In huge black type was the headline, *Promising music student commits suicide at Ballard Heights.* The article didn't have many details, but it seemed like a straight forward suicide. A young man named Andrew

Cole hung himself. His roommate had moved out shortly before the death which was hypothesized to have increased Andrew's feelings of depression and anxiety.

I scrolled past the article and found a video of the news channel segment on it. I hadn't brought headphones but I clicked the play button anyway. A pop-up offered subtitles which I accepted. A demure woman stood in front of an apartment complex. It was classic grayish Washington weather. Behind her an apartment was closed off with yellow crime scene tape. She repeated the same information that was in the article.

I paused the video. One thing it had that the article didn't was a perfect shot of Andrew's apartment. 1B. That number, 1B, was the apartment I lived in. For a brief moment I thought it could be a coincidence, then I double checked my living history dates. I lived in 1B when Andrew killed himself.

"Oh fuck." Beside me a middle-aged man scowled at my curse. I glared back until he finally looked away.

I hit play again to finish out the remaining thirty seconds of video. An older couple came on screen. The text on the bottom said they were Lenora and Richard Cole, Andrew's parents. They spoke about the tragedy of their son's death and how they would just like to mourn in peace.

Sure. That's why they agreed to a news segment; not because they wanted to mourn in peace, but because they wanted their twenty seconds of run time.

I typed their names in Google and spent the next twenty minutes scouring the internet for anything. She had a Facebook account that was private. Eventually I found a church blog that had an old post for an evening social hosted by the Coles. Lenora's number was at the bottom, asking for members to call with what they'd bring to the event.

It would be surreal to call these people out of the blue and ask if they knew anything about a guy named William Grigg. Fuck, what else was I supposed to do? I felt compelled to contact them. If they had nothing, fine. It wasn't a setback seeing that this was a shot in the dark. If I *had* been the roommate, they might tell me something useful about myself. I jotted down the number with plans to call after I left the library.

My fingers hovered over the keyboard. I wanted to search my parents' name, but something held me back. After this many years, they'd moved on. Why wouldn't they? I willingly submitted myself to tests for drug rehabilitation. I'd been a drug addict. That meant I caused them pain. They'd been living their lives without me, probably happier. Who was I to waltz in, the clusterfuck of problems I am, and put myself in their lives? I was still a mess, still addicted to drugs, and would still be a problem.

The self-help books would tell me I'm worth it. That it was low self-esteem making me think I didn't deserve happiness or second chances. Fucking self-help books. The evidence was always stacked against them.

Screw it. It didn't do anyone any harm for me to just look. I typed in my mother's name. There were plenty of Rachel Griggs. Even taking into account she'd look older than in my memories, none of the work or social profiles were her. My search for my father, Samuel, yielded the same results. I added words like 'death' and 'obituary' as search terms.

Nothing.

Disappointed, I logged off my library account and went outside. A few men I saw earlier approached me for some oxy, which I obliged once we found a more discreet spot. I tried pushing some bennies on them, but they weren't interested. If I really wanted to sell all my stock quickly, I'd go to the overpass. If the sea of tents was there, I'd have my inventory gone in a heartbeat. Not for optimal price, but at least it would be gone.

First, the phone call. I got my clamshell piece of shit cell out and typed in Andrew's parents' number. On the third ring, nerves almost got the best of me. Then a soft woman's voice came on the line and I knew I had to follow through.

"Hello?"

"Hi, is this Mrs. Cole?"

Hesitance on the other end. "Yes, who is this?"

"My name is Donovan Holloway." I smashed the first two names together that I could think of. "I went to school with your son Andrew."

"Oh, I see. You know, Andrew…"

"I know. I'm sorry to bring up painful memories. That's why I'm calling though." I took a breath. My brain was on autopilot trying to find an excuse. I should've thought about it more before calling. "Me and a few others wanted to do a memorial for him."

"A memorial? It's nearing nine years since he died."

Shit. "Yes. This is for next year. Ten years is the right time for a memorial we thought. We've been thinking about it a lot."

On the other line, she sighed. She sounded relived. "Andrew didn't have too many friends. I'm sure he would be so happy to know people still have him in mind after all these years. What is it you need from me? Photos and such?"

"Photos would be great. I was hoping to get a few words from you about your son, things like that." The words came out before I really thought about what I was doing.

"That's lovely. You can come over whenever you like. We're retired so not much to do but haunt the house." She laughed. "Can you take down our address?"

I didn't have a pen, but told her to go ahead. They lived in Mt. Vernon. I had no clue where it was, but told her I'd be there tomorrow sometime in the afternoon. She gave me a pleasant goodbye and hung up.

The self-help books would be proud of this. They had to give me a little credit. I was actively looking for answers, seeking my true self. Yeah, I was doing it in a less than impeccable way. Something was better than nothing.

The library was still open. I returned and waited for a computer again, then found directions to Mt. Vernon. It was a two hour bus ride north. I wrote the directions down too, taking some level of pride in my collection of notes, and headed to the overpass. Tomorrow would be an all-day affair.

I thought of Olivia's Immaculate Car and how the trip would probably be cut in half if we drove together. Then I remembered she thought I was a lazy fuck-up. That, not for the first time in my life, I'd made a bad fucking decision.

With the drugs weighing heavily in my pocket, I walked up the hills to the overpass to help other people keep making their bad fucking decisions.

CHAPTER 16

There was no such thing as a good bus ride. It can be mediocre, bad, dangerous, smelly, or neutral. Once, I'd almost been stabbed. I'd seen every kind of bodily fluid known to man excreted, spewed, or released on the bus. Neutral was definitely as close as you can get to a good bus ride. That morning on the way to Mt. Vernon, I discovered another type; agonizingly boring.

The first hour of the journey was on I-5, a bland stretch of freeway that passed dozens of cities. There were two other people on the bus the entire time I was there, which killed my chance of people watching. One was an Asian kid glued to a tablet, the other an old bearded man who was passed out drunk or dead.

Traffic was in reverse, delivering all the worker bees to city centers for the day. When I finally arrived at the Everett transit station, I waited a half hour before my next bus came. No city I'd ever been to was like Seattle, where all you had to do was turn your head an inch to spot a crazy squatter, a punk, or some other character.

Everett was quiet and dull. It was close to the water and I heard seagulls cawing overhead. It made me turn inward to my thoughts which was never a good thing. Six cigarettes later, by the time the second bus arrived, I was grateful just to move ten feet onto the bus.

At least the second leg had some scenery. I didn't leave

Seattle often. There was no reason. Now I was reminded of the beauty Washington had to offer. As I left the gray, flat city the scenery turned to lush forest and grasslands. I let my forehead rest against the window, rubbing the humidity off it every so often, and watched it pass by. This area was definitely the kind of place someone would retire to. Remote, pretty. Quiet.

The bus dropped me off in the center of Mt. Vernon. I walked twenty minutes to the Cole's house. During that time I fussed over the shoes I chose, my teeth, my smoke laden clothing. What if they realized I was a fake? I chose my cleanest pair of dark jeans, a plain gray shirt, and brown leather jacket Donovan gave me that had always been slightly too small. I looked presentable. Like everyone else. Sort of normal was the best I could do.

They lived in a small one story house in a retirement community. Despite it being winter, their lawn was perfectly kept. A flashy blue picket fence enclosed their yard, with a hand painted sign proclaiming 'Welcome' hanging off the gate. Red and white Christmas lights were woven into the fence. Dozens of little Dutch girl statues lined the walkway to the door. I looked for signs of a dog and saw none. I unlatched the gate and entered.

During the bus ride, I'd worked out more details of my back story. I was confident I could make this work.

A much older version of the woman I saw on the video opened the door before I even rang the bell. Lenora Cole was willowy and soft, her white hair back in a low bun at her neck. She wore a button up dress, tights, and slippers, like she'd teleported from the late 1950s to here. Her eyes, a clear but watery blue with droopy eyelids, met mine and she smiled.

One of those fragmented memories I had from my childhood came up. It was my own grandmother on her deathbed. Some incurable disease was eating away at her. I don't know if anyone told me what it was. I'd been ten, maybe eleven. I was angry that my parents brought me to see her. That would be how I saw her from then on in my mind; an ashen face, muscles and skin sitting too close to her bones. Now, almost two decades later, it was the only memory I had of her.

"Donovan, it's so great to meet you. Please come in." She stepped aside and invited me into her home.

I took a deep breath and smiled back before entering, letting the thought of my grandma drift away. I tried to remember how Olivia acted when we first encountered Brian. I wished I'd paid more attention. "Thanks so much. What a lovely home you have."

"Oh, we do our best. I get my retirement and Richard has his pension." Lenora moved by me gracefully. She stopped a few feet away and looked pointedly at my shoes. "Shoes off please."

Feeling embarrassed though I couldn't pinpoint why, I slid out of my shoes and set them by the rest next to the doormat. "Sorry about that."

"No problem. I like to keep the house very neat. Now, would you like something to drink?"

A whiskey would be nice. I had to stop myself from saying it out loud. She didn't give me any options so I agreed. Lenora led me into a living room where I expected to see sofas covered in plastic, but was startled to find a hospital bed with a frail man lying in it. He was hooked up to wires and tubes. Machines emitted beeps and whirring noises. There were two sitting chairs across from him. In the corner of the room by a window was a sparse fake Christmas tree.

So much for setting aside traumatic childhood memories.

"This is Richard," she said as she guided me to one of the chairs. "He suffered one too many strokes and requires full time care now. I hate the thought of putting him in a home, so I take care of him."

Her voice dropped at the end of her sentence. I saw right through her in that moment. The tiredness, the OCD house. She had to take control where she could. A house doesn't fight back. It can be exactly what you want it to be. I did the same with my own body; I could put whatever substance I wanted in it. It was my choice.

"I'm sorry. It's good of you to take care of him." It was all I could think to say. Lenora smoothed her hair back and walked away. I wondered if she got many visitors.

Being in Richard's presence made me feel uneasy. His eyes were closed and, based on the giant tube going down his throat, the movement in his chest was involuntary. Not quite alive, but not quite dead. It was cruel to keep him around. Selfish. I wondered how Lenora justified it. Did she think he'd come around?

Fuck, maybe he did. Maybe he woke up sometimes and was lucid. I didn't know. I leaned back in the chair, looking anywhere but at him. There were dozens of photos on the wall. Many were of Lenora and Richard in their youth. Both were attractive and lively. The rest were of Andrew. Him playing guitar or piano, dressed up going to prom with a pretty girl. Laughing beside his father on Halloween. I wanted to see the pictures and suddenly remember him. Anything to fill in the blank space.

"I hope you don't mind coffee. I know a lot of young folks drink tea these days, but nothing is better than a nice cup of java." Lenora came into the living room baring a giant metal tray with a fancy coffee press and two mugs. There were sugar cubes, a pitcher of cream, and delicate crumbly cookies that resembled pressed sand. She set it on the coffee table between our two chairs. "The cookies are spritzers. Been in my family for generations. Does your mother bake?"

I cleared my throat and got into Donovan Holloway mode. "Yes, she is a great baker."

"Wonderful. Cream or sugar?"

"None, thank you. I like it plain."

Her smile twitched when my hands came up to retrieve the cup she'd poured. "What happened there?"

I looked down at my own hands and saw the string-like scars. Scars I hadn't made up a story for. "Oh, well, it was a childhood accident. I was so young I barely remember."

"Terrible. Kids think they are invincible, don't they. Do you have any?" She sipped her overly sugared coffee. Her gaze eventually moved to Richard, then back to me. "I see you don't have a wedding ring though."

Would the personal Q&A ever end? Is this what normal people did when they first met? I wasn't sure. Almost all of my conversations consisted of asking what a person wanted, giving them a price, and telling them to come back soon. I took a long drink of coffee to reorient myself. "No wife or children yet. I'm thinking about proposing to my girlfriend soon. I have a good feeling she'll say yes."

That hit her. Her face lit up again. "That's lovely! So wonderful. I wish Andrew had the chance to meet a lovely young woman and get married. I would've loved to have grandchildren. But I only ever had him."

"I'm so sorry about your loss." I jumped at the chance to shift the conversation. "Andrew was such a great person. He loved music so much."

"Yes, he was talented. He wanted to go to Juilliard as you might know, but his father always put so much pressure on him to go to the University of Washington. That's where both of us went way back when. Sometimes we worry that's why he took his own life, because he felt like he wasn't living his dream."

"I don't think so," I said, searching for something to say to make her feel at ease. "Some people just have thoughts that weigh them down so much, they feel like ending their life is the only solution to take that weight away. It has nothing to do with us."

Straight from the self-help books. At least they were good for something.

"I suppose so." She was quiet for a moment. "Anyway, let me tell you some things about Andrew's childhood. That might be nice to have in your memorial."

I'd come prepared, having purchased the little notebook from the dollar store I kept telling myself I wanted. I retrieved it from my pocket and set it on my knee to write. Lenora told me sprawling tales of Andrew as a baby, when he first started playing music, his first girlfriend. Eventually her stories came to when he moved to Ballard, where she stopped.

"Do those stories sound good? I hope they'll be useful for your memorial."

"They're great," I assured her. "I think everyone will appreciate them. I know it's difficult, but would you mind telling me about Andrew's time in Ballard and school? I just feel like it might give everyone closure to know the whole story. We were never told much beyond how he died and haven't been able to find his roommate."

I was nearing dangerous territory. What I wanted to know might be things Donovan Holloway *should* know as Andrew's friend. I worried at any moment Lenora would realize I wasn't who I said I was and kick me out or call the police. I relied on her desire to talk about her feelings and worries rather than think too deeply about me.

"The whole thing did happen fast, didn't it? Well, Andrew moved to that Ballard apartment just before fall quarter started. The university had no room in housing. Andrew planned on finding a roommate because even that apartment was too expensive for one student. About a month later Ethan moved in."

A wave of dizziness swept over me. My chest tightened up and my heart raced at the sound of my own name. According to the credit check William Grigg lived in the apartment and that's what I expected to hear. Who gave me the name Ethan Knight and why? When? Why did I believe that was who I was?

"Was his last name Knight? Ethan Knight?"

"Knight?" Lenora pursed her lips in thought. "I don't remember. I don't think I ever heard his last name."

"Did you ever meet him?" I regretted the questioned right away. If she had met me, maybe she'd remember now.

"No. Richard did once when he drove down to drop off some of Andrew's things. He said Ethan was unusual and might do drugs, but Andrew got along very well with him. Andrew told me Ethan never missed his half of the rent. Did you know Ethan at all?"

I fidgeted in my seat. "I never met him. I only knew Andrew from class and when we went out, but never went to his place. Do you know where Ethan worked, or if he went to school? I'd like to try and find him in case he wants to speak at the memorial."

Lenora poured herself another cup of coffee and topped off mine.

"I don't think he worked. Andrew said he had trust fund money that paid for his rent. I know he didn't go to school. I'm sorry, Donovan, it's hard for me to think about things too close to when Andrew died. I hope you understand."

I wanted more, but knew she had nothing left to give. I suppose I did get some answers. I did live with Andrew, I didn't go to school. Somehow my rent was being paid for even though I didn't work. That was a possible avenue to explore; where had I been getting money from? Was it possible to get some records from the apartment complex? Olivia would know what to do. This was out of my expertise.

"Of course, I understand. Thank you so much for everything."

She smiled and nudged the plate of cookies towards me. "You haven't tried one of my cookies. Have a few. There's one other thing I have for you."

I obliged, hungry from the long trip, and ate four by the time she came back. They were dry and sweet, but tasted good. She handed me a wooden keychain in the shape of a buffalo with two keys hanging from it.

"We put all of Andrew's things into a storage unit right after he died. Whatever the police didn't keep. Richard and I planned to go through it all, but he had his first stroke shortly after and, well, things fall to the wayside. If you wanted, you could take a look. It might be nice to have some of his old drawings or instruments at the service. It would make me happy to know someone finally went through it. It's the self-storage on Broadway in Everett."

"I will." I took the keys and stashed them in my pocket. "I think that's all I need. You've been so helpful, thank you."

Lenora stayed standing. It felt like a cue to leave, so I stood. "When is the memorial? I'd like to come. I'm sure I can find a caretaker for the day to watch Richard."

I glanced at Richard, his chest still rising and failing with forced breath. "Well, it's still a ways away. We're working on the details, but as soon as I have a definite date, I will give you a call."

"That sounds fine," she said. She escorted me to the front door and watched as I put my shoes on. "Come by any time. It was nice to have some company."

I opened the front door and stepped outside. After what I just did and discovered, I needed a cigarette. Lenora's request made me feel even guiltier. I'd have to add manipulating and giving false hope to an old lady to my resume of shitty things I'd done. But the lie was still going and I told her I'd come by again when I had the chance, all the while knowing I'd never set foot in the house again.

CHAPTER 17

On the way to the bus stop I checked my phone, hoping to see something from Olivia. There was only a voicemail from Donovan asking if I'd sold my Whiteout yet and how much I got for it. I deleted the message and told myself I needed to come up with the money for it, or toss it and come up with a good story why I didn't have it.

The storage unit was somewhere in Everett. I used the time on the bus to consider if I wanted to go there, ultimately deciding I had nothing better to do. That small hope of finding a clue, anything, was always there. Now that I knew for certain I'd lived with Andrew Cole, there was a more compelling reason to keep looking into it.

Olivia was mostly right in the parking garage when she said I was in this for myself. I was in it for myself, but also because I wanted to do right by Skid's memory. I needed to be the person he thought I was. Going to the storage unit in hope of finding more information on myself was what I *should* be doing.

I used a map at the transit station to find Broadway and walked there. Everett seemed more alive now, with people returning from work. Cars filled the streets and pedestrians, though not as many as Seattle, populated the sidewalks.

A half hour later, the sky was growing dark and rain picked up just as I arrived at the storage unit facility. It was two stories and painted an odd combination of purple and orange. The front of the building sported a clock tower. It was self-service with multiple entrances depending on which block you needed to get to.

I wandered a while before I found the C aisle, which stretched down the entire length of the building. Most of the units there had narrow doors, though there were a few larger ones. My footsteps echoed. Energy saving lights turned on as I approached.

C12 was one of the bigger units. I unlocked the padlock looped through the storage unit's built in lock, then the next. The door clattered as I pushed it up. There was no light inside the ten foot square room, making me rely on the hallway light as I took in the contents.

There was a bedframe and mattress propped up against one wall. A couch and desk were against the other, two empty bookshelves behind the couch. In the center resided stacks of boxes and some black lumpy garbage bags I figured might have clothing. It was strange to think no one had been in the room since Andrew died. In a way, it was a bodiless tomb. An entire facet of a human being stored in one place.

I took a deep breath, then entered and opened the box closest to me. It was full of textbooks. Music mostly, then math and a few art history. I heaved the box to the side, feeling more confident, and searched the next one. More books. One contained board games, the other action figures. Andrew seemed to be a bit of a nerd. Between talking to his mother and going through his things, I began to feel like I knew him.

Fuck, I did know him. I just didn't remember.

Dust was thick on all the boxes, making me sneeze

and cough as I sorted. Eventually I sat down on the couch, sending another plume of it up. I realized how exhausted I was. The day seemed never ending and I still had at least an hour and a half left before I'd be back at my apartment. When I first left the Cole's house, I felt a sliver of optimism. Now that was fading. I knew more than I did, but I didn't see how it would put me any closer to finding out who was behind Whiteout.

I needed something to take the edge off. Just something small. I fished around my pockets for the plastic baggie of Xanax I'd brought along in case things got rough. My body was already relaxing as I popped the round orange pill in my mouth and dry swallowed it. I worked up some saliva to wash it down, then leaned my head back on the couch.

I saw myself smiling next to a beautiful blonde girl.

At first I thought I accidentally took LSD, then I realized it was a worn photograph taped to the underside of one of the shelves on the book case. I reached up and touched the picture, still unsure if it was real. I picked at the tape and pulled it free, sitting straight as I studied it. It had been folded and unfolded many times based on the fine, crackled lines throughout it.

An odd feeling came over me, similar to when Olivia gave me William Grigg's missing person report. The guy in the photo was me, but at the same time wasn't. It wasn't a version of me I knew, yet there I was. I tipped the photo closer to the light from the hallway for a better look. I wore a tan knitted hat and a heavy winter jacket. I looked young, perhaps seventeen at most. It was snowing, flakes gathering on my shoulders and the fuzzy ball that topped my hat.

Next to me was the girl I sometimes saw in my dreams.

Not the redhead, but the blond. Her hair was long, to her waist, and she wore pink earmuffs. Her eyes were a vivid, piercing blue. She wore no makeup but had a fringe of thick black eyelashes, her cheeks flushed from the cold. The side of her face was pressed against mine.

We were happy. God, we looked so happy. I would've given anything to be back in that moment. To even *remember* that moment.

I turned the photo around. On the back the name *Sarah B, the only one for me* was scrawled.

Her name was Sarah B. At one point, I liked her. Maybe I even loved her. She might've loved me back. A painful jolt went through my heart. I would never know those feelings again. At least I had it once.

I folded the picture and tucked it into my pocket, then searched the rest of the bookcase. There was nothing else. Had I hidden the photo there? Why would I have done that? To keep it from Andrew? Or someone else?

With newfound motivation to search Andrew's belongings, I started on the boxes again. There were six left, stacked in pairs against the wall, and two guitar cases. I grabbed one of the cases by the handle and lifted it up. The case wasn't closed properly and the guitar tumbled out of it, hitting the ground.

"Shit," I muttered as I went to pick it up.

My hand closed around the neck. I felt dread overtake me, strong and sudden, even against the haze of the Xanax. I flipped the guitar over, a beautiful light colored instrument, felt the metal strings beneath my fingertips. Some part of me told me to stop, begged me not to look at it. It wanted me to turn away.

I set it face up on the couch and ran my hand across it. I looked at the scars on my hands, noticed what a perfect match they were to the strings.

And then it came back to me, fast and hard like it was happening real time. The memory of killing Andrew, locked away for almost a decade, finally came back.

CHAPTER 18

My eyes flash open and I'm in a room I'm not quite familiar with. I feel strange, like my brain is on overdrive taking it all in. Somewhere outside the room I hear musical notes. At first the sound doesn't bother me, but they keep going. Someone is tuning a guitar.

I know the someone. His name is Andrew. I try to bring up his face but it's blurry in my memory. I can't make out all his features. His eyes and mouth melt into dark shapes on his face. Everything I know about him is hazy, like I'm trying to recall a dream but the more I do the farther it slips away. Maybe his name isn't Andrew. How did I get here?

I was sleeping. I'm under the comforters of a twin bed but I don't remember how I got here. There's a green digital clock on a nightstand next to me that reads 9:34am. Next to that is an orange prescription bottle with a name on it. Ethan Knight. That doesn't sound like my name. I'm not sure what my name is.

Instinctively, I reach out and snatch the bottle. Shake it. Empty.

My mouth is dry. I taste something strange, not quite metallic, lingering on my tongue and cheeks. I sit up and push away the covers, swing my legs over the bed. My head feels bulbous and sensitive.

The same thought keeps repeating in my mind; where am I? Where am I?

I feel like I should know the place but I don't. It's a memory. I've been here before but not really. The tuning won't stop and I wish it would so I could think clearly for a minute. I crush my hands against my ears but I can still hear it. Note after note. None of them quite in key.

When I stand I have to brace myself against the wall before I open the bedroom door. Outside Andrew has guitars around him, his back to me at the dining room table. It's too fucking early to tune guitars. I wish he would stop. I can't think. My vision is pulsing now. Andrew is bigger, then smaller.

I'm sweating. I feel it dripping down my forehead. There's a tightness in my chest that won't go away. It's going to cave in. My breathing quickens. Andrew's body is distorted. His limbs are long. The tuning is grating. I think my ears are bleeding. He's trying to kill me.

Suddenly I'm walking across the room. Andrew is asking me what's wrong, what's wrong. There are strings like cobwebs littering the table. I grab one and wrap it around my hands. He's moving away from me but I still hear the tuning. That's how I know he's a monster because he makes the noise without actually doing it. His mouth is opening and closing but I keep hearing the tuning.

The strings cut into my hands. I'm bleeding.

I rush the monster, knocking him to the ground. He gets on his knees to crawl away. I jump on his back and wrap the guitar strings around his neck. I pull hard, as hard as I can. If I squeeze hard enough it will be quiet and I'll have a second to think. Fuck I need to think. I need quiet so I can remember why I'm here.

The monster stops moving. His eyes are bloodshot, his

swollen tongue pushing out of his mouth. The strings cut so far into his neck I can't see them anymore. I unwrap the wire from my own hands, feel the sting of pain as they dislodge from my skin. I'm crying now, sobbing as I look at the body. What have I done?

Time blisters. I'm lying on the couch shaking when two men come into the apartment. I don't know how long it's been. They call me Ethan—that must be my name then—and tell me it will be okay. I tell them I need more pills, because that's important I think, but they say no more of those.

"Jesus, just give him some Whiteout until we can get this cleaned up."

I want to kill them but I'm shaking too hard. I can't even stand.

"We aren't authorized to do that, they're trying to get him off it. We need to take him back."

They're going to take me somewhere. I need my picture. What picture? My head lolls as I look around. There's something I'm missing. I can't leave without it.

"For fucks sake, give him a benzo then, he's having a panic attack!"

They give me three oblong orange pills. They say it will help me calm down and shove a whole bottle of it into my hands. Soon the world is going dark. They wash the blood off me and lead me out of the apartment. Everything is getting fuzzy. I'm feeling warm. I want to feel like this forever.

CHAPTER 19

The shrill ringing of my phone broke me out of the memory. At first I wondered why my eyes weren't working. I opened them and saw nothing but darkness. Then I realized I was lying on the ground in the storage unit and the automatic lights had turned off. I couldn't remember the last time I was in that kind of stillness. It was dark and unmoving, like I was floating in a void.

I sat up and found my phone. The faint glow illuminated the boxes around me. I didn't let my gaze settle on the guitar. Not after what I'd just remembered.

The number wasn't one I recognized. I hit the green answer button. "Who is this?"

"It's Trisha. Can you meet?"

I looked around myself, dazed. I didn't know how long I'd been out, or if there were even any buses left to Seattle. "I don't know. I'm in Everett. I'm kind of fucked up right now. What's going on?"

Her breath was ragged on the other end. "If we're going to do this, we need to do it tonight."

Mustering my energy, I stood up and felt my way to the hallway. As soon as I stepped out, the lights came on and blinded me. I squeezed my eyes shut and took a deep breath. My body was exhausted, like the memory had taken everything out of me. For the first time, I didn't want a Xanax. The men who came for me played God, tossing me pills with no concern for what it did to me. They gave me drugs like parents put their toddlers in front of the TV. Whatever you had to do to shut them up.

"Do what? Fuck, Trisha, I don't even know what you want."

"My guy, the supplier, is home alone tonight. His family is overseas. If we're going to get him, there won't be a better chance than this."

"Get him? You mean kill him?"

She was quiet.

"Dammit, I never said I was going to kill anyone." Anger boiled up inside me. Trisha's assumption pissed me off. The adrenaline was a balm for the pain and I let it overtake me. "In fact, if you don't tell me what you know, I'll tell Donovan you're still pulling tricks and want to escape him. How do you think that will go?"

"Jesus, E, really? Who do you think he'll believe when I say you've been coming on to me for years and were jealous when I wouldn't run away with you?"

I wasn't sure. But she was right. It came back to me being dependent on Donovan. Trisha picked the right person to try and manipulate. I had nothing beyond my drug dealing and what he offered me. She had power and information over me and that made me hate her.

Trisha didn't need to screw me to get me to do what she wanted. So many times before I recognized she wasn't the same girl anymore. This time the realization settled. The Trisha I used to know was dead.

The truth was, I'd been played. Now it was up to me to turn it into something else.

"Okay. What do I do?"

"I'm going over there around twelve tonight once my shift here ends." She gave me the address of a suite in downtown Seattle. "Call me at this number when you get there. If you still have Whiteout, bring it. You'll have him, I'll have my money, we'll both be happy. Got it?"

I sighed. The night would never end. I needed a few hours to process the fact I'd strangled a completely innocent person with my bare hands. It looked like I wasn't going to get that.

"I'm on my way. Trisha, if you fuck me over, I'm going to end you."

It was past midnight by the time I arrived at the suite. I'd been unconscious for an entire hour in the storage unit, then the rest of the time was spent navigating the nightmarish public transportation system. There I experienced more of my least favorite thing; agonized waiting. Plenty of time to think about what I was going to do, what the worst thing that could happen would be. The time I'd been craving to think about Andrew was available, but I found myself avoiding it.

Underneath it all I felt something I typically didn't dare allow myself; hope. Hope that I could finally get answers. An affluent guy living in this part of Seattle, supplying Whiteout? He'd know someone else in the hierarchy. Maybe *he* was the person behind it all. I could get the answers I wanted and end everything once and for all.

I stopped at my apartment to get my gun. It was a last minute decision that added time, but I felt better knowing I had it with me. Then, finally, I was standing outside the building. The spotless glass front door was locked. The reception desk inside was unattended. I got out my cell and dialed Trisha. No answer. A minute later, a text arrived.

Down in 5.

The gun dug into my hip. I tugged my jacket down to cover the gun more, then thought of how obvious I looked. Fidgeting, glancing around. The epitome of suspicious.

Beside me, the door chimed and whooshed open as Trisha came out. I hadn't seen her in regular clothes for years. She wore no makeup and her hair was pulled back into a ponytail with a baseball cap. She sported jeans, sneakers, and an over-sized Seahawks championship sweater. Not what I expected for a dancer having a seductive night with a rich guy. She spared no pleasantries when she saw me.

"Do you have any Whiteout?"

Of course I did. I'd been carrying it around with me since the day Donovan gave it. "Yeah. Why?"

"Give it to me. I need it."

"He already knows you're here. He'll assume you're the one that ripped him off."

"Then he won't remember you."

It seemed too thoughtful of her, but it was true. I pulled the little plastic bag out that had all the Whiteout, including the one I'd taken from Skid's tent, and fished one out for her.

"I want all of them."

I took my hand back, clenching the baggie tightly. "No. You don't need all of them."

"I do. I'm sure I'll need the rest of them at some point. You want to get answers from this guy or what?"

Giving them to Trisha was better than selling them to

random people on the street, I supposed. I surrendered the bag. It was easy to convince yourself when you had no options.

"Great. You'll wait outside of his place. I'm going to slip this to him and I'll get you once it's working."

"What exactly is the plan here?"

Trisha led me to an elevator where she pushed the up button. It opened right away, still on the first level. It was granite and dark hardwood inside. Fancy.

"It takes about ten minutes for the drug to work. He likes to be tied up during sex. He'll be gagged." She hit the top floor button. "He'll probably get scared fast, then he'll tell me the code to his safe. I get all my money and go. You can do whatever you want with him. Interrogate him or whatever."

Something felt off, though I couldn't pinpoint the specifics yet. There was something in the way she talked about him that made me feel uneasy. Too much of the pronoun game. Who was *he*? She'd yet to say his name once in either of our conversations.

We stepped off the elevator on the twenty-sixth floor and went to the end of the hallway. I hung back while Trisha knocked on the door gently. Chastity opened it. She wore red lipstick that was smudged on the right side of her mouth. A long men's robe covered whatever she had—or didn't have—on underneath.

Trisha handed Chastity the pill. She shut the door without saying anything and slipped back into the suite. Trisha beckoned me over and I stood with her outside the door.

Maybe my expression gave me away, but Trisha leaned

over to me and whispered, "Don't worry. This is the guy you want, Ethan. I swear. He's the one that gave Whiteout to Donnie."

I itched for a cigarette as we waited. Wasted time checking my phone twice, watched as twenty minutes crawled by. What would Olivia say about this? Would she have known who lived here in this apartment, told me it was a waste of my time? I wondered if she would have a better plan of attack. Mine hinged on the mercy of a stripper. Some part of me wanted to find a critical piece of information and give it to Olivia. Make amends. I wasn't sure how I could go back after our fight unless I had answers.

Trisha's face was tilted down. She stared at the gaudy printed carpet beneath her. I studied her. She was going through so much to escape Donovan. She was risking her life, as well as Chastity's and my own, to get out. Olivia risked her life trying to find answers. It seemed like anything worth knowing or having also brought the chance of a quick death.

A thought struck me. "Is Donovan that bad?"

"Not any worse than the rest of us," Trisha said. "Not when you really think about it."

Chastity opened the door, startling both of us. She flashed me a smile then turned to Trisha. "I got him tied up really good. He thought it was Molly."

"Let's get this over with. Put some clothes on, Chastity." Trisha pushed past her into the suite.

We entered the apartment together. Chastity closed and locked the door then disappeared down a hallway immediately to the right. The place was nicer than anything

I'd seen before. Like Kaylee's, the living space was open and connected directly to the kitchen. The floors were a grayish stained hardwood, counters white granite. The lights were dimmed low, reflecting gently off modern looking furniture that was all leather, glass, and metal. There were champagne glasses and empty bottles on the counter. Pieces of lacy yellow lingerie and a sparkling red dress were scattered in front of the living room couch.

The outer wall of the suite was all window. A thick mist covered most of the city, blurring lights. Even my favorite cliché landmark, the Space Needle, was obscured.

I followed the sound of grunting down the hall into a spacious master bedroom. Bedding was rumpled on a king sized bed with most of the comforter sliding off onto the ground. Our mark lay on it, both wrists tied over his head onto the wrought iron headboard above him. A pang of anxiety ran through me as I pictured Kaylee's body instead of his. My breath caught in my throat. I shut my eyes but that made it even worse, so I opted to stare straight at him.

He was in his mid-forties at best with a pudgy stomach that jiggled every time he moved against his restraints. There was a tattoo over his heart of an old woman. It was distorted now, the victim of body hair and stretch marks. Fingernail marks, still slightly red, trailed down his chest and shoulders. There was a bona fide ball gag in his mouth. Spit dribbled from it as he tried to talk. I jogged my memory to see if I'd seen him in newspapers or his face plastered on buses. He seemed familiar, but no name came to mind.

The room was huge, almost the size of the living room. There was a sofa facing the bed and a bar built into the wall. It reminded me how badly I needed a drink.

Trisha sat on the side of the bed talking to the mark. In the bathroom adjacent to the master bedroom, I saw Chastity pull jeans and a plain hoodie from a backpack. Her shapely curves disappeared as she dressed, the mirrored walls reflecting every angle of her.

"Chuck, listen to me. Listen to me," Trisha said and slapped him lightly on the face. When he didn't comply she hit him harder, enough to snap his head to the side. "I want the code to your safe. If you give it to me, we all get out of here safe and sound. If you don't, I'm going to have my friend here cut your dick off. You got it?"

Tears streamed down his cheeks. He looked at me, his eyes searching and begging all at once. I shrugged.

"Open the closet over there and push back the clothes in the center."

Following orders from a stripper? What was the world coming to? I gritted my teeth and did as she ordered, walked over to the closet and opened it. I had to do my part and then Chuck would be mine. All the pretty fabrics inside oozed money. Pinstriped suits, stiff-collared dress shirts, and silk ties. It smelled like leather and fine cotton. I shoved everything aside, revealing the metal door of a safe.

"The faster we get this over with, the sooner you can be on your way," Trisha told Chuck. "You got me?"

Chuck nodded, his double chin turning into four. Trisha smiled and reached around his head to unhook the mask. It left angry red indents all around his face where it'd been secured. Chastity didn't joke around.

"Chastity," was the first thing out of his mouth. He had a thick accent that reminded me of Donovan's. It was definitely Russian. "I thought you loved me!"

I couldn't suppress my snide giggle. Trisha glared at me, but her face melted quickly and she rolled her eyes instead, the hint of a smile tugging at her lips. Chastity came out of the bathroom, fully clothed, and smiled at Chuck.

"I love you, baby. I love your money more."

He looked at each of us one by one, then wailed loudly. Trisha's hand snapped out to hit him again. "This can go real easy if you just tell us the code."

"Okay, okay. 49852," he muttered.

I punched in the code. A little light by the handle flashed red. I tried it one more time just in case.

"Not working," I said. "You sure that's it?"

The mood in the room shifted. It was tense before, but easy. All threats. Then Trisha pulled a gun out from somewhere beneath her sweater and pointed it at Chuck's head.

"I'm sorry! I swear, I-I'm just nervous. For God's sake, get the gun away from me!"

Up until then I'd separated myself from what was happening. Trisha getting her money didn't affect me. It was a just a step on the path to get to Chuck, who dealt Whiteout and might have answers for me. But accidents could happen when a gun was involved. Accidents that might stop me from getting what I wanted.

I was about to tell Trisha to calm down when Chastity stepped in. "Cool it, okay? I'm sure Chuckie is just really nervous. Right sweetie?"

She sat down on the other side of the bed and reached out to stroke Chuck's sweat covered face. He pouted and nodded. "That's right. I changed it last month. I just forgot. It's 49855."

"Ok, 49855." I typed the numbers in. Again, the red flash, but this time accompanied with a series of beeping noises. I questioned my shaking hands and punched it in one last time. The light flashed green and something within the safe made a loud *clunk* noise.

Trisha took the gun away from Chuck's head and moved over to me. It was still in her hand, but her finger was off the trigger. She gestured to the handle.

"Open it up. Fast."

Inside the safe was a grid of narrow boxes with small handles, much like a vault. Trisha pulled one out and crouched on the floor to open it. There were bundles of hundred dollar bills. She broke into a huge smile.

"Chastity, get your bag. Hurry up." Trisha looked up at me. "Pull the rest of those out and help us. Then we're out of your hair, okay?"

The first decent thing Trisha had said all night. I complied and began pulling out the drawers. Some contained jewelry, while most had neatly bundled hundreds. I kept waiting for one of the drawers to contain his Whiteout stash, but none did. Chuck watched with horror as the women stole all of it. I almost felt bad for the guy.

Almost. Because in the world I knew, you did what you needed to do to survive. Even though I was hard on Trisha and Chastity, I understood them. The suffering, the endless battle to get ahead. You couldn't pull yourself out of the gutter when you were chained to it. Bad things happened to good people, but they also happened to bad people. Chuck made himself a target. He fell in love with a stripper, he supplied people with a horrifying drug. He was getting what was coming to him.

All the drawers had been emptied and Chastity and Trisha were on their knees stuffing it into the bag they brought. Chastity cooed and awed at the jewelry. With nothing else to do, I walked around the bed and leaned on the nightstand. It was my turn.

"Where's the Whiteout? Who are you getting it from?"

"What are you talking about?"

"Don't be stupid," I chided. "Who's supplying you with Whiteout?"

It was about the same time I realized Chuck wasn't playing dumb that Trisha shot me and someone broke through the front door.

CHAPTER 20

I'd never been shot. That I knew of. The pain was concentrated at the area it grazed me just in the outer flesh of my shoulder. Blood seeped from the wound down my arm. I dropped to my knees and crawled to the bathroom. It could be worse. Six inches inward and it would've hit my throat.

Down the hallway I saw three men enter the apartment. One immediately came down the hall while the other two moved deeper into the suite. They had sub machine guns.

I thought of the beeping noises, my incorrect entries on the safe. Had it triggered something? Was it an alarm? These guys weren't police. They wore regular clothes and hadn't announced who they were. Cops didn't carry those kinds of guns, did they?

Once in the bathroom I slammed the door shut and backed up against the giant bathtub, sitting against it for support. I withdrew my Glock. I had one extra mag. I wasn't sure it would be enough against three guys. My hands were shaking uncontrollably. I wish I'd taken something earlier to dull my senses.

It was quiet for several seconds then gunshots sounded from inside the room. Trisha fired wildly—I recognized the caliber—and the fast automatic fire of the other gun answered. It ended as fast as it started. There were sounds of movement. I stayed put. As far as I was concerned, everyone outside was the enemy. The more that were killed, the better. Maybe I'd get out of this unscathed.

Then a dozen rounds shredded the door and shattered the mirrors. Shards rained down around me. I aimed at the door, chest level, and fired five shots. Something thudded outside. I hoped it was a body.

Somewhere farther away in the apartment more gunfire rang out. Then a scream. I edged away from the line of sight of the door towards the toilet in case someone sprayed another volley into the room again.

I let the minutes pass. No one came for me. When I strained and listened I swore there were still footsteps outside.

Shit. I couldn't wait forever. I was a sitting duck in the bathroom. As far as I could tell, there were two options. I either cleared the apartment and questioned Chuck, assuming he was alive, or I made a run for it. I'd come too far to run, even though my survival instinct begged me to.

My grip was tight on the Glock as I crouched and moved towards the door. I reached up and flicked the bathroom lights off. Light from the bedroom streamed through the bullet holes in the door. If anyone was coming, I'd see their shadow first. I waited for something to block the light. Now closer to the bedroom, I listened.

Someone right outside the door was moaning. It didn't sound like one of the girls. Definitely masculine and in pain. I grabbed the door handle, flipped the lock, and pushed the door open. It traveled about halfway before hitting a body. It was one of the men. Blood flowed in a weak trickle from a wound in his neck. His white t-shirt was saturated red around his upper chest.

His submachine gun was slung around his shoulder, but his hands were loosely pressing against the wound on his neck. I leaned forward and peered down the hallway. It was empty.

Chuck was still on the bed. He appeared unharmed. His eyes were shut and he was whimpering.

I pulled the gun from the dying man into the bathroom. I had no idea what it was, but figured out how to drop the magazine. Only ten rounds left. I was better off using the Glock, which I was more familiar with. I slung it around my shoulder anyway. Better I have it than anyone else.

The wounded man took in a long ragged breath then his body went limp. Dead. He stared upwards at the ceiling, his eyes unfocused. Less blood leaked from his wound. I stood and dashed across the open area that exposed the hallway to the bedroom, closer to the closet. Trisha, Chastity, and their bags were gone.

A voice came from the hallway. "Mr. Melnikov, you in there? Cheslav?"

Fuck me.

I stared at Chuck, now wide-eyed and staring right back at me. Cheslav Melnikov. Chuck was his American nickname. That was Donovan's uncle. Donovan's dad's fucking brother. That's why he looked familiar. I'd seen him one time, years ago. A person looked different sweaty and naked with a gag in their mouth.

Trisha convinced me to screw over the brother of one of the most powerful men in the city. A man who could destroy me.

A man who probably knew nothing useful about Whiteout.

"I'm here!"

I brandished my gun at him. "Shut the fuck up. Not another word."

So many moves I'd made since I woke up from my four year blackout had to do with protecting my world. I dealt drugs. At the end of the day, I got those drugs from the Melnikovs. I existed because of them. Whether I killed every person in the apartment or not, they'd find me. They'd kill me.

Fuck Trisha. Trisha deserved to go to hell. If she thought they wouldn't find her, she was wrong. I'm sure she thought she was being careful by using Chastity, by wearing that baseball cap and those clothes. By giving Whiteout to Chuck so he wouldn't remember her.

She assumed I'd let Chuck live. She knew I was the only one who had Whiteout besides Donovan and wanted it for her own use. If she got it from another dealer, word would get back to Donovan. But me? She'd tricked me fair and square. Really, I should've known better.

A thought popped into my head that put even more dread through me. What if Chastity hadn't given Chuck the Whiteout? What if he remembered my face?

"Mr. Melnikov, is there anyone in the room with you?"

My attention snapped back to the present. I needed to get out of here alive. Chuck had done nothing to hurt me so I wasn't going to kill him.

"I'm not going to hurt you, Mr. Melnikov. I don't want to. Those women tricked me. They said you know about something you don't." I took a deep breath. "Tell your men to stay there, okay? Look at me, I swear I won't do anything if I don't have to."

Wheels turned in Chuck's brain. An eternity later he nodded. "What do you want, then?"

"I want to get out of here alive. Can you help me with that?"

Chuck frowned. "You killed Dimitri. When they see that, they'll kill you. They'll kill you no matter what when they see me tied to the bed, no matter what I tell them."

So be it. I pointed the gun at Chuck and shot him in the foot. The shot went higher than I intended, around his upper leg. His body flailed wildly and he screamed for help.

I crouched behind the end of the sofa farthest from the doorway and waited. In seconds a man peeked around the doorway into the bedroom, the muzzle of his gun sweeping the room. I stayed put and waited until he ventured farther into the room. Once I had a clear shot, I came up and pulled the trigger.

My first shot hit the wall beside him, drawing his attention briefly. I had the element of surprise and kept firing, correcting my aim enough to get two shots into his chest. He fell sideways, firing his gun as he went down. The shots hit the floor and climbed the wall to the ceiling.

I prepared myself for the last man, closely watching the door, but no one came.

Chuck was hyperventilating, lost in his own world of pain and fear. I dropped my mag and loaded my spare, then left the bedroom. There would be more on the way.

There was no sign of the women as I left the suite, but another man lay dead in the living room. I exited the apartment and took the stairs instead of the elevator down each floor.

I holstered the Glock and tried to calm myself as I

exited the building. Somewhere across town sirens were wailing. I forgot there were hundreds of people living in the building who would have called the cops.

My shoulder was bleeding. I looked like hell and felt like it, too. I couldn't get on the bus. I couldn't walk. I couldn't call Donovan. I imagined how that conversation would go. *Shot your uncle and killed two of his people. Helped your girlfriend escape you. Can I get a ride?*

I crossed the street and took cover in an alley where I pulled out my phone and dialed the only person who could help me.

The only question was if she would.

CHAPTER 21

"Hello?" Olivia sounded tired. I'd woken her up. I hadn't thought about how late it was until I heard her voice. "Ethan?"

I cleared my throat. "I'm in trouble, Olivia. A lot of fucking trouble."

"What happened?"

"I followed up with Trisha. She screwed me over." I felt panic welling up and tried to breathe deeply, to slow down my words. "I can't go home. There's cops everywhere."

"Ethan, where are you?" There was shuffling on the other end. I imagined her throwing covers back and getting out of bed. "I'm coming to get you right now."

I couldn't remember the exact address of the building. My body was still pumping adrenaline to try and mask some of the pain from the gunshot. Yeah, it was a surface wound. It still hurt like a bitch. I dreaded what it would feel like once I had a minute to calm down. I looked around the alleyway for some clue as to where I was. At the end of the street was a noodle shop with apartments above it. The buildings on either side of me were nondescript. I gave Olivia the name of the noodle shop in case it sounded familiar.

"I'm only five minutes from there. If you start walking north you'll be at my apartment complex. I'll start walking to you now and we'll probably meet halfway, okay?"

"Okay," was all I managed before I hung up.

The sirens were closer now. As I left the alley I saw red and blue flashing lights turn the corner a few blocks down. At least they were coming in the opposite direction from where I was heading. I tried not to look conspicuous, but was sure that made me look even more suspicious. Plus the bloody clothes were hard to hide. All I wanted to do was clutch my shoulder, but that would draw attention to it.

It took three minutes of fast walking before I spotted Olivia. The street was empty at this hour and she stood out, wearing a bright pink overcoat and a cream hat. She jogged towards me, her breath giant white plumes in the cold air.

When we reached each other, her eye went straight to my shoulder. "Oh my God, you're bleeding! Why didn't you tell me, I would've brought the car. We need to get you to a hospital!"

"No!" I looked around, aware of how loud I'd shouted. There was a UPS store beside us that was closed. Shops and restaurants on the other side. "It's not that bad and you know I can't. For now just take me to your apartment. It's just a deep scratch."

She was skeptical. Her face looked harsh with no makeup under the unforgiving streetlights. "If that's what you want. Come on, I'm just around the corner."

I followed her two blocks to a gated apartment complex. She pulled a card from her pocket and slid it through a panel on the gate. We walked through a well-lit courtyard that sat in the middle of the U-shaped complex. She led me down a path to a single glass door with another keypad. Behind it was a stairwell. Once in, we climbed one flight of steps to the second story. Olivia's apartment was the first by the door.

"All I know about first aid is what I learned in summer camp in high school," she said as we entered. "And I don't have much in the way of medical supplies. I hope you don't need stitches. I'll pass out if I have to stitch you up."

Olivia kept talking. Maybe a nervous habit. I stopped listening because I was too busy studying her apartment.

It wasn't what I expected. Knowing what I did of Olivia, I expected something pristine. Everything dusted, everything in order. Calculated. What I saw were books scattered everywhere and potted plants lining each available windowsill. The kitchen was a mess; dishes and pots were stacked in the sink and more than a few wine bottles rested empty on the counter. A yoga mat was set up in a small area by a brick fireplace. Every single light in the place was on.

And it was hot. The temperature must've been close to 80 degrees. Olivia tossed her jacket across a couch and kicked her boots off beside it. She had on loose cotton pants and a plain long sleeved shirt.

I didn't like it when my predictions were wrong. It made me feel out of control, and that was the last thing I needed at the moment.

"I'll get whatever I have. Please don't get blood on anything."

She disappeared into one of two doors connecting the living space to what I guessed were bedrooms. There wasn't much I could do without dripping blood somewhere, so I stood like an idiot exactly where she left me.

When she returned she had a brown bottle of rubbing alcohol and dishcloths. She handed them to me and pointed to the barstools at the kitchen counter. "Sit over there. Do you need help?"

"No, I guess not." I sat down and took off my jacket, folding it in a way that wouldn't dirty anything. Not like the place wasn't a mess already.

I pulled my t-shirt off my shoulder to assess the damage. The wound didn't look as bad as it hurt. The bullet grazed about two inches of the top of my shoulder. It had bled and stung, but now that I looked at it and realized how minor it was I felt embarrassed. If I told someone I was shot, it would be a gross exaggeration.

"How is it?"

Olivia stared at me intently, arms folded across her chest.

"Not bad. I'll be okay." I poured alcohol onto the dishcloth and dabbed at it. It stung like hell and I wondered if it was worth it. A tiny bit of fresh blood surfaced. "Thank you for helping me."

"I didn't have a choice."

"Great, thanks."

She stared out the window. I searched for something to say, to fill the space. Then, for once, I decided to step up. Even as the words came to me, I was impressed with myself. Without worrying about whether it would come off badly or point out I'd acted wrong, I did it.

"I'm sorry for what happened the other day, Olivia. I took some low blows. It was how I felt, but the delivery was bad."

Olivia pursed her lips. "So, you're saying you were right, but you said it wrong?"

"That was a shitty apology. I'm sorry. Unconditionally sorry."

She was quiet as she sat on the bar stool next to me. Her face was neutral, but reminded me of when she first confided in me about her past. It was the real Olivia, the one that was hidden from most. "Apology accepted. I'm sorry for backing off the way I did. I needed time to think and you pushed me too hard. Considering the circumstances, I don't think that conversation could've gone any other way."

I laughed in relief. I'm sure it helped that we both knew, on some level, we were in it together. As much as I picked at her lifestyle, I knew I had an ally in her.

"I did do what you said. I used my social security number to look into my living history." The moment of levity was already clouded by the memory of Andrew Cole.

"And?"

"I killed someone."

"God, are you serious? How did you find that out?"

I focused on dabbing at the bullet wound again, gathering up the words to describe what I'd done. The easiest way was to start from the beginning with finding the article on the apartment, and my encounter with Lenora. Then the guitar that triggered the memory of killing him. I told her everything in complete detail, sparing no expense on the sensations I remembered while killing him. If Catholics felt that kind of relief during confession, I understood why they did it.

It hurt to tell her, to admit I murdered someone like that. The others I had killed in self-defense. Andrew was from confusion, almost against my will. Saying it aloud made it more real, but that's what I needed.

"That's..." Olivia threw her hands up and slid off the stool. "Well, it's extremely messed up. How does Trisha fit into all this?"

"She doesn't. I woke up in the storage unit because she was calling me, saying this was my best chance to come talk to that guy. It turns out she was just using me to get Whiteout and some cash to disappear. I don't really understand her whole plan. It sure as hell fucked me up though."

She went to the oven and set the temperature. The appliance whirred to life as it heated. I dreaded how much it would increase the apartment's temperature. Olivia opened the freezer side of her fridge and withdrew a pizza. There was something about her and food I didn't mind.

"You okay with Deluxe Toppings?"

"Sure."

After she tore the pizza from the cardboard and plastic, she leaned on the counter opposite of me. "Do you think they'll trace the incident back to you?"

"Yes. If there were security videos anywhere they'll get them. I left him alive, so whether Chuck was on Whiteout or not, they can find me. One thing's certain, I can't go to Donovan. My connections are limited at this point."

"What are you going to do then?"

I didn't know what I was going to do. My career just crumbled around me in an instant. Soon I'd be hunted down and killed for what I'd done. It didn't matter that I was tricked. I knew the only solution was to leave Seattle forever. The farther away I got, and the more they tried to find me with no results, the more likely it was they'd forget.

For the time being, I still wanted to find whoever was behind Whiteout. I still wanted answers, for myself and Olivia. I diverted the conversation since it was moot anyway. "Don't worry about me. I'll figure it out. What about you? Have you had any breakthroughs on the case?"

We shared a smirk at the sleuth reference. The oven beeped and Olivia tossed the pizza in, set a timer, and resumed her position next to me. Her mood sobered. "This morning Kaylee's father made calls to all of her closest friends and family to report she was missing. As of right now, she is just a missing person case."

"Fuck me. Must've been a top notch cleanup crew. Did he say anything else?"

Olivia bit her lip and made a gesture somewhere between a nod and a shake of her head that looked like she was making circles. "He said there was no evidence as of yet that she was harmed, so the cleanup must've been good. Or—"

"Someone in the SPD is covering things up," I finished for her. "We suspected people were involved like that."

"You said Andrew Cole's death was ruled a suicide, right?"

I found myself staring at the scars on my hands. An image of them bloody and fresh popped into my mind. "Yes. The article I read online said it was and the parents believed it was, too."

"There's a definite connection here, Ethan. Your friend's death was covered up and so was Kaylee's. She was probably on Whiteout and Andrew was connected to the drug through you." Olivia fidgeted in her stool then slipped off it, going to the fridge. She pulled out two Diet Coke's and handed me one. I would've liked something a bit harder, but accepted it anyway. "These cover-ups have been going on for a long time. Think about yours; you killed that man because you were coming off the drug and were unstable.

They made it go away. Kaylee had a breakdown after weeks of anxiety and suspicion, gets murdered, and they make it go away. Or are in the process of it at least. Do you know what I'm seeing though?"

I swallowed a gulp of the flavorless soda and realized how thirsty I was. I took another pull and suppressed a belch. "What?"

"When you were coming off Whiteout, you went crazy." She paused. "No offense. You did. You got violent and harmed someone. I've been drugged before and came off it okay. Granted I was at home when I woke up, but I was okay. The kid you told me about was confused, but not intentionally violent. Kaylee didn't hurt anyone, just freaked. I think the drug has evolved since you were on it. It's better now."

"Great. A better version of something that's already too dangerous. D.P. went under around the time I woke up. If they were out of business, then…" Olivia looked at me expectantly as I came to the same conclusion she must have. "Someone kept working on it. Any idea who?"

She ran her finger around the edge of her soda can. "The trail goes cold there, detective. I spent hours researching D.P. but for once the internet isn't giving me anything. There were a few medical journals on some drugs they developed, but nothing suspicious. That's why I think we need to go to the D.P. building."

"How can there be nothing? There's always something online."

"Not this time. They were a small company as it was. They took down their website, none of their drugs are still being manufactured. Legally, that is. They're just another company turned to dust because of the recession."

"Okay, I believe you. So we go to D.P. and dig around their files. What do we look for?"

"Anything we can follow up on. Best case scenario we find the names of their board of directors, lead drug engineers. We can look into them and see what they've been up to." Olivia paced back to the oven to check the pizza. It seemed she always liked to keep busy. "I could see the guys who originally designed it keeping it for themselves or something. I don't know the exact ins and outs of drug manufacturing."

"Sounds good to me. When do we go check it out?"

"I left early today and said I was sick, so I can call out tomorrow with no questions asked. We go first thing in the morning." She glanced at my jacket on the counter, then at me. "Can you go back to your apartment?"

"I'm sure I'll be okay for tonight. I should probably pack a few things and be ready to bail out if I need to."

It was an outright lie, but I didn't want to impose on her. The thought of staying at Olivia's place made me feel uncomfortable even though I bet she'd agree to it if I asked. I'd spent my fair share sleeping under overpasses and in parks. I'd be okay.

"Great. I'll pick you up outside of your apartment around 9:00am and we'll head over." The timer beeped. "But first, we eat."

CHAPTER 22

It wasn't just cold, but wet. My exposed skin felt damp and chilled. There was a nipping bitterness that made my lips chapped and my eyes hurt. When we reached the parking lot, its shadow blocked what precious sun there was and the temperature dropped another few degrees. Everything was tinted a bluish white hue from the winter sun.

My neck and back were stiff. The wound on my shoulder ached. After Olivia dropped me off at my apartment the previous night, I gathered up clothes, blankets, what drugs I had left, and anything else that fit in my one duffel bag. I'd been ready for a gun fight the entire time and was almost let down when no one showed up to take me out. I went to the convention center park, a quiet place with tons of nooks and crannies to sleep in. I traded an oxy for a good sleeping spot in a service shed and got two hours of sleep at best. Between the concrete and the near freezing temperatures, it was one of the worst nights I'd had in a while. That said a lot.

It would've been more convenient if I told her to pick me up at the park, but I didn't want to scare Olivia. After I woke up, I made the trek back to my apartment. When she picked me up I stashed my bag in her trunk. She looked as rested and well dressed as ever.

We drove into a part of Seattle I rarely ventured to anymore. The entire neighborhood was in shambles.

Nearby office buildings stood empty with plywood boards over their windows and vandalized "do not trespass" signs plastered on every fence and entrance. This area had gone to hell years ago. It was overrun with homeless and drug addicts, or anyone looking to evade the police for a while. I'd been there before to collect drug money or teach someone a lesson. I'd passed the very building a dozen times and never thought twice about it. Another gang had claimed the territory recently and I hadn't been back since.

And all that time, it likely held the secrets to my past. The universe had a sick sense of humor. Part of me appreciated it. The other gave it the finger. I wondered what my fucking self-help books would think about that.

"Is it even safe? It looks really beat up," Olivia said, drawing my attention from my philosophical thoughts.

"We'll be fine. Come on, let's get in there." I crossed the empty parking lot to the front doors. Olivia followed quickly behind me, her sneakered feet slapping against the concrete. The crowbar she brought from her car looked out of place in her hands. It was shiny without any signs of use.

The door had a chain around the handles with a rusted padlock that had already been cut once and hung just by its crook on the chains. I pulled the chains free and they clattered to the ground.

When I stepped in, I knew right away that the building had guests recently. The scent of urine soaked into concrete assaulted me with a hefty smack, smelling humid and intense despite the cold. The black and white checkered floor was littered with beer cans, cigarette butts, and the occasional used needle. Some of it looked fresh, only just discarded. And we were only in the lobby.

Having learned my lesson at Chuck's, I withdrew my gun. I wasn't taking any risks. Olivia didn't like the gun, I was certain—I saw the look of disdain on her face—but it was necessary. She reached into her pocket and took out a flashlight she brought from the car.

It was dim inside the building. Little light filtered through the cracks between the boarded windows. The interior stretched back past the lobby into a hallway. To the right were open elevators, gaping black and empty. A stairwell door stood adjacent to them.

"This place is huge. Where do we even start?" Her voice echoed. Something shifted down the hallway. A chair sliding, I figured. Or an animal scurrying away? No other sounds followed. It worried me, but I let it go.

I paced around the lobby and quickly found what I was looking for. Behind a dusty plastic plant against the wall, a sign had fallen. I used the edge of my jacket sleeve to wipe away the grime. It laid out each of the floors. D.P. Pharmaceutical Industries held the entire third floor. I took the lead and went up the stairwell by the elevator. Olivia lit the way behind me, making my shadow tall and jumpy as we ascended. In the closed space the smell was even worse. I wanted to cover my mouth but I kept my grip on the gun and my gaze ahead.

I'd lost my breath by the time we reached the second story but Olivia was fine, toting her crowbar and looking around eagerly. The door to the lobby of the third floor was halfway off its hinges and left a small triangle of space underneath. I holstered the gun for a moment to lift it up for Olivia to go under, then followed.

The third story wasn't as destroyed as downstairs.

Maybe others weren't keen on going all the way up here either. Not that there weren't signs of vandalism. Food garbage littered the floor and graffiti was sprayed across the wall separating the elevator from D.P. A giant floor to ceiling glass window was shattered to the right, letting in ample sunlight. There was water damage and tufts of moss growing near it.

"It's funny, when I thought of this place I pictured a big business tower about a hundred floors high made of steel and glass. Lightning crackling overhead." Olivia made that small *hmph* noise. "Not this. There's something terribly anti-climactic about it."

"I'd rather deal with this than that. More manageable."

We walked around a large reception desk built into the ground in front of two wooden double doors. These were padlocked and, unlike the entrance to the building, still secure. There were four loops of chain around the handles in addition to two locks. The door was scratched and beat up around the handles. It looked like someone tried to get in before with no luck.

"You didn't happen to bring a lock cutter too, did you?" I joked as I inspected the door. The bottom right side of it, closest to the window, was waterlogged and rotting. "I think this might give. Hand me the crowbar."

I took the offered crowbar and gave the door a few test hits. Soggy wood flung off in shards. The door was weak there. If I could get a big enough hole, we could crawl through. I hit it a few more times until it gave, then used the pry end of the crowbar to work off larger chunks. By the time I was done there was a hole just over two feet around.

I got onto my hands and knees and peered into the

room. Dozens of cubicles dotted a bright room, lit by skylights evenly spaced every five feet above. There was a thick coating of dust on all surfaces, including the linoleum floor in front of me. Inside, there were fewer signs of vandalism.

My aching body protested as I got onto my belly and shimmied through the hole. Dust came up around me and elicited a few sneezes. Once on the other side, I waited for any signs of life.

"Looks good in here. Come on through."

Olivia grumbled, though I'm not sure what she said. She pulled herself through the hole and was on her feet in an instant, dusting off her jacket. One side of her face was smudged with dirt where it had pressed against the floor.

"Let's walk around first and get a feel for the place. Then we'll start digging," she suggested.

"Split up or stay together?"

I caught her eyes flicker to my shoulder. Maybe my close call had her rethinking our safety, too. "Might as well stay together."

We looped around the cubicles first. It reminded me of a documentary on Chernobyl that Donovan made me watch while we were strung out on cocaine. Everything left exactly the way it was, toys and school things set down never to be picked up again. A ghost town. This place was similar; there were family photos on desks, comic strips. Desk chairs with musky cushions, dull mugs who hadn't seen coffee in a nearly a decade. There were no computers or phones left behind. The only thing that ruined the image was the garbage strewn about.

The cubicles were in the center of a U-shaped

configuration with doors spread along the rest of the walls. Olivia and I peeked into each one and found personal offices. Two doors led to small labs, one to a room full of cages, and another two were packed with filing cabinets and cardboard storage boxes.

"If we're going to find anything, I bet it will be here," Olivia said as she entered one of the storage rooms. She tugged a cabinet drawer. "Locked though. Think we can get them open?"

"We're in it now. No going back."

The cabinets in the room had dates on each drawer. I found one that was dated two years before I began my trials, and jimmied it open. Inside were undamaged folders organized by the month. I pulled out January and set it on top of the cabinet, leaning it towards the window. It was all numbers for a mood stabilizing drug. I found another folder for a sex enhancer. The third folder was for Whiteout, the words 'Working Title' in parentheses next to it.

Percentages of test subjects who experienced side effects of Whiteout. 100% anxiety, 14% nausea. The list went on and on. There were summaries under each statistic outlining the severity of the side effects. It was interesting, but not useful. The entire cabinet was organized by year. I bet each would have more of these. I went through and broke open each one.

I took satisfaction in knowing for certain D.P. created Whiteout. This is where it started. Now we knew for sure.

"Hand me that, I want to look, too." Olivia took the crowbar and pried open a drawer of her own. She pulled out stacks of folders and soon we were lost in reading.

"You find anything?" I asked Olivia as I scanned

statistics. I'd found a folder of stats from my first year of testing. Even though nothing pointed to me directly, I was part of those numbers. I wondered if I was part of the remaining 4% who experienced nausea. I knew I was part of the 89% who experienced violence when tapering off.

"Kind of. These are all personal files of test subjects. Their basic information."

"I'm surprised they didn't shred all this."

Olivia hefted a stack of folders out of her cabinet and set them on the ground. "I'm not. If the building was seized like that article said, it makes sense. The bank didn't get around to clearing it out, and there you have it."

I moved on to a stack of filing boxes next to the cabinets. The boxes were taped shut. I peeled up the tape and shuffled through them. They were all financial reports. Nothing I cared about. Again, I went through each box just in case something tricky had slipped in. By the time I was done, my vision was blurred with numbers.

That's when I realized Olivia hadn't spoken or moved in minutes. "What's up? Did you find something?"

"Yes. I suppose it's nothing new. It's just..." she handed me a folder. The tab read *William Grigg* in neat capital handwriting. "I found yours. I didn't look at it."

I cleared my throat and took the folder. "Thanks."

"Do you need a minute?"

I waved her away. "No, it's fine. Keep going through files. We need to finish up in here and hit the other room."

Before I even opened the folder I made a deal with myself; there was nothing in there that would change what I wanted. Nothing in there would stop me from finding out who was behind Whiteout and what happened to me.

William Grigg was, as far as I was concerned, a different person. I might have some of his fragmented childhood memories, but I was not him. Not anymore.

Whatever I found was a fact. That's it.

I came face to face with that other version of me when I opened the folder. I stood unsmiling against a white wall. My face was waxy and there were dark circles under bloodshot eyes. My blackish hair was matted and greasy. The photo was so different from the one I found of me and the mysterious Sarah woman. I had no doubt the image with Sarah came long before this one.

Beneath the photo was a hefty stack of papers. The first set was a human trial contract and disclaimer that was a quarter inch thick with nothing but fine print. As I flicked through it I saw the initials W.G. on each page and a matching signature throughout. There was no question; I'd agreed to the trials. I did submit myself voluntarily. My parents had said that much in the missing person report.

Under that was a profile of me, similar to the missing person report but much more detailed. This had my blood type, past medical issues, and vaccinations. There was a personal history outlining confrontations I had at school, what subjects I had aptitude for. Near the end was a drug history. It said I started exploring marijuana and barbiturates in middle school, then moved on to painkillers by the beginning of high school. Near the end of high school I tried heroin at a party and got hooked.

The "current" status report said I had been addicted to heroin for almost a year. My parents and girlfriend gave me an ultimatum to get sober or they'd abandon me. My intent of going into the trial was to get some cash and hopefully become addiction-free.

There was a list of items I surrendered upon entering the trial. Clothing, shoes, wallet, an unused needle, cell phone. A photo. It had to be the one of me and Sarah B. What else would it have been? The question was, how did I manage to get it back and hold on to it during those four years?

Another half inch of papers included treatment history for the course of two years. What dosage of medication I was given daily, my vitals, comprehensive tests, reading assignments. Not a page mentioned ice baths or tubes down my throats or acid. There was nothing about abuse or inflicting of pain. Then again, there were still two years of blackouts unaccounted for.

"Are all the records you've seen so far just two years' worth?" I asked Olivia.

She jumped when I spoke. I realized how quiet it had gotten while I was absorbed in my file.

"So far, yes. They all cover a two year span. Maybe the rest of the results are in the other room?"

I flipped through more of my daily reports. "Might be. I wonder if—what the fuck?"

The knot twisted so hard and fast in my stomach I thought I was going to vomit. I felt lightheaded.

The last page in my document was a photocopy of a death certificate.

My death certificate.

CHAPTER 23

I wondered if William Grigg was my twin. Maybe we both went into Whiteout trials and he died after two years. Ethan Knight got the raw end of the deal and his trials extended longer when things got rocky with D.P. Or what if I was dead? What if I was dead right now and in my own version of hell? I'm sure I deserved it.

"Well, obviously this is fake," Olivia said after studying the death certificate. "The most compelling reason being that you're right in front of me."

Her declaration startled me. Of course I wasn't fucking dead. I wasn't a twin and I wasn't a ghost. My brain went wild and had a knee-jerk reaction when faced with bad news. Someone declaring me dead was bad news as far as I was concerned.

I fished out a cigarette and lit it. The nicotine helped soothe my mind and my shaking hands. It wasn't until I sucked half of it down that I spoke. "What's the date on that again?"

She told me. I thought about the missing persons report and when my parents stopped looking for me. The dates went together perfectly. Someone must've told them I was dead and that's when they stopped inquiring about my case. Not because they'd given up. Because they thought I was dead.

"What's the cause of death?" I asked.

"It says here you were found dead of a drug overdose. Body found in Olympia, too decomposed for identification. Says your remains were identified through dental records and notice was sent to the parents."

"Okay, so someone made me dead. Why? Why would they do that?"

Olivia paused, then crouched down and rifled through the folders she spread out on the ground. "Ethan, a lot of these people have been reported dead. There must be a connection."

"Take any files with death certificates. We can read their backgrounds and see if anything matches up." I flicked the ash from my cigarette and stood. "Let's finish up in here and check out the other room, okay?"

It took another half hour before we were done with all the files in the first storage room. Some of them were waterlogged from a leak in the ceiling, but I suspected they were more of what we already read. Olivia gathered a stack of ten test subjects who had death certificates in their folders. All of them were photocopies. There seemed to be little connection between them on first glance, except they died over the span of two months.

The second room of filing cabinets wasn't as packed as the first. I felt a mixture of relief and nervousness. If we were going to find something more, it would be in this room. At the same time, we were at the end of the line. What we'd found so far was somewhat useful, but not as much as I wanted.

We were quiet as we searched through the folders. It was a lot of the same as the first room: profiles of people, financial reports, summaries, pay stubs. Nothing incriminating. The profiles in this room were of a new crop of people. D.P. hadn't signed on people who only had drug addictions. There were gambling addicts, chain smokers, college dropouts looking for money, widows. People from all walks of life.

"Yes! Ethan, come here and look at this."

I set down the folder of a middle-aged woman and navigated around the junk on the floors to Olivia. She had one of the hundreds of financial reports in her hands that I'd looked through in the other room.

"It's nothing. Just numbers on the company," I assured her and turned to move back to my work.

She frowned. I felt her judgment pass over me as though it were a blanket sliding over my body. She pointed at the bottom of the last page where there were four signatures. I'd seen them before on the other documents but they meant nothing to me. I assumed they were just money people. Accountants.

"These reports have to be signed by the president of the company and anyone else important. These names are the people who owned this company."

"How was I supposed to know that?"

"Don't get defensive about it. We found it, that's all that matters." Olivia said. Her tone changed and I knew the conflict was over. "Jonathan Draper was the CEO of the company. I already knew that name, plus 'Draper-Paulinsky' is the company name. He died five years ago from a heart attack. That doesn't mean he wasn't involved in any of this, but it's likely a dead end."

She caught my accusatory look. "I forgot to tell you last night, I'm sorry. It wasn't important since he's dead. There's two other names on here. Christian Paulinsky and Rupert Fearnley. Like you said, there are no titles under their signatures. I'll see what I can find."

Olivia dug her cell out from her never-ending purse and started typing. I wandered back to the profiles I was looking at. After reading enough of them, I felt a connection to all the people. Unity was a strange feeling, but as I read their dosages of Whiteout, the time they spent there, I couldn't help it. I reached back deep into the filing cabinet for the last folder.

"First search on Christian Paulinsky says he works at Microsoft in accounting. Found him on LinkedIn. Looks like his whole history is in finance so…damn, he lives in China. Unless we're going to fly over there or harass him on the internet I doubt he'd be a good lead."

My breath caught in my throat when I opened the folder. It was the redheaded girl from my dreams. Even with the harsh lighting in the photo against that blank wall she was smiling and bright. She was so young, barely an adult. Seeing her without the burns made me look at her differently. She and Olivia had the same shade of auburn hair, the same dimples in their giant smiles.

"Rupert Fearnley looks more interesting. Found some kind of portfolio website for sculptures. He has a studio downtown. We should go see him."

I looked up at Olivia, the memory of the redhead's burnt face in my mind. Her smiling, telling me everything would be okay. They were so similar. Olivia had a sister that left at some point. Where did she go?

Olivia was still talking about Fearnley when I came up beside her, folder in hand. She took one look at it and her body swayed. She dropped her phone and brought both hands to her head, which she clutched in a white-knuckled grip.

"Oh God, it's her." Her breaths came in rapid inhales. "It's her. It's really her."

"Is this your sister? What is this, Olivia?" She'd kept things from me before. I wouldn't be surprised if this was another secret she thought wouldn't matter, or wanted to keep private. "Is this why you're after Whiteout?"

"No." She sunk to the ground, sitting on her heels. "Well, it's not the only reason."

Here it came. What I'd been waiting for since our argument in the parking garage. I felt the truth coming and it made my stomach churn. It was the resignation on her face paired with the fact she wasn't getting any oxygen from her quick breathing. Panic attack.

"Okay. Calm down. You need to breathe or you're going to pass out." I breathed in and out audibly, slow and loud to give her a baseline. Soon she was steadying herself. I took the chance to look at the rest of the folder.

Her sister's folder was thinner than the others. She had a different name. Lanna Price. Her basic medical information was inside. Written in the current status report was "substance addiction" without any specifics. There were only a few months of summaries on her Whiteout dosage and vitals. I opened the biggest document, the contract, and found the initials L.P. and a signature.

I sat down next to Olivia, wedged between a stack of boxes and a cabinet. I wanted answers. If I got high and mighty, I'd say I deserved them. She had unknown motives she couldn't avoid explaining to me any longer. She went quickly from shocked to numb. Her gaze was unfocused, her hands clasped in her lap.

"I knew this is what I'd find but I still can't believe it's true. They must have given her a new identity. Like how William Grigg became Ethan Knight. Lanna Price is Laurel Holloway."

"Enough, Olivia. What aren't you telling me?" My patience was running out. "You tell me everything *now* or I'm gone."

Then it all came out in one steady, long stream. Her voice was flat. Mechanical, like she was reciting something she had memorized for some time.

"When I was growing up I hated being at home, because of all the problems with my family I told you about. I took on every extracurricular activity I could to cope. It got me out of the house, helped ensure I'd be able to go to college early, wherever I wanted to go. I worked myself as hard as I could." Olivia picked at her fingernails. Her voice was thick. "Laurel handled things differently than me. She was only a year older but she seemed to carry the burden of our family's problems much worse than I did. She fought my dad constantly, nagged at my mom. She had a lot of boyfriends and made it known that she had sex with them."

"She rebelled. That sounds normal enough to me," I offered when Olivia took a lengthy pause. Though I failed to see any connection yet, I waited for the rest of her explanation.

She shook her head. "Not when those boyfriends included Dad's associates. Clients, other lawyers. Instead of going after them—I mean, *they* were the ones having sex with an underage girl— he blamed Laurel for it. Like he couldn't call the police or stop them. He always called her a slut and a tease. Dad hated her. He made her leave when we had people over. Always had an excuse: Laurel is at a soccer game. Laurel has an art class."

"How did you find out about this?" I asked. "Did she tell you?"

Her shoulders hunched forward. Olivia threaded her fingers through her hair and clenched it. She was fidgeting. Her unease was tangible. I had to make a conscious effort not to let it get to me. "Yeah. She told me everything."

"What did your dad do about it?"

"He made her disappear. When I was fifteen I remember waking up and walking by her room, and the door was open. She wasn't in there. Her closet was empty. It was surreal. I asked my mom where Laurel was. She said she got early admission into a two year study abroad program in Italy. I knew right away it was a lie and asked her if she was sure. She said to ask Dad if I had any questions. She knew I wouldn't. She knew I'd never ask him anything."

Olivia went silent and the minutes crawled by. Until I couldn't take it. "So she never came back? Or called or something?"

"Eventually my mother told me she ran away with a boy, but didn't give me anything else. Dad kept up the lies. Told people Laurel was doing great, got a scholarship to stay and finish her bachelor's in Italy. Then her master's. Then she was going to get married and live there. He created this whole world. I was so confused about it when I was young, then when I got older the lie had been part of my life so long, I was locked up. I couldn't do anything."

Now I was starting to connect the dots. "How did you

know he put her here? When I handed you that folder, you weren't surprised. At all."

"I couldn't tell you everything when I first met you. I didn't think you'd believe me. Or trust me. When I read your blog and met you in person, I knew you weren't the kind of person who believes in good people." She frowned as she looked at me. "That, and I was afraid. I didn't want to put all my cards on the table right away."

I stilled. "What are you talking about?"

"Weeks after she disappeared, I got a letter from Laurel. It didn't have a return address. It wasn't very coherent. She said she was being held captive and experimented on. She couldn't escape. They were giving her a drug that caused blackouts. She wrote about how she lost days and weeks of time. She'd come out of these blackouts, beaten and sure she'd been raped."

A tremor ran through my body. The fury I had towards the people involved with Whiteout tripled. "And?"

"She'd traded sex with a security guard while she was coherent to get the letter to me. Laurel said she missed me and was afraid she might die. I couldn't write back, but every couple weeks I would get a letter from her. She'd talk about the experiments, how you couldn't trust anyone. Except there was one guy she thought she loved, who made her feel less afraid."

"Let me guess. William Grigg?"

"Yes," Olivia confirmed. "You were Will in the letters. She wrote about how you disappeared for a while but came back and you insisted your name was Ethan Knight. You didn't remember her. In her last letter she was desperate. She said she feared for her life more than ever. She was losing more of her memories every day from the drugs they gave her. She wanted me to find her, but also to help you. She loved you."

I rubbed my eyes as my brain tried to make sense of all the new information. This was too absurd to be true. Yet I remembered Laurel. I had good feelings in my dreams when I was with her. Granted they always ended in pain and suffering, but never because of her. Maybe I had met her. Maybe we did love each other.

One thing about Olivia's story didn't work for me. "Why have you waited so long to find me?"

"You didn't matter. You were just some name, some guy. I spent years trying to find Laurel. Once I realized it was pointless, I threw myself into my job. Hid that fucked up, surreal part of my life and pretended it never happened. Then I started having blackouts of my own. They were just like Laurel described, down to the metallic aftertaste when she woke up. I couldn't ignore it anymore."

"And then what?"

"Then I started looking for William Grigg and Ethan Knight. I thought maybe you and Laurel had escaped and were with each other. Or maybe you knew something. Then I found your blog. How you described your blackouts, your name. I knew you were the one Laurel talked about." She groaned. "I read on your blog about your connection with the drug world. I talked to so many people on the street looking for you. I thought I was going to get mugged and killed before I made any progress. That's how I found your apartment. Someone from under the overpass told me."

Everything clicked; how Olivia magically found me,

how she had my missing person report. All this time she knew who I was. She'd been leading me along. Fuck I was easy.

"Okay. I believe you. I would've liked it if you told me all this right when you met me."

"I was going to, but our first meetings didn't give me the best impression of you. You barely believed me when I told you I was having blackouts. Would you honestly have believed everything I just told you?"

"I have no idea," I answered truthfully. "Now I know. Thanks, I guess, for helping me figure out who I was. For filling in some of my blank spots. We'll get through this."

Like me, avoidance was Olivia's best defense mechanism. When things were so bad that the effort required to fix them seemed impossible, just ignoring the problem all together seemed like the best answer. She couldn't find her sister, so she buried everything to do with her. She couldn't imagine telling me the truth, so she hid it from me. Unfortunately for Olivia, she couldn't avoid what I was about to tell her. And while I should have been stunned at the news, I was focused on the best lead we'd found since the start.

I thought of the best way to phrase it, but there was no way to break it gently. "Your dad put Laurel into the Whiteout trial."

She nodded. Barely a tilt of her chin. "It seems like the perfect place to get rid of someone you don't want around. Laurel said Dad didn't take her there himself, but she knew he was behind it."

"He knows about Whiteout, Olivia. Somehow he knew about this and had enough power or connections to get your sister in it."

It was futile to ask if she'd talk to her dad because I knew the answer already. Her father's secret had been tucked away for too many years to get a straight answer from him even if she tried. And she wouldn't try. Even though I never met him, I couldn't picture her having a big confrontation with him. If he was as dangerous as she said, their conversation might end up turning violent.

But I had to ask for my own sanity. "Is there any way you could talk to h—"

"No. And don't push it," she snapped. "I can't."

"Fine. We won't," I conceded.

"I've tried looking into him, just so you know. I've followed him after work, tried to hack his bank accounts. By hacking I mean password guessing. None of that is as easy as it looks on TV."

"I never thought it was."

Olivia sat still. She hadn't shed a tear or lost control yet, but I saw her chest heaving up and down with her weighty breaths. She was thinking now. Her brow was furrowed slightly and she clenched her jaw. She seemed to tune back into reality and reached out for her phone resting on the stack of folders from the other room.

"Something isn't right with all of this. I think we've been trying to find the wrong answers."

"Wrong answers?" I had to stand. My knees were cramped from sitting too long. "We're trying to find out who's been making and distributing Whiteout. How is that wrong?"

"It isn't. I mean, we're missing something. How did my dad get involved in this? For what purpose were these death certificates made? And since we know at least yours is fake, how did that happen?" She rolled her shoulders and stood. "I say we take everything we can carry to the car, then go straight to Fearnley's. His studio is open for viewers until 7:00pm. We have a few hours. We should go in, see what he has to say and go from there."

The plan was fast and loose, but I didn't mind. I felt like the hazy picture we'd been forming was almost clear. The faster we moved, the faster we'd finish this.

CHAPTER 24

Rupert Fearnley had his last name cast in the ten foot tall metal doors to his studio. The doors took an irritating amount of effort to open, and I wondered if there was some kind of artsy intent to it. I'd never been in an art gallery before, but that seemed like something an artist would do. Make you feel an emotion you weren't anticipating.

The first thing I noticed were metal sculptures of humanoid figures scattered throughout a single giant room. The floor was a pale wood that looked washed until it was almost white. Wall dividers hung on thick metal cords from the ceiling. Directional lights focused only on the sculptures, casting most of the space between in darkness. It echoed loudly as we walked. There wasn't a single person visible in the studio.

"What's our story?" I whispered as we browsed. I kept an eye out for Fearnley.

"I'm still thinking about it," Olivia said. "I'll come up with something. Don't worry."

Shit. The smooth talker didn't have her story yet. We spent an hour dragging boxes of files into her car at D.P. They weren't particularly heavy, but the cardboard was weak and we could only manage one or two boxes at a time. Then she spent thirty minutes fixing her hair and touching up her face, both messed up from the hard labor. Maybe if she spent less time doing that she could've devoted more energy into how we were going to get info out of Fearnley.

"I see you've found Juniper."

I jumped at the sound of a male's voice behind me. The man was at least 6'5" and wore an outfit complete with a sweater vest and bow tie. His receded hairline almost reached the round of baldness at the crown of his head.

"Oh," he murmured. His face went slack as I faced him. That flash of confusion disappeared as quickly as it came. He smiled pleasantly at us and reached his hand out to me first. His eyes were locked onto mine and eventually I gave up the unsolicited staring contest and glanced at the ground as I shook his hand.

He didn't look at the scars on my hands once. He shook Olivia's hand then placed his hands behind his back.

"I'll admit it, I'm the artist," he said. "Rupert Fearnley at your service."

There was something about him I didn't like. Or maybe my ego was bruised since he managed to sneak up on us like a cat and made me feel like a scorned kid.

"I'm Katie Knight and this is my friend Oliver Smith."

"Great to meet you. Normally I have an art major volunteer roaming the space," he said. He looked around the giant room like he'd never seen it before. His eyes came back to me and stayed there even as he spoke to Olivia. "But they're having finals right now, I believe. So it's just me. Are you interested in purchasing, or just out on the town? Studio hopping is such a stimulating date."

Sure it is. I looked at Olivia. *Now what?*

"Actually, I'm a student myself. I was hoping to talk to you about your work." Olivia put on her million dollar smile. The picture of innocence. "If you have a moment?"

She'd been carefully ambiguous on what she was studying or what she knew about his work. Let him fill in the blanks. It was the technique I used on her when she first came to my apartment. Her words must have resonated with him because he clapped his hands together and grinned.

"Fantastic. I was just about to take my late tea. I'll lock up the front door and we'll go upstairs. The downstairs is my studio, upstairs is my living space."

"Very classic design," Olivia said. "What a wonderful thing to have your art so close!"

I wanted to puke. The contrived pleasantries were killing me.

Fearnley excused himself and went to the heavy doors. Once he was out of earshot I leaned down to Olivia's ear. "I hope you know what you're doing."

"I do," she whispered. "Just...I don't know, follow my lead. That's what they say, right?"

We stepped apart and looked at his sculptures. My mind wanted to be too many places at once. I kept thinking about Laurel and Sarah. Then Fearnley. And whether it was a waste of time or not, how to convince Olivia we should interrogate her dad.

Once Fearnley was back he led us to a door at the opposite end of the studio that opened to a spiral staircase. Fuck me, I was done with stairs for the day. The week, actually.

The staircase lead to a long hallway that appeared to span the length of the studio downstairs. There were doors on both sides, as well as windows on both ends that showed the walls of the surrounding buildings. Not much of a view.

He led us down the hallway to a room with vaulted

ceilings. Everything felt rich. Dark wood floors, plush red rugs, swirling vintage wallpaper. There was a small couch and two big easy chairs that made me realize how tired and stiff I was. I wanted to sink into one and not move for days.

"Please, take a seat. I'll fix us a tray. Do you have any dietary restrictions?"

"No, but thank you for asking," Olivia said. "We're both fine."

"Great, I'll be back shortly." With that he stalked off in his quiet way out of the study.

This guy was too much. Late tea? Art studio? From his mannerisms to how he spoke and what he wore, he was quite the character. It was hard to believe he could've been involved with Whiteout. Yet something still nagged at me. When things looked too perfect, it was because they weren't. This was a great, carefully put together facade, but one that could have rot and secrets behind it.

"Do you have a story yet?" I asked Olivia.

"Yes, kind of. It should be good enough to get us somewhere." She paused. "But, Ethan, us being here might've been a bad move. If Fearnley is still involved with Whiteout, he's most definitely going to be suspicious of us. He might tell someone we're digging around. We could be putting ourselves in a lot of danger."

"Shit, you're right." Everything we'd done so far had been discreet. Investigating my past, going to D.P. Brian wouldn't tell anyone we were there. We were never this close to the source. And that was exactly why we had to keep going. "Things are going to get hot soon. We have to be ready for it."

Ready for what? What was Olivia's goal? It was a

conversation we needed to have.

If one of her goals was to find me and fulfill her sister's last wish, she'd succeeded. The issue of her getting drugged was something entirely separate that still had an ambiguous outcome. What was she going to do once she knew the truth? My fate was already decided for me when I decided to help Trisha. I couldn't stay in Seattle anymore. The Melnikov family was tricky. They'd let you think you got away with something, then swoop in and gut you like a fish when you least expected it. I wasn't going to live with that.

I could've left when we finished at the D.P. building. I knew my real name. I knew I was in the Whiteout trials, confirming what I suspected all these years. What kept me with her was a need to fill in the remaining blanks. I'd been tortured and given a fake identity. Who did that? Why would they do that instead of kill me? At one point the Whiteout clinical trials were legitimate. Where did it go wrong?

The sound of glass clattering drew my attention. Fearnley came in with a silver platter complete with a delicate tea pot, cups, and cookies. It was the upper crust version of what Lenora Coles brought to me. I liked her setup better. It had coffee and the cookies didn't look like piles of dirt patties.

He set the platter down on a coffee table in front of us, then settled onto the edge of one of the big chairs. He took his time pouring, asking if we wanted cream or sugar, then handing us each a cup. The guy was all about theatrics.

"The wafers are vegan. Coconut oil, chia seeds, organic fair trade cacao nibs, and agave with a base of almond meal.

Help yourself."

No thanks. I wasn't picky, but part of me felt like I'd be contaminated with pretentiousness by even a bite of the cookies.

Olivia smiled then sipped her tea. "Thank you, we will. Is this chamomile ginger? What a unique flavor combination."

"I grow and dry the combination myself in the summer. I've got a greenhouse on the roof." He gave her a sheepish grin. "I admit, I do have some unusual hobbies. Now that I've gotten the pleasantries out of the way, what can I help you with, Miss Knight?"

I went ahead and let Olivia take the lead. I wouldn't say I was the brawn of the operation, but Olivia's charm and speaking skills would always trump mine. Instead of talking, I sipped on my tea, wishing it was coffee, and checked out the hundreds of hardback books Fearnley had lined up on his bookshelves. Most of them looked like self-help books on stress, coping with guilt, recovering from loss. I'd read most of them myself. Scores of them were on medicine and ethics. I wanted to draw a conclusion from that, but there were novels, too. Cookbooks, art history, sculpture. He had a bit of everything.

"We wanted to talk to you about your time at Draper-Paulinsky Pharmaceutical Industries," Olivia said. She didn't give a reason yet. I had a feeling she was testing the waters.

Still, I was impressed she cut to the chase so quickly. I lowered my cup to the table and gave my full attention to the conversation.

Fearnley's smile faltered at the edges and his eyes

narrowed. His shoulder tensed and lifted towards his ears. "Here I was excited you were interested in my sculptures. D.P.? I haven't thought of them in so long. That was a different part of my life. Why are you inquiring?"

"I'm sorry, I didn't mean to disappoint. I'm actually studying to be a drug engineer. I'm sorry if you were confused." The lie sounded smooth and natural, and pegging the remark at the end helped. Unlike Fearnley, Olivia kept her attitude up perfectly. "I've had a dream of creating something to help soldiers with PTSD. Of course, I wanted to see if there was a precedence for something like that. After months of research I came across a bit about the Whiteout clinical studies and your name."

Fucking hell, it was paper thin. Drug engineer? If Fearnley asked her any occupational questions we were screwed. And she left herself open for more questions. That didn't really give Fearnley an answer as to why we were here. The more questions people asked, the more likely they were to find the lie. Fortunately for us, he filled in the blank himself.

"And you were wondering why we ended it? I figured all of this would be on the internet somewhere. What a huge amount of trouble you must've gone through tracking me down."

I wondered if he was accusing us in some underhanded way. There was something off about the way he was reacting, like he saw right through us but was playing along for the hell of it. I couldn't pinpoint exactly why I thought that. I had a static sensation along my skin. A sense of unease.

"Exactly. Could you give me some background on your time there? I'd just like to get a feel for all of it if that's okay with you." Olivia took a sip of her tea and made that tiny *hmph!* noise she so often did when she strongly liked or disliked something.

Fearnley studied his teacup. Glanced at me, then back towards Olivia. My palms were sweating and I was very aware of my heartbeat.

"I'm guessing you know about Jonathan Draper, then. I was his assistant at D.P. He had a brilliant staff of drug engineers on his team. Our first year of Whiteout testing showed promise. It wasn't magic, but when people took it they tended not to remember what they'd been doing. But while they were on it they were high functioning; not what you'd see with Rohypnol or something of that sort. At some point the company was under scrutiny by the FDA, which was the start of the downturn."

"Why was that?" Olivia asked.

"Our IRB," he paused and look at me pointedly, "Our Institutional Review Board, questioned the ethics of Whiteout testing."

I scowled. "The ethics weren't questioned until *after* the testing began?"

"No. I'll admit, Draper wasn't the most adoring of the laws of informed consent. I don't believe we broke any laws, not directly, but the way in which we presented the drug might have been a bit in our favor for gaining approval from the FDA to move forward with human studies." Fearnley freshened everyone's tea as he spoke. "Whether you end up working for a big or small pharmaceutical company, be aware that they're made up of people who will do anything they have to in order to get what they want."

He was playing mind games with us. I was sure of it.

Olivia sent me a reprimanding glare before returning her focus to Fearnley. "I'm sorry to interrupt, Rupert. Do you remember anyone who was on the IRB for Whiteout?"

He paused and thought. "We had at least six boards while I was at D.P., one for each of our drugs. We had the minimum requirement of board members for Whiteout. I remember because I'm the one who originally sent requests out. We had a physician named Jeff Whittingstall, a community coordinator named Wanda Christoph. There was an attorney. I don't remember his first name, but I know his last was Holloway. Eventually a Dr. Kidd replaced Whittingstall. There was a professor from the chemistry department at UW. And of course, Donald Stettler. His concerns focused on environmental repercussions."

Olivia didn't flinch at the name of her father. I suppose we already knew he was involved. At least now we knew *how* he was involved. Still composed, she asked, "Did the trials end when the company shut down?"

Fearnley finished nibbling on one of his dirt patty cookies. "Of course. Those last few months were anarchy. The FDA wanted to shut down D.P. for too many violations involving Good Clinical Practice and Human Subject Protection. Both of which I'm sure you're familiar. Once the Whiteout trials were under question most of our financial backers pulled out. Our other drugs were put under scrutiny. We ended all of our trials after the stock market crashed. The bank seized our building, God I remember how awful that was, and the rest is history."

"That's so unfortunate. I'd imagine Whiteout could've been a very useful drug had it been properly researched and tested." Olivia set her teacup down. She shifted to the edge of her seat, her hand on her purse. "I suppose there's still room for me to pave the way and try making it again though, right?"

"There's always something newer and better on the drug market," Fearnley agreed. He tidied up his tea tray and stood, signaling our time was over. "Pharmaceutical companies have to stay in business somehow."

I clenched the armrests and sized up Fearnley. This is what we were leaving with? We had a guy who was *there* when Whiteout was being tested, who was obviously mind fucking us, and we weren't putting any heat on him? His wording, his attitude, pointed to something else. Didn't Olivia see that?

"What have you been doing to stay in business all this time?" I gestured around the study. "Something lucrative I'd imagine. You pay for this place with your sculptures?"

Fearnley studied me. His right hand went to his neck, but he dropped it when he noticed he'd done it. "Yes, I do."

I wasn't done. "Great part of Seattle, too."

"It is."

"Expensive?"

Olivia reached out to my shoulder. I shrugged her off and leaned farther back in my chair. Fearnley was unmoving, his gaze fixed on me.

"Whiteout seems like the kind of drug that would do well on the streets. But for a nicer clientele. Someone who has a lot of money to spend and something important to protect. Don't you think? Imagine what men of power could get away with."

"Perhaps it would've been, the important word here being *would've*." Fearnley finally took a step towards the door. "I think it's time for you to leave. I shouldn't have let you stay after you brought up D.P. That's extremely private information."

"But you did. Guilty conscious maybe? People asking around about something you've been keeping secret for nearly a decade, profiting off of. Dirty money never feels good." I sprung out of my chair and strode to the bookshelf. "No amount of books will ever help you get rid of that feeling. Trust me, I know."

Olivia sat stone still, her hands still clutching her bag. My style of information gathering was very different from hers, but in this case it was the only way we'd get more if there was anything. Olivia got us in. I was grateful. It was my turn now. And part of me knew Fearnley might've been telling us the truth. Maybe he didn't know anything about Whiteout. Maybe he did make all his money off sculptures. My bluff could be for nothing.

Or maybe not.

Fearnley took two more steps to the door. I closed the distance between us and grabbed him by the arm. "You know why we're here. Admit it. You've been waiting for something like this to happen."

I was going out on a limb, but I was all in. My gut told me Fearnley was hiding something. If brute force was the only way to get it out of him, so be it.

"I was just trying to be helpful! Jesus, you're going to break my arm!"

"Whiteout is on the streets. People are dying. The worst things it could be used for are happening *right now*. Don't you feel at all bad about that?"

He took a deep breath. When he spoke, his words were

forced. I'd broken something in him. Planted the seed. "It's time for you to go. If you promise not to come back, I won't call the police."

"Why would you do that?"

"Please, *please* just promise me and go." Fearnley shook his head, his eyes squeezed shut. He pointed at the door with one limp hand. "Get out of here."

CHAPTER 25

"**W**hat was that?"

Olivia was livid the moment Fearnley shut the doors to his studio behind us. Her cheeks were flushed red.

"He was hiding something."

"Where did you come up with that? Just because he's different than you, he's hiding something?"

"We're playing the class card again, huh?" My laugh was bitter at best. "Nice, Olivia. I thought we were over that. When he saw me, he…I don't know, he recognized me or something. He kept staring at me."

We were already at her car. She flung the driver's side open into the road, eliciting a honk from an angry driver passing by. Olivia ignored it and slid into her seat. I got in the car.

"Staring? That's a terrible reason for what you did. And I'm not playing the class card and you know it. The second we went in there you were defensive. I admit, Fearnley was a little odd. He's an artist, they're always a little off. But your outright accusations were poorly handled."

I leaned back, replayed what just happened. I didn't regret it, but I might've handled it better. Hindsight being 20/20 and all that. If only I had been in a mindful mental space, I could've controlled my reaction. Fucking self-help books.

"There was something up with him. Plus, Fearnley

didn't seem interested in reporting us. I think we'll be okay. We have more names now, too." I put my seat buckle on. "Let's go back to your apartment. We'll look over the files. We should make one of those boards with names and strings showing connections. What do you say?"

She tried to keep her scowl but it dissolved into a reluctant smile. "Sure, Ethan."

Olivia and I had different frameworks for everything. Some parts aligned and others didn't. When they didn't, sparks flew. Neither of us could handle being undermined, or having a situation suddenly go out of our control. Especially when we thought we had it under control to begin with.

The better part of the drive consisted of us making little jabs at Fearnley's sculptures. Olivia even spoke in Fearnley's voice about tea and how delightful it was. She told me about an art exhibition she put on pro bono for a college friend. His art consisted only of sculptures made of beer cans from frat houses. It was supposed to be a serious commentary on hazing and the dangers of fraternities. It became a popular destination for the very frat brothers it disapproved of. They took pictures of themselves with their phones and stumbled around the exhibition drunk. It was the first time we talked about something that light. I liked it.

"I'm starving," she announced as we pulled into her parking garage, laughter still on the edge of her voice. "Let's order noodles. I need to check on some work stuff first, then we can get down to business."

Olivia had a handy folding dolly we stacked the boxes on and one of my bags. I shouldered my backpack and hauled everything to the elevator for the short ride to the first floor.

Her apartment was exactly as I saw it last. Even the cardboard circle the pizza had been on was still on the counter by our empty Diet Coke cans and the bottle of rubbing alcohol. I wheeled the files to the counter and started clearing space.

Olivia kicked off her shoes and pulled out her cell. Either she knew the noodle place number by heart or she had it on speed dial, because in a second she was placing an order for four different dishes.

I sat awkwardly at the counter, not sure what to do with myself, until Olivia slipped off to her room to check into work. I opened the boxes of files and stacked them neatly on the counter by type.

The profiles of the ten dead people interested me the most. Now out of D.P., I noticed the strong smell of musk and rot emanating from the papers. I found a pen amongst the junk cluttering Olivia's kitchen counters, and began circling anything noteworthy on the profiles as I read.

All the patients were of different ages, genders, and backgrounds. What unified them was their history with drugs. Some were addicted to hard drugs like heroin and meth, while others were pill poppers. One was an alcoholic. A few of them had specific notes on remaining family, but many had no family ties. The kind of people no one would miss.

I browsed through all of the consent documents, but the legal wording made no sense to me. It was like they were written to confuse. All I gleaned from it was a promise that Whiteout would help addicts get clean with little strain on their psyche. I wondered if this was some of the unclear wording Fearnley mentioned.

Forty minutes later Olivia came from her bedroom when the doorbell rang. She'd changed into loose pants and a sweater again, despite the sweltering temperatures in the apartment. She brought the takeout to the kitchen and set it on the floor while she tidied up a space near the fridge.

"You've been busy. Find anything?"

I leaned back. My eyes had a hard time readjusting to things farther away. "I just checked the last death certificate. It looks like you have to have a doctor or coroner sign off on it before it's official. Guess who signed every single one of these?"

Olivia finally set down the takeout on her cleared spot. "Who?"

"Dr. Kidd. The guy Fearnley said was on an IRB for Whiteout. Although I'm still not sure what an IRB is."

"Institutional Review Board. They're supposed to monitor clinical trials to protect the human participants." Olivia set up all the takeout boxes side by side and got two plates from a cupboard. "I was invited to be on one last year to provide a non-scientific humanitarian point of view. Do you want some of everything?"

"Sure, thanks." I thought about the IRB and laughed. "Fuck, they didn't do a good job of protecting the participants did they? I have a fake identity and no memory of my past."

Olivia set a heaping plate of noodles in front of me with a fork stuck in the side. I caught a piece of noodle that threatened to fall overboard. I took a mouthful of noodles and savored the spiciness, the warmth. It wasn't until I was eating that I realized how hungry I was. She retrieved more of the wretched diet soda from the fridge and gave me one of those, too.

"Maybe they didn't know what was happening. My dad must have, since he was on there and put Laurel in the program." Olivia pushed food around her plate.

I stopped eating and straightened up. "Hey, are you okay?"

"Yeah. I mean, I knew he wasn't a good person. Now I'm just seeing how bad he was." She laughed weakly. "Anyway, I've met that Wanda Christoph. She's the most compassionate woman I know. She'd never let anything like that slide. Plus, at some point the FDA *did* try to shut D.P. down so the boards did their job. What I'm wondering is if my dad was swaying the board or helping to hide things. And Dr. Kidd. He was on the board and signing off on these death certificates. Which, by the way, we don't know if all of them are fake or not. Some of these people could've died."

I speared a shrimp with my fork. "True. I guess we could do the missing person angle again? Do what I did to track myself down?"

"We could." Olivia gained more interest in her food and started eating again. "Hopefully if I go to the police station this weekend I'll be able to find what I can and hand it off to you. I can't take more time off work."

"The mayor thing, right? Election party or whatever?"

"It's a gala to announce his running for Senate. He'll also have a chance to start working the crowd for financial support, too. People have a good time, see him in a great light, they're more likely to show support. It's all politics really." She paused and laughed. "Literally all politics. But, what I mean it's a social game."

"I get it."

I finished off all my food and got seconds by the time Olivia finished her first plate. When she was done, she hopped off the bar stool and headed towards her room. "I'm going to grab my laptop. We'll check online for those people first, just in case."

I set my plate in the sink and turned back to the files. What we'd learned took a bit of the self-centered loathing from me. I used to think what happened to me was unique. Someone was out to get me. They made me suffer, tortured me. That wasn't the case. Other people were victims. From what I'd read about myself I wasn't particularly bright before I lost time. My parents and the girl, Sarah, cared about me. Apparently I didn't care about them or myself enough to get clean. I was wasting my life before and I continued to waste my life after. Was there anything I'd truly lost that I didn't bring on myself?

The thought hit me hard. Hard enough that I started opening cupboards in search of hard alcohol. Olivia's cupboards contained a bunch of healthy foods—why did she eat so poorly when she was with me?—that I probably couldn't pronounce the names of. After yielding no results, I went to the freezer. It was a treasure trove of ice creams and frozen pizzas. Then I spotted it; a frosted bottle of vodka. It hadn't even been opened.

I heard murmuring from Olivia's bedroom. It sounded like she was on the phone. I bet she'd say yes if I asked for a drink anyway, so I took the bottle and cracked it open. The ice cold liquid fogged the glass I poured it into. I knocked the shot back, then another, and poured myself a reasonable looking portion before returning the bottle to the freezer.

Heat spread from my throat into my core, then began to work its way down my arms and legs. That familiar tingly feeling washed over my head and my eyes smarted. Now all I needed was a cigarette and I'd be in good shape. I wandered over to the couch where I sat and studied Olivia's stuff. Closer to her room, I heard her talking. It was hushed, too quiet to make out words.

She had books on meditation and happiness that I recognized or had read myself. They were well worn, with dog-eared pages and sticky notes popping out of the edges. Just as I was about to reach out and pick one up, Olivia came from her room.

"That was Kaylee's mother. They found her body." She noticed the glass in my hand but didn't say anything.

"Jesus, are you serious? How did that happen?"

"She said they found her car turned over off the road on I90 towards the mountains this morning. It had caught on fire so the funeral will be closed casket. Coroner identified her by her dental records. Funeral is tomorrow morning by the way." Olivia fell into the couch next to me and tucked her legs beneath her.

"Tomorrow? That's a fast turnaround. Don't these things take a while?"

"Normally," she agreed. "Knowing her parents, their money, and track record with generous bribes, the timeline is possible."

People and their money. Must be nice. "Any idea why she was headed out that way?"

"According to the police she had snow gear in her car, like she was going snowshoeing."

"Is that something she did by herself?" I asked.

"Sure, it's possible, but the Kaylee I knew was a city girl. She didn't care for the outdoors and she certainly wouldn't go off by herself snowshoeing. Not like I told that to her mother. Naturally, she's devastated. Plus since the police came to her with this, she has no reason to suspect they're lying."

"Good point. No one except the people behind it, and us, know the truth." As I spoke an idea came to me. "You and Kaylee hang out in the same circles, right? You have most of the same friends?"

"There's a lot of overlap. We do have a few associates each who don't know each other."

"It's safe to say they'd be at the funeral tomorrow, right?"

Olivia grimaced. "What, do you think the killer will go to the funeral? Even if they did, what makes you think we'd know who it was?"

I took a deep breath. "This is the part you aren't going to like, but hear me out. You told me yourself you're drugged during these events where a lot of people are present. Tomorrow, those same people will likely be at the funeral. What if there was a way to find someone we know for certain is involved in this?"

"You're right, I don't like where this is going."

"What if we used you as bait?" I said it out loud anyway.

Olivia dropped her head back against the couch and rubbed her face, keeping the palms of her hands over her eyes. "God, Ethan, do you realize how desperate that sounds? You want me to knowingly put myself into danger."

"Well, you were going to go the funeral anyway, right? Just don't take any of your precautions. At the reception, drink and eat anything and everything people bring to you. Make it easy for them. I'll stand by and if you go off with someone, I'll follow. We could catch a guy in the act of trying to abduct you."

"What about *me*? Who knows what he'll do to me if he takes me and manages to escape you. And what would you even do if it seemed like someone was abducting me?"

She wouldn't remember what happened to her anyway, but I didn't point that out. It wouldn't do us any good. I did admit she was right on them escaping.

"Nobody has a clue what we know—"

"Assuming Fearnley didn't make some calls," she interrupted.

"Right, assuming he hasn't—and since nobody knows what we're doing, they have no reason to be suspicious. However they've done it before, they'll do it again." Still, Olivia wasn't convinced. I broke down the plan step by step, hoping it would reassure her. "Imagine we're at the reception. If there are lots of people there, maybe I can slip inside. Otherwise I'll wait outside somewhere with a good vantage point. You start walking off with a guy. Maybe you're suspicious of him, maybe you aren't. You go with him anyway. But I'm right behind you the entire time. Once things get dicey, he tries to get you in a car, I'll step in and save you."

She snickered. "My Knight in shining armor."

"Ha-ha. I'll give you that one," I laughed. "What do you think?"

"What will you do? No offense, but if you're popping up out of nowhere asking me to come with you, whoever I'm with will be very skeptical."

"We play your original cover story. I bump into you, tell you I've been trying to get a hold of you because of some big issue with the charity outreach program. I'll ask if I can talk to you privately. We step aside, then you go back and say you're terribly sorry but something has come up. Perfect."

"Not perfect, but it's passable," Olivia admitted. "It will get me out of dodge."

I sipped at my vodka, pleased with myself. It was an aggressive plan. If it worked, we'd have a face and name of someone who was behind Whiteout. That would put me even closer to knowing what happened to me. Maybe I could put an end to Whiteout, then get out of Seattle forever. Fuck, I might even try to start a new life somewhere if I had it in me.

Putting an end to Whiteout. I wasn't sure what that would look like. I'd killed in self-defense. Andrew was an entirely different situation. I couldn't see myself carrying out premeditated, coldblooded murder. I could, however, see myself hiring someone else to do it. The people using Whiteout now, and the ones who tortured me before, deserved to die. When I thought of Skid's death—of Kaylee's brutal murder—that conviction was even stronger. The drug just hit the streets and it didn't seem like there were many points of contact to get it. If whoever was behind it was uprooted like a weed, *that* would put an end to it.

Olivia didn't want to tarnish her reputation by going to the police with what happened to her, but she still wanted justice. Everyone won with my plan. The people behind Whiteout had to go.

I finished off my vodka and set it on a coaster on the

cluttered coffee table. It was time to test the waters again, see if Olivia's tune had changed. Maybe I could get her on board with my plan.

"We're getting close, Olivia. Last time we talked, you said you just wanted to know who the men were so you could avoid them, not confront them." I tried to be delicate with it. "Is that still the case?"

She tilted her face towards me. For a moment it seemed those piercing blue eyes saw right through me. Then she blinked and turned away, eyes focused on the fireplace. "I don't think so. After we saw Kaylee like that, the idea of doing absolutely nothing is horrific. Where is the justice in that? Once we find out who is involved, we—sorry, I—can take it to the police. Maybe not SPD, but someone higher up. The FBI or something, I don't know. Someone needs to do something about it. They can't get away with this."

I wanted to tell her what I was going to do, but couldn't. Olivia still wanted structured, approved justice. I had a feeling she wasn't down for vigilantism. She might like the results once it was over. If she knew now, though, she would try to stop me. She'd say it wasn't right. Olivia proved herself more complicated than I thought, but I still trusted my gut. She wouldn't like what I wanted to do.

So I wouldn't tell her. We'd go through with our plan, I'd find names, and end them.

"Ethan?"

"Sorry, what did you say?"

"Thank you for helping me." She reached across the space between us and set her hand on my shoulder, then gave it one quick squeeze before returning it to her side. "Thank you for everything."

CHAPTER 26

My body is wrapped in wires, from my toes to the top of my head. They cut into my flesh and make it bleed. The pressure on one of my eyes is so intense, I know it will pop soon. The wire will cut into it and it will ooze out. I deserve this. I see Andrew's face and he's crying. Crying because I murdered him, because life was unfair and life did its work through me.

The wires release and I'm on the ground in a black, infinite space. Cuts on my body sing with a pain so pure my brain can barely comprehend it.

Laurel is beside me. I know her name now. Her hand is stroking my body, smearing blood across my skin. She is telling me about her father, her family, her school. But it's getting harder and harder to remember them. The drugs make her memories stretch and tear. Soon she won't remember any of them. She smiles and says, maybe then I can restart my life. We can look at it as our lives being taken away, or we can see it as a real second chance.

I tell her about Sarah. I remember her, her beautiful hair and laugh like chimes. The only light in my dismal life. I used to have a picture of her. A man gave it back to me when I went to the apartment. Then I killed Andrew.

I knew they'd come and take me back. I knew in time, there would be so many holes in my memory eventually it would be nothing. I taped it under the shelf and left her behind. They'd take it away from me when they found me again.

Time bends. I'm lying in the back of a van. The carpet is sticky. I can't move my legs. I hear someone up front say they're sorry. So sorry.

I smell the ocean. I feel their hands as they haul me out of the van. I'm finally going to die. It's going to be over.

Everything is cold. I can't breathe. I'm sucking down salt water and it's filling my lungs. I kick my feet but they're stuck. Tied to something. I kick and kick. I'm free. I'm going up. I suck in fresh air. I'm floating in the ocean.

I'm alone.

When I woke up, my body was paralyzed. Only my eyes worked and I stared at the unfamiliar landscape around me. Too much golden light streamed into Olivia's apartment. Self-help books stacked on the coffee table blocked my view of the fireplace. The faint smell of soy sauce and egg noodles lingered.

The dream had been more coherent than any other. There was still a surreal quality to it, things that obviously couldn't have happened, but the rest? It resonated as a memory, not fabrication. I was sure this was what my buddy Plato was talking about when it came to anamnesis. I had talked to Laurel. I had left that picture behind. Someone tried to dump my body. While the memories were useless, they were something. With no drug to grab and dull my pain, I lay instead. Let the miserable feeling of being sober wash over me.

I hated mornings. Or rather, waking up. My brain had so much time to keep working, churning, while I was asleep. It always came up with worst case scenarios, and other depressing thoughts, that it was excited to present to me the second I came to. The confidence I had about my plan last night, the conviction I had to kill whoever was behind Whiteout, looked like a lot of work now. It seemed like it would be too hard to do, had too many risks. I was also aware of my tiny roll of cash, barely a grand, that would need to get me through…well, I didn't know. Probably a long time, and with an alcohol and cigarette habit that wasn't much.

I shook the foggy memory of the dream away and sat up. Last night, when she offered me the couch, I accepted. I had plenty of nights sleeping on cold, hard surfaces headed my way. In the meantime, I'd take where I could get. Plus, Donovan had called me and left a voicemail about his uncle. He couldn't keep his voice straight as he asked where I was, how I was doing, and told me to come by his place soon. He stopped by mine and I wasn't there. Where was I?

Staying at Olivia's place was safe. I needed that. Her couch, though a bit too short for me, was a better sleep than my mattress back at the apartment anyway, and here there was no threat of being murdered in my sleep. She'd given me multiple blankets, though I didn't use any due to the desert-like temperatures she kept the place at, and a clean soft pillow.

The godly scent of coffee hit my nose. I forced myself off the couch to investigate. A space had been cleared on the kitchen counter and a coffee maker I hadn't noticed before was plugged in. It blubbered away happily as it dripped coffee into a pot. I was surprised I slept through the sound of Olivia setting it up.

"This thing, like that vodka you guzzled, was an apartment warming gift. Never used it but I figured we might need an extra boost this morning. Grabbed some coffee beans from the store down the street."

Olivia wore a black knee-length dress that had sleeves down to her wrists. It scooped around her neck, showing her pale skin. Her hair was turned up in a towel and her face was, incredibly, without any makeup. Her eyelashes and brows were so pale they almost faded into her skin. I had to give her kudos for the expertly applied makeup she wore every day.

The funeral was soon. Caffeine wasn't the only thing I'd need to get through today.

"You've been up for a while?"

"Of course. It's almost eleven." She went into the kitchen and pulled down two mugs from the cupboard. "I've been to the gym downstairs, bought the coffee beans, showered, and I'm getting ready to go now. I put some clean towels in the bathroom if you need to take a shower."

I became aware of how itchy my unwashed clothes and body were. "Yeah, that sounds good. What time is the funeral?"

She poured two mugs to the brim with coffee and handed me one. No tea drinking today.

"Two. There's a service at a church downtown, then everyone will go to the cemetery up in Queen Anne. After that is a reception at the parent's house about ten minutes away from the cemetery." She blew on her coffee and took a sip. "Plenty of opportunities for someone to kidnap me."

I wasn't sure if she was trying to be funny or not, so I drank deeply from the mug instead. The coffee was too hot to gulp, but felt good and woke me up. It tasted like money. Knowing Olivia, the beans were expensive. I savored it.

"All right. If this works, we'll be in good shape. If it doesn't, we'll continue on the investigation track. Sound good?"

"Works for me. I feel like I should be wearing a wire or something." Now she laughed and I returned a smile. She set her mug down, barely touched, and headed off to get ready.

I finished mine and the rest of the pot before taking the offered shower. The bathroom was all blue tile and porcelain appliances. It felt awkward being in there amongst the dozens of hair and body products, so I opted for a fast rinse and put on some of the few clean clothes I had in my duffel. Even after I was done it took Olivia another hour before she declared she was ready.

Her hair had been put up into some kind of bun and she'd pinned a piece of lace into it that settled over her eyes. It looked retro. I wondered if she'd gotten it for the occasion or if she'd been to a lot of funerals. She consolidated whatever she needed from her huge bag to a small black purse to match her outfit.

"I'll have to drop you off away from the church, then I'll park. We don't want to be seen together. Wait outside the church, or come in if that's possible. I guess we don't have any choice but to drive together to the cemetery." Olivia grabbed her keys from the kitchen as she led me out of the apartment. "I'm trusting you, Ethan. Don't let anything happen to me."

"Don't worry. We don't know for sure if someone will try to take you. The reception will be a better time than the funeral itself," I assured her.

Soon we were in the car and driving downtown. Olivia dropped me off two blocks from the church. I knew it well; they served food to people in need every other week. It had been a great hunting ground for people looking to score. I had a skull cap, pulled low to my eyebrows, but wished I had sunglasses, too. Any one of the Melnikov family could spot me. Now that I knew they were looking for me, it made being on the streets dangerous.

The street across from the church had cafes and shops. I went into one of the cafes, reasoning that since it had the best view of the church it justified grabbing a coffee and donut. I parted grudgingly with ten bucks for the goods and settled into the front of the shop by one of the windows, next to two teenage girls yapping about their upcoming Christmas break.

Kaylee's funeral drew a huge crowd. Masses of people entered the church over the half hour before the funeral started. Olivia was one of them. She'd buddied up with another woman that looked her age. Everyone was dressed in black or dark gray, save for the few attention grabbers who opted for something bolder.

I expected to see someone and know right away, *yeah, that's a killer.* But none of the people who entered the church stuck out. In fact, they were all the same to me. Similar haircuts, similar suits. They carried themselves the same way. Any one of them could've killed Kaylee or was drugging Olivia.

My phone buzzed. It was a text from Olivia.

So far so good in here. Funeral starts in five.

For the next hour she'd be safe and I had time to waste.

I grabbed a book from a take-one-leave-one bookshelf the cafe had and read. It was poetry, something I didn't care for, and I found myself reading the same lines over and over. I was worried about Olivia. About what could happen.

One of the girls next to me tried to start a conversation with me about the book—they'd read it in one of their classes—and I indulged them. As the hour came to a close and I saw people coming out of the church, I bid the girls farewell and left the cafe.

My body tensed as I walked out and spotted Olivia with a man her age exiting the church. She had her hand on his arm as they walked. There was a smile on her face that I recognized as genuine. He hugged her, his hand coming up to the exposed skin of her upper back. He lingered, but eventually pulled away. My gut tensed. Something wasn't right.

The two started down the street together. I took the risk and jaywalked across the street, hoping no eager cops stopped me, and trailed behind them. I let myself get closer until I was only five feet away. That's when I spotted it.

It was no bigger than a dime and was stuck on her upper right shoulder, partially obscured by her dress. The color would've matched her skin had she not been so incredibly pale. I was sure it hadn't been there before. The suited man had to have placed it on her when he hugged her.

It was time to put my plan into action, but first I wanted to see where he would take her. We neared the parking garage where I knew Olivia left her car and they kept going, turning left at the corner. More storefronts with apartment buildings above them. Further down the street the buildings grew taller and turned into high rises near

Fifth Avenue. We were blocks away from Westlake where I first encountered Kaylee.

They stopped outside an old building with a wood façade and giant windows. There were lots of old retail spaces like this around town. Where once there had been a single business per building, now the buildings were often converted into multiple office spaces or boutiques. This particular one was split in half. The right side was Raven & Holloway Law Group. The left was under renovation.

The guy Olivia was with was patting down his pockets. Olivia was fine. She didn't act nervous and kept close by him as they chatted. For someone who was worried about getting drugged, she was being awfully friendly. I worked up some saliva to coat my dry mouth and swallowed.

"Miss Holloway?"

Startled, she turned around and faced me. Her eyes widened and smile faltered. "Oh, hi. How are you?"

"I'm okay. I've been trying to get in touch with you about the outreach program. We have a small funding crisis and I needed your help."

Her friend eyed my beat up my jeans and jacket. I hoped it helped my case instead of raising more suspicion.

"I've been at a funeral, I'm sorry." Olivia's brow furrowed. She glanced at her companion. "Hugh, I'm sorry. This is Oliver Smith. I'm working with him on an outreach program for recovering addicts. Do you mind waiting for a moment while I speak with him?"

"Olivia and Oliver? What a coincidence." He laughed, pleased with his observation, then he waved us away. "Of course. I'll wait here, no rush."

Olivia led me out of earshot and leaned forward. "What

are you doing?"

Not what I had expected. "I'm saving you. That guy is drugging you."

"Jesus, Ethan. I've known him since I was a kid. There hasn't been a single opportunity for him to drug me."

"He's watching us, so don't touch it. I saw him stick a patch to your shoulder. That's how they're getting it to you. Through the skin. That way you can't stop them. They probably take it off when they put you back in your apartment." I watched the mix of confusion and denial spread on her face. "Olivia, where is he taking you? The parking garage was a block back."

"His father has been friends with mine since before I was born. Hugh said his father had a condolence gift dropped off at the office and we were just going to grab it." She paused and squeezed her eyes shut. "I'm so gullible. Why am I so fucking gullible? He used to date Kaylee. About a year ago. He'd have her security code. Kaylee doesn't change things like that."

"Calm down. You had no idea. Just go back and tell him this is urgent and you have to help me out before you head over to the reception, okay?"

She nodded quickly and took a deep breath. "I can do this."

"Olivia, wait." I stopped her from leaving. "If he tries to hug you, let him. He might be trying to remove the patch and we don't want to give him any reason to be suspicious."

Another quick nod and she headed back. As I predicted, Hugh hugged her again. Now that I knew what to look for, I saw him peel away the patch as he kept her in his arms. I wondered if it had been on long enough to make her forget the incident, and what she'd feel like coming off it.

She returned to me and kept walking. I followed. She was upset. I wanted to let her take the lead on this. "What do you want to do?"

"He wanted me to go in the office for some reason." She was angry now. Betrayal did that to a person. "So let's wait until he leaves, and we'll see what he has in there."

CHAPTER 27

We walked back to her car and waited in hope that Hugh went to the reception as he said he would. Olivia was lost in her own thoughts. To know a lifetime friend, who she didn't suspect at all, had slipped her Whiteout must be earth-shattering. So many things had been turned upside down or straight up torn apart in her life since I met her. I was impressed with how well she was handling it.

Then again, Olivia already had a crack in her life she dealt with since her earliest days. Her public image versus her life at home. The rigidity and perfection she had in her office, in her appearance when she walked out the door. Then, chaos everywhere else.

Our brooding was interrupted by Olivia gasping. "*Ugh.* That taste." Her fingers went to her lips. She looked at me. "Ethan? Where? How'd we get to the...oh, hell."

More like oh fuck. I went to set my hand on her shoulder but thought better of it. Olivia's breath was shallow, her chest barely rising and falling with each quick inhale. "You're safe, Olivia. You're with me. We're in your car."

She wrapped her arms around herself. "Tell me what happened. I need every detail."

"Take some deep breaths, okay? It hasn't been long. You haven't lost much time. You're coming off Whiteout right now."

"I know I am! I don't remember coming here!"

Olivia was panicked, but not nearly as bad as Kaylee had been when I first met her. Or myself, or what I imagined Skid's friend was like. The patch had been on her for less than ten minutes, which indicated it was likely an extended release formula. She hadn't received a large dose of the drug yet, and I bet that was why she wasn't going ballistic.

You pick up a few things about drugs after seven years of pushing, if you're so inclined.

"They have another delivery method for Whiteout. Not the pills like I've seen. A guy put a patch on you outside the church."

"Who? Who did it?"

"Hugh."

"No." Olivia launched into the same conversation we had less than a half hour ago. Hugh would never do it. He was a family friend.

After I relayed the conversation I had with her while she was under the small dose of Whiteout, she went silent. Then, "Thanks. Thanks for saving me."

"You going to be okay?"

"Yeah. It's just weird. As I'm sure you know. One second I'm walking down the street, then I'm here with you and you're filling in the blanks. At least I have that much, right?"

"Right," I agreed.

"Anyway, he's gone by now, I'm sure." Olivia grabbed her purse and slid out of the car. "Let's head back."

I followed beside her. "You have a key to the office?"

"Surprisingly, yes. It's only because my dad finds it more convenient to give me one so I can run the occasional errand for him than a matter of trust. If the alarm system deactivate code is still the same, we should be in good shape."

On the way back to Raven & Holloway, I kept an eye out for Hugh but he was nowhere to be seen. If he did go back to the reception, we'd have plenty of time to look through the office.

Olivia unlocked the front door and satiated the concerned alarm system.

It was like every other reception area I'd been in the past few weeks. Big desk in the middle of a well-lit area. There were waiting chairs. Double doors flanked either side of the desk. One had Raven & Son in a gold plaque, the other Holloway. Behind the reception desk were glass shelves full of awards. Some were framed images, others little statues. To our left was a hallway that offered a bathroom and an emergency exit to the street behind the building.

"I suppose we should check out Hugh's office first," Olivia said. She went to the door and pressed it open.

The room had two giant ornate desks. Father and son, I guessed. Nothing was out of place. Pens, laptop, the obligatory family photo. Bookshelves offered thick, hardback books that looked too decorative to ever be read. I went to the desk closest to us. It had drawers on both sides. I pulled open the first one and found files. They were all case files, the kind of shit I certainly shouldn't be looking at. Olivia went to the other desk and started rummaging, too.

"While we were in college Hugh asked me out a lot. We went on a few dates, but I just didn't like him. I told him I wasn't interested. We were great friends growing up, but just friends." The story coming from Olivia was more to herself than me, but I listened. "He didn't take it well.

He said he really thought we had something special and he'd thought so since we were children. The whole thing was so awkward. I wanted to stop being friends all together, but he insisted we not let our friendship be ruined because of him. Here we are, years later. The occasional awkward lunch date. I see him at parties if his father is there. And now, to think what he's been doing."

"Don't blame yourself for not suspecting him. It's not your fault," I assured her. "I saw him; he's charming as fuck. We don't expect the people closest to us to be the ones screwing us over."

We lapsed into silence as we looked over the files. Like the organization of the room, nothing in the documents was out of place either. I got on my knees and ran my hands around the underside and lips of the desk.

I heard Olivia's heels click-clack towards me. "What are you doing?"

"Checking for anything secret taped to the desk somewhere, I guess." I laughed as I groped around underneath. "Nothing to lose, right?"

"I'll check the other one." I expected her to see some humor in it, but she was dead serious as she crouched down and started checking the other desk.

Neither of us found anything.

Olivia collapsed into the heavy red leather chair at the desk and sighed. "What was he going to do when he brought me in here?"

I had ideas, but I wasn't going to share. Instead, I shrugged and sat in the other desk chair. Fuck it was comfortable. I leaned back and let it hug my body.

"We should check your dad's office and the receptionist

desk just in case. I'm not sure what we're going to find here, but we can't leave knowing we didn't look everywhere we could." I tried to veer her off the subject. Not because it wasn't important, but because we needed to focus.

"Right." She hauled herself out of the chair and straightened items on the desk that had been bumped.

I did the same and found her at the reception desk. It had no drawers, just a laptop, and didn't take long to look over.

"I'm going to stop by the restroom. I need to rinse my mouth out. Head into my dad's office and start looking," Olivia said. "Meet you there in a second."

While the Ravens' office was ornate and vintage, Mr. Holloway's was austere. The desk was made of steel and glass. Two metal filing cabinets rested against the wall behind the desk. There was an abstract painting of blue and white swirls that held no visual appeal. There wasn't a single family photo anywhere. Two blue metal chairs faced his desk. Despite the small leather cushion on them, they looked incredibly uncomfortable.

I went to the filing cabinets first. They were locked. His desk drawers were locked as well, save for the top right which had a jumble of office supplies.

Just when I had given up, Olivia finally showed up in the doorway. Her face was pale. She leaned against the door frame.

"You okay?" I asked. "You were gone a while."

"I found something. You need to see this."

She led me down the little hallway in the reception area to the bathroom. It was ten square feet at least, and decorated more in the Raven fashion. There was a second door adjacent to the toilet. It gaped open. I expected to see a broom closet, but it was a whole other room. It was beat up. The wood floor was missing boards, the walls were peeling, and the whole room was lit from an ambient glow coming from cloudy plastic hung over the windows. Pallets of tile and constructions supplies took residence in the corner by a closed door. Another door directly across from me was open. This was the left side of the building that was under renovation. The two sides were connected by the door Olivia opened.

I reached out and pushed the door shut. The door itself wasn't hidden. Though painted the same tawny shade as the bathroom, it was obviously a door. It was strange, I had to admit.

"Why is this door here? It's a weird place for it."

"It is. This didn't used to be a bathroom, it was a janitor's closet with a sink. This is a historic building, almost seventy years old. Four years ago the owner sublet this part of the building to my dad for his practice and they remodeled."

Olivia opened the door again and walked into the room with the construction supplies. "This room provides shared access to the basement for both sides of the building. Dad planned on removing his door to it and walling it off, since he'd never have use for the basement and he wanted to turn it into a bathroom, but the owner wouldn't let him do it. Said it would be defacing a historic part of Seattle or something." Olivia rolled her eyes, apparently finding the story ridiculous. "So he installed little metal strips on the top and bottom of the door to stop it from opening, painted over it and took the doorknob out as an act of defiance, saying it was as good as a wall now."

"Sounds like more trouble than it's worth. The door is open now, so that means…?"

"I haven't been here in months. The last time I was here, you couldn't get through this door. Now you can. What if Hugh was going to take me in *here*?"

"If he wanted to take you into that side, why wouldn't he just do it?" I asked.

Her eyebrows rose up. She brought her fingertips to her temple. "Because, I wouldn't do it. If we were on the street and he suggested we go in that way, I'd get suspicious or put up a fight. But I'd willingly come in here, then he could force me wherever he wanted once I'm out of sight."

It made sense. Charming Hugh wouldn't want to risk anyone they knew seeing them go into a shady building. If anyone did spot them, they'd see longtime friends going into their father's law office. Nothing suspicious there.

I stepped into the room. It smelled dusty and vaguely of stagnant water. The stacks of tile looked like they'd been there at least a few months, with a thin coating of dust across them. I went to the door by the tiles and opened it. There was a narrow stairwell. A single bare bulb on the bottom of the steps revealed a concrete wall that went left and right.

"There's a light on," I told Olivia. "Does anyone own this building?"

"I don't know. Do you think someone's in here?"

I paused and listened. If there was someone downstairs, they were being quiet. I withdrew my gun. "No, but I'm not taking any risks. And I'm going to find out. Stay behind me, okay?"

She nodded and kept a good distance behind me as I

started down the stairs. The temperature dropped quickly as I descended. I became aware of the scent of piss and a coppery undertone that had to be blood. I led with my gun, keeping it level as I hit the landing and checked both my sides. To the left was a small, empty alcove. To the right the basement opened up to shelves of old junk. Paint cans, tools, boxes. What stuck out was a wooden chair in the center, a rope hanging loose on each arm and leg.

The basement appeared to wrap around the staircase into the other side of the building. I moved close to the shelves and strained to catch any sounds. It felt empty, but I didn't let my guard down.

As I turned a corner, I came face to face with fresh plywood. This half of the basement had been walled off completely. There was a closed door in the center, with a latch above the doorknob. The latch had two padlocks.

Yeah, we definitely found something.

I steadied my hands, willing their nervous shaking to stop. Behind me, Olivia started to breathe faster. I dropped one hand to the locks and inspected them. They were combination locks. And both were already open.

Before I pulled them off, I turned to Olivia and looked her hard in the eyes. "Olivia, we have no idea what's in there. You need to be ready for the worst. I'm not going to ask if you can do this, because I know you can. Ready?"

"Yes. Open it."

I unhinged the padlocks and set both on the ground. Then I opened the door.

"Holy fuck."

I expected something bad. I had a few ideas inspired by movies on what a torture room would look like. What

I saw was worse, because it was real. My mind went wild presenting me with images of what could've been done there. The suffering, the cruelty.

My hand was on autopilot. I reached into my jacket pocket and pulled out a plastic bag. Concern for my gun set aside, I holstered it and pulled out two Xanax. At least I thought that's what they were. It didn't matter; in that moment I needed something to blur the edges. I swallowed them dry and felt them catch in my throat. After working up more spit, I swallowed again and felt them travel down.

The room was about fifteen square feet. The walls and ceiling were padded with thick, wavy soundproofing panels. Pushed against the corner was a bare mattress, stained with blood and other bodily fluids. There were rings coming from the ground and wall with cuffs attached to them to keep the victim restrained.

Watching over the scene was a camera on a tripod. It was plugged into a power outlet in the wall. The screen was open and ready to use. Behind it was a set of floodlights, set onto the lowest setting but still casting blinding light onto the scene. A metal stool was near the tripod. There was a spiral bound notebook sitting on top of it.

To my right was a wall of rusty metal lockers. It looked like the room was built around them. Black plastic tubs were stacked in front of them with lids hiding their contents.

Olivia moved past me into the room and picked up the notebook. She only looked at it for a second before handing it to me. "I can't believe this."

She could. She just didn't want to. I took the notebook and flipped it open to the middle. Printed in neat handwriting were names of girls on the left side and dates on the other. Between this data were names, but they didn't make sense. Eagle, Herring, Azure, Captain, Bolt. The first two could be connected since they were birds, but the rest didn't fit in. Considering where they were, they had to be code names.

I was looking at a page from two months ago. I turned to the most recent pages and my gaze fell on the latest entry. It was for Olivia. The code name was Herring. Hugh Raven was Herring. It made sense in a pathetic he-thinks-he's-clever kind of way. I wondered if his father was in on it. Father and son code named after birds.

Besides Olivia's name I recognized Kaylee, but no others. Olivia appeared sporadically, but Kaylee came up nearly every week. Only one other girl, Miranda, showed up as often as Kaylee. I flipped to the front of the book and saw that the dates had started a year ago. Did it mean that's when this whole operation started? Or it was it just when they started logging?

It wasn't any of my business to look, but I did. As I flipped through the pages I looked for Olivia's name. Two names kept coming up: Herring and Captain. At most Olivia had been drugged twice in one month, otherwise she was the least used of any of the girls. If I were her, I'd find it reassuring, but since I didn't know if she wanted the information, I kept it to myself.

"It's a log," I started to say, then realized Olivia probably guessed that much. "Do you know anyone named Miranda? Olivia?"

She was fixated on the bed. Her eyes were impossibly wide. When I set my hand on her shoulder she finally looked at me. "No. How much is Kaylee on there?"

"A lot," I said. "I think these are code names for the other people involved. Does Azure, Captain, or Bolt mean anything to you?"

A nod. Suddenly her body was in motion and she darted from the room, then fell to her knees by a workbench. She dry heaved, then regained enough composure to say, "Azure was our dog."

"Who is it then?"

Her answer was cut off by the sounds of footsteps upstairs.

CHAPTER 28

My gut told me to run, but the only way out was up the staircase. Then the instinct to fight came over me. I had a gun, I knew how to use it. I could shoot down whoever got in my way and make a run for it. After fighting Melnikov's guys, I knew I had it in me to win a gunfight.

The third option, my least favorite, made the most sense. I needed to know who each of the men were. I was confident Eagle was Hugh's father. Olivia knew who Azure was. That left Bolt and Captain. I wanted to take out everyone involved in Whiteout. Until I knew all the players, I had to avoid direct confrontation.

The internal dialog took place in seconds. I grabbed Olivia's arm and hauled her up. There were few places to hide outside of the room. The shelves offered no cover. We went into the last place I knew either of us wanted to go.

My heartbeat thundered in my ears. It made my whole body pulse. I wondered if the Xanax didn't work anymore, because it sure as fuck wasn't relaxing me.

I shoved aside one of the black tubs and opened the locker. It was narrow, but empty and deep enough for Olivia to fit in with room to spare vertically. I pushed her in. "We have to hide. Be quiet, Olivia. Whatever you do be quiet, okay?"

I didn't wait for an answer and closed the locker on her, then returned the black tub to its original position.

The door to the room was still open. It was impossible to get the locks back on and hide, but I shut the door anyway hoping no one would read into it. I opened the locker next to Olivia's. Ropes and chains hung from giant hooks. Shit. I opened the next one and found a ratted jacket hanging inside. Good enough. I squeezed myself in. My body pressed against it and I smelled motor oil and dust. As quietly as I could, I pulled the locker door shut until it clicked.

My head pressed painfully into the locker ceiling. If someone out there didn't kill me, I'd die of claustrophobia or a panic induced heart attack inside the confined space.

With the door to the padded room shut, it felt oppressed and quiet inside. I was aware of my own labored breathing and tried to stay it. Four narrow slats, angled downward, provided my view of the room. The tubs, tripod, stool, and edge of the mattress were in my field of view. Olivia would have a similar view where she was. I needed her to watch— as painful as it might be—because she was our fastest way of identifying the men.

I heard the door swing open and multiple sets of footsteps enter the room. Two men dragged the body of a woman. They tossed her on the mattress. I saw black high heeled shoes, black tights, and the hem of a black dress. Whoever she was, I'd bet anything they got her from the funeral.

"Didn't plan on doing this today, but since the slot opened up." The voice was older, deeper. Definitely not Hugh. "Cross out yourself and Olivia and put me down for Julie."

"I bet you're really fucking pleased with yourself about that." The second voice was Hugh. I recognized the tone, the snobbery. "It was my turn with Olivia. Who knows how long I'll have to wait now. No one screams like that girl."

"She's no Kaylee."

"Jesus, you're insane. No repeat of that or the Cap is going to destroy you. You almost destroyed all of us. You break the rules too much. If we hadn't found her running around Westlake, who the fuck knows what would've happened. And the markers!"

"How was I supposed to know she'd go postal from smelling markers?"

"Maybe if you didn't draw on her every fucking time you had her she wouldn't have been triggered by it." Hugh kicked the wall of the room with a soft thud. "And you *know* we only bring them here and we only kill one if we all agree. You did the messiest kill ever in her fucking apartment. The cops investigated me when the parents reported her missing, you know that? Because I used to date her."

My body felt like it was going to tear itself apart from the inside out. Kaylee's murderer was there. Two of the people I held accountable for Skid's death, for Olivia's suffering, were right there. I was aware of the Glock's presence against my hip, pressing hard between me and the locker wall. I wanted to unload every round I had into them.

"Don't knock it until you try it." The older man grunted as he knelt down. I saw more of him now. He wore a tailored suit and was unbuckling his pants. "You don't know what power feels like until you have someone trussed up like that."

Hugh snickered. "I know what power feels like. I keep your videos."

The older man was quiet for a minute, then said, "Get

out. I'll call you when I'm ready for you to take her back."

Hugh said nothing more and left, closing the door behind him. The older man stood and walked behind the tripod and adjusted the camera. His pants sagged low on his hips. He shimmied out of them and placed them on the stool, followed by his jacket then the rest of his clothing until he was buck naked.

The girl moaned and shifted. "Where am I?"

"Did you say something, slut?" The man went to the top of the bed, out of my line of sight. "You acted so sweet at Kaylee's funeral. The crying had everyone fooled but me. I know you're a tease. I know you don't care about anyone but yourself. I know..."

His trail of profanities continued into incoherent mumbling. The girl was sobbing now, her cries cut off occasionally by him hitting her. Eventually he stripped her clothes off and climbed behind her. The screams shifted, the pain different now.

My stomach clenched into a hard knot. I squeezed my eyes shut and wished I could cover my ears to block out the sounds of the twisted bastard raping the girl. His name calling, his grunting, the sick sound of flesh slapping against flesh.

What the fuck was I doing? This wasn't me. I wasn't going to let this happen.

Just as I was about to open the locker door, I heard Olivia's open first. The man kept going, oblivious to what was happening behind him. I slowly pushed my door open and unholstered my gun.

Olivia stood behind the tripod, her gaze fixed on the man and girl. He rooted at her like an animal, one hand on the back of her head pressing it into the mattress. Olivia turned to face me. Tears streamed down her face. She held her hand out to me. At first I was confused, then saw her hand reaching for the gun.

I let her take it. She took a deep breath, then was in motion. She blocked the edge of the floodlight which caught the man's attention first. He turned but was blinded, then I'd imagine everything went dark as Olivia slammed the butt of the gun against his temple. She dropped to her knees and began removing the manacles from the girl, who was too overwhelmed to speak. I picked the gun up from the floor where she dropped it.

"Get the chair from out there," Olivia said. "Tie him up before he wakes."

It took me a second before I followed her order and stepped out of the room into the remainder of the basement. Even the air out here felt lighter than in the torture room. I gulped in deep breaths of it as I went to the chair we saw earlier and dragged it back into the room. Olivia had the girl's dress back on and her arms wrapped around her.

"It's okay, Julie," she murmured. "We're going to get you out of here. Just stay calm, okay?"

I pushed the tripod aside to make room for the chair. The naked man was twitching so I picked up the pace and lifted him into it. Moving unconscious bodies was much harder than I thought. He seemed heavier than he should have and his limbs flopped as I settled him. I tied the ropes around his wrists and ankles and looked to Olivia.

"Do you have anything I can give her?"

There was no more Xanax. I had some uppers, but that was the last thing she needed. "I have some pain killers.

That's it."

"Give me one. Turn the floodlight on him."

I searched my pockets and found my last Oxy and handed it to Olivia. Whatever her plan was, she seemed to be confident. The girl knew her or trusted her, because when Olivia held the pill up she took it and swallowed it.

"Olivia, what are we doing?" I asked. "What are we doing with *him*?"

She looked away from the girl at the man. Her glazed expression finally shifted into pure anger.

"That's Azure," she said. "That's my father."

CHAPTER 29

For years my life had been about me. My suffering, my misery, my unknown past, my trauma. There was nothing outside of it. No one could know those things like I did. No one could know the horror of losing years of your life, of not knowing who you were. Of seeing scars on your body and not knowing where they came from.

Olivia's pain wasn't the same as mine. I didn't try to quantify or qualify it. I saw the agony on her face and for the first time ever, I empathized. I was not in this ordeal alone, and neither was she. Whatever she needed, *whatever* she needed, I would do what I could.

I continued to wait for Olivia's lead. She retrieved her father's phone and sent a text to Hugh saying he was taking the girl back himself and there was no need to come back. Then she stared at him for nearly ten minutes. He'd been awake for half of it. He yelled for help at first, then quieted down.

The girl sat in the corner beside the mattress. She drifted in and out, the pain killers making her loopy. Olivia stayed by her side until her father woke up, then she stood beside me watching him.

The first thing I'd noticed about him was that Olivia looked nothing like her father. His hair was black, peppered with gray, and his complexion was more olive than hers. The only thing they had in common were the eyes, a shade of light blue that seemed to glow. His brows were furrowed low into a scowl. He glared past the floodlight with hatred so pure I felt needles prickling my skin.

His chest was still slick with sweat. Wiry gray hairs sprouted from his upper body and stomach. I'd tightened the cords on the chairs as far as they would go. His arms were red from where they rubbed against his skin.

"What the fuck is this?" He struggled against his restraints and tried squinting through the blinding light. "Who the fuck are you?"

Olivia leaned over and whispered in my ear. "Ask him whatever you want. I need a minute, okay?"

I nodded, glad to have the chance for some interrogation. "Tell me who's supplying you with Whiteout."

A vein bulged in his neck. "How do you know about Whiteout?"

"Does it matter? Tell me who's giving it to you." I didn't care about hiding behind the floodlight any longer. I came forward and pressed the muzzle of my gun against his head. He didn't shy away from it, but pressed into it instead. I lowered the gun and backhanded him. A dribble of blood went down his lip.

"Do you think you can intimidate me? I'm a professional intimidator, you sorry piece of shit. When I get out of here, I'm going to destroy you."

"When you get out of here?" I laughed. "You're an optimist."

I hadn't put a second of thought into the looming issue of what we'd do with her father when we were done. The motherfucker deserved to die. I planned on killing everyone else involved. But he was Olivia's father and that wasn't my decision to make. I still held the same cards, but couldn't play them the same way anymore. Not for him.

"I don't know how you got down here or what you think you know, but you're screwed. My people will find you. They're going to end you for this, whether I live or die."

"So protect the brotherhood then, that's your story. Do you think Hugh Raven would protect you like this, Mr. Holloway? We already know half of your fucked up clan. You'd just be saving us time if you told us now."

A flicker of hesitance went across his face as I used his real name and Hugh's. It felt good to be on the delivering end of information reveals. He stared at his lap. I thought he was crying as I watched his shoulders move up and down, then realized he was chuckling.

"They wouldn't protect me. They've been out for me since the very beginning, God only knows why. You caught one of us, but you caught the least important one."

Olivia took a step forward, but I stopped her. "Are you sure you want to do that? Once he sees you, there's no going back."

"I know," she said. There was resignation in her voice. Something I'd never heard before.

When Olivia walked into his field of view in front of the floodlights, his body went still. The hell beast I'd just spoken to melted away. I saw the mask go up, just like his daughter did. They had more in common than their eyes. "Livvie? What are you doing here?"

She unhinged the camcorder from the tripod and held it in front of his face. "Did you know what they were doing to me?"

He tried to look away from her, but Olivia reached out

and squeezed his chin in her hand. Her nails dug into his flesh. She repeated her question two more times. Then, "I want to hear you say it."

"Yes!" He choked on his own blood and spit as he said it.

Olivia released her grip and walked away, her back to him. She returned the camera, then wrapped her arms around herself and took a deep inhale. I stayed out of the way. Unlike with Fearnley, this was all her. I wouldn't dare interfere with this moment unless she wanted me to.

"Why? Why would you let them do this to me?" She pointed at the mattress where the other girl had been only moments ago. "Do *you* do *that* to me?"

"Jesus, no, Livvie! I'd never touch you like that. Please tell me you believe me."

"How could I? You're a monster. You're abusive, sadistic, and insane. You're a rapist. You're a murderer. How could I believe anything you tell me? You sent Laurel away to the drug trials. You lied to everyone about it for years."

At the mention of Laurel he clenched his jaw and spat on the ground. "Your sister was a whore. Do you know how many of my clients she managed to fuck? How many associates? She was trying to destroy me. Do you think I could've gotten as far in my career as I have if I let that go on?"

"You're out of your mind," Olivia shouted. She took a slow breath. "No, Laurel shouldn't have let those men take advantage of her. That should never have happened. But doesn't any part of you see that *they* were wrong to accept her advances to begin with? They were committing a crime.

You should've called the police. You should've stopped them. You didn't care."

Holloway sneered. "Laurel was a little slut through and through. I don't blame them for what they did."

"It's your fault! Laurel was trying to destroy you because you were destroying other people's lives. Our lives. She was a good person and you threw her away like she was trash."

"She *was* trash. *You* are my good daughter, Livvie. I love you. You're the one that made me proud."

"Are you fucking serious?" Olivia threw her arms into the air and turned in a circle. "Look at this place! You say you love me, that I make you proud, and you're letting men drug me, do things to me. How does that make any sense?"

"I had to. You don't understand, when I was on the board for those Whiteout trials, I saw a way to get something I need. I need to do these things or I don't feel whole. The Whiteout makes it so I can get what I want without hurting people."

Olivia was right. He was truly insane. All of the people involved were power hungry lunatics who got off on controlling and hurting people. Holloway was trying to play Olivia. I saw it clearly; he was trying to make himself look like a victim to his own desires. He wanted to look like a saint for using Whiteout so people wouldn't remember the pain he inflicted on them.

"Tell me how you managed all this. Tell me everything and I might forgive you." Olivia turned the table. I was proud of her. Assuming she wasn't telling the truth about forgiving him.

"So you know about all the trials? The IRB?" Olivia gave him a nod. He grinned. "You're smart. You should've been a lawyer like I said."

"Shut up. Just tell me what you know."

"Halfway through the trials, we blackmailed Draper to forget everything to do with ethical research and do all he could to make a better version of Whiteout. Off the records. He'd been abusing his participants since the very beginning, so we had a lot on him. He selected a group of people who had minimal outside connections, a history with drugs, and contacted all their families with fake death certificates, runaway notes, you name it. Anything to make them disappear. The IRB was told they'd voluntarily withdrawn from the program. No one questioned it. It was all tidy.

"He experimented on those ten for the next two years in addition to others. The official participants were treated well, but the only reason why was because of what Draper was doing off the record. The actual subjects received the lowest doses of the drug, underwent harmless psychology and intelligence tests. Nothing truly useful. The real gains came from the dosages of Whiteout given to the ten, the physical tests. Of course, by the time he was done, the ten were destroyed mentally. We learned a lot from them. About how to use the drug most effectively, how to avoid forming triggers."

Olivia looked at me, then to her father. "What did you do with those ten?"

"Most of us voted to kill them. Some were already dead, no one would care. But Draper and his fairy assistant Fearnley suddenly developed a conscience. They told us the ten would never remember what happened to them, especially if we got them addicted to drugs again, which helps prevent the brain's attempt at repairing itself, so they tried to integrate them back into society. Halfway houses, mental institutions. It was a terrible idea."

"Fucking hell it was a terrible idea," I spat. How could their plan to save us include getting us addicted to drugs? "You should've killed them all. Would've been more humane."

"That's exactly what I'm saying!"

That wasn't what I meant. Not really. I felt blood rush to my face. I clenched my jaw to keep from spewing anything else.

Olivia ignored both of us, her gaze fixed on her father. "Keep talking."

"It was a huge clusterfuck. Fearnley assured us he knew what he was doing and would do it right. He had already given them new names in the off-the-record trials after we faked their deaths. More stupidity. He treated them like pets. Had too many feelings for them. He should've numbered them like we told him. It turned out, when he restarted their new lives, he used their old social security numbers to try and get everything in order. Applications to apartments, unemployment. They weren't legally dead so the numbers were still valid.

"But it doesn't work like that; to do it right they needed new *identities,* new social security numbers, new towns, everything! We didn't know how piss poor of a job Fearnley did until one of them strangled his fucking roommate Fearnley came crying to us. We had to swoop in and clean up the mess ourselves. Not just that one, but *all* of them. Imagine if the cops got involved? It would come back to us. We'd be screwed. We took the ten back, ran a few more months of trials, then tossed some of them in the Sound, staged deaths for the others so they couldn't be identified."

My dream. The salt water, the drowning. That was my cleanup.

Ten lives and they thought they could toss them out like garbage. I was one of them. I was a stepping stone in the grand plan for some corrupt rich people to have Whiteout for themselves. The life I forged after I woke up was one given to me out of pity, and one created recklessly. I almost knew everything I wanted to find out when I started this whole thing with Olivia; all the who's and why's. The answers I'd found made my life feel more meaningless than ever before. I might've learned empathy being with Olivia, but that didn't magically make me okay with myself. I still hated myself. I was still worthless. If anything, what Holloway was saying made my perceived worthlessness more solid.

Fuck the self-help books. Some people aren't meant to have happiness. There was no coming back from this.

I willed myself to postpone an inevitable breakdown and focused on Olivia and her dad. On the feeling of the gun in my hand, the musty smell of the room. Anything but what was going on inside my mind.

"And me? How did you get me involved in this?" Olivia asked.

"Look at yourself!" he shouted. "You're sweet, you're a princess. You're exactly the kind of girl they want. I told them no, that you were my daughter. They said if I didn't let them take you, they'd cut me off. They'd frame me and end my career. My life! At first the videos were fun. We watched them after, shared them. Then they were blackmail."

Her face sparkled with tears. "Who are 'they'? Who wanted me?"

"I'm not going to tell you."

"The hell you are!" She screamed. She backhanded him. The rings she wore tore up the skin on his cheek, drawing more blood. He sat, stunned, staring at the dirty floor. Olivia came over to me and held out her hand. "Give me your knife."

If she expected me to tell her not to kill him, that it wasn't going to be the justice she wanted, she was wrong. If I were her, I'd kill him in a heartbeat. I reached into my back pocket and withdrew my folding knife. She turned and went back to her father.

"How long did you torture Kaylee for?" She flicked open the knife. "Do you think you can last that long?"

"Livvie, please. You're being ridiculous. We can move on from this. You can't *torture* me."

Her voice was flat. "Ethan, find a gag. I'm sure there's one somewhere in here."

I was outside of my body as I searched for one in the black tubs. I found a black leather gag. It had bite marks on it and a smudge of blood. I went to her father. Olivia raised her hand to stop me.

"I will carve every word you called Laurel into your body, like you did to Kaylee, and when I'm done, you will tell me the names of everyone involved in this." She pressed the tip of the knife into the flesh of her father's chest. "Do you understand?"

"You wouldn't. You don't have it in you."

She lowered her hand. I forced the ball gag into his mouth and laced it tightly around his head. The image of

Kaylee was so strong in my mind that bile threatened to come up. I stepped back.

Olivia pushed the knife hard enough to draw blood. "You're in for a surprise."

CHAPTER 30

In the end, Holloway didn't give us anymore names. Olivia had some kind of monster inside her, not as corrupt as her father's, but dark nonetheless. It allowed her to slice words into his flesh without shedding a single tear, getting sick, or stopping. She'd taken the gag off after the first few minutes, realizing he couldn't tell her what she wanted to know. That forced us all to listen to his screaming. I was the one who stopped her after her father had fallen unconscious.

When I set my hand on her shoulder, I broke her out of a daze. She looked at me like she didn't recognize me. There were flecks of blood on her face. Her hands were drenched in his blood. It struck me that I didn't know Olivia as well as I thought. Each time I thought I had her pegged, I was proved wrong. She was dangerous. She was a force to be reckoned with.

Even though she messaged Hugh saying not to come back, we couldn't stay down there forever. Someone could come down at any minute. It was too risky, and since Holloway was out we weren't getting anything out of him.

"We need to leave. What are we doing with them?" I gestured to the girl and the father.

Olivia grabbed her dad's jacket and wiped her hands on it. "I know where she lives. We'll take her to her apartment and wash her up, put her in bed. She won't have to remember any of this."

Good thing her not remembering was in our favor, too. "And your dad?"

"Do you have anywhere we can hide him?"

"No. Donovan's family is after me. None of the places I'd go to are safe for me anymore." I took a deep breath. "Olivia, do you want him to live or die? Knowing that would help us figure out what to do."

Instead of answering me, she went to Julie and helped her up. The girl leaned against Olivia and blinked slowly. "Where am I?"

"This is a bad dream, Julie. You'll wake up soon, okay?" She stroked her hair.

"Does that mean Kaylee's not really dead?"

"Yes, sweetie. She's just fine." Olivia guided her out of the room.

She wanted time to decide, but we didn't have that, not when we had a hostage. I popped the memory card out of the camcorder and slipped it in my pocket. We'd left the thing on the whole time accidentally. There was something morbidly ironic about there being video of Olivia torturing her father, just like I imagined Hugh had a video of her dad torturing Kaylee.

I closed the doors to the lockers and surveyed the room. Save for Holloway on the chair, there was no obvious evidence of our presence. I picked up the gag from the floor and put it back on him, then dragged him out of the room while still on the chair. The fucker was heavy. Olivia stood with Julie in the other part of the basement.

"I'm going to get my car. We'll put him in the trunk and take him to D.P. I don't want to kill him." Olivia offered no explanation for why she didn't, but I had a feeling that pressing the matter wouldn't get me far. "Stay here with Julie. I can't have her walking around like this. I'll pull around back."

"Fine," I said and came to take Julie, who stumbled as she switched from Olivia to me. I waited until Olivia was gone to help Julie sit on the floor, then pulled out a cigarette. "Do you mind?"

Julie blinked hard and frowned. "Smoking is so bad for you. It's the twenty-first century, buddy."

"I know," I said, cigarette between my lips. I lit it and inhaled. The first smoke after being deprived felt the best. It was never enough. I sucked the thing down and lit another.

"I never liked Mr. Holloway," Julie said. She watched him from the corner of her eye. "He's creepy. I kind of—I'm not surprised I'd have this nightmare. If I'm dreaming can't I control what's happening? Can I fly right now?"

"Dreams don't always work like that," I offered.

The answer satisfied her. She brought her knees to her chest and rocked back and forth. I felt like a monster. It was unfair to lie to her, but everything that just happened to her was unfair. Her situation was too familiar. Did I want to know the gritty details of my 'off the record' Whiteout trials? Probably not. Maybe. The experience didn't define me, so technically I didn't need to remember it.

Experience didn't define me? Fucking self-help books. I made a mental note to lay off them.

While he was still unconscious, I got Holloway out of the chair and dressed him. Dressing him was even harder than putting him in the chair, but dragging him around naked sounded even worse. He groaned and flinched as the material ran over the cuts in his skin. There was a thin layer of blood across his whole body that obscured most of the words. When I finished dressing him, I bound his wrists behind him with the cordage from the chair, then returned the chair exactly where I found it. I'd get his ankles once we were at our final destination.

By the time I was finished Olivia was back and Holloway was awake. He didn't struggle, but watched us like a hawk as we helped Julie up. Olivia led her upstairs, leaving me alone with him.

"It's time to go. I'm going to get you to your feet, then you're going to help me get you into the car. If you don't, you're dead. Nod if you understand."

Holloway nodded. His forehead scraped against the concrete, leaving a sweat and blood stain behind.

I slid my hands under his armpits and helped him to his feet. He was dangerous, and I was ready to do what I had to if he tried anything stupid. I kept my gun pressed into his back and made him take the lead out of the basement and into his office where the exit door hung open. The Immaculate Car waited for us, barely humming, with the trunk open.

Julie was in the backseat. Olivia stood by the trunk.

"Get in."

He made a guttural, pathetic noise. Holloway looked at me then to Olivia, then the trunk.

The alley was empty. Cars and the occasional pedestrian crossed either end, but none paid any attention to what was inside. Eventually someone would, so I gave Holloway a shove towards the trunk. He gave in and sat on the edge of the trunk, then brought his knees up and rolled back. It was a tight, uncomfortable fit. Good.

Olivia slammed the trunk closed. "I can't believe any of this. I can't believe what I just did or what I just saw."

"Don't think about it too much. We have to think about what we're going to do." To emphasize my point I went to the passenger door and opened it. "Let's get Julie home, okay?"

She nodded and rolled her shoulders back. "You're right. Let's go."

Inside the car the three of us were silent. I watched Julie in the side mirror as she looked out on the street. There were bruises starting to form on her cheek and temple where Holloway held her down. I knew they were fingertip shaped, but would anyone else guess that just by looking at them? Maybe they'd fade by the time she woke up. Then she wouldn't have to struggle against what she was seeing versus what she remembered.

"Where does she live?" I asked, suddenly in need of filling the quiet.

"Near the convention center. I'll take her up while you wait in the car. Then we're taking him to D.P."

I tapped my fingers against the arm rest. I wanted to ask what we were doing with her dad, but figured her time alone taking care of Julie would give her a minute to breathe. No matter the decision, keeping him in D.P. wasn't as easy as she thought.

"Oh, I'm home," Julie's lofty voice stated.

"We're here." Olivia parked the car in a loading zone. "Drive around or find somewhere more discreet. I don't want anyone hearing him if he starts kicking around. Come back in a half hour."

I did as I was told and switched to the driver's seat. The

Immaculate Car practically drove itself. With Olivia and Julie gone, I felt self-conscious in it. Certainly a cop would question why a guy like me was driving a car like this. There was a difference between the fashionable homeless look many Seattleites sported, and the *actual* homeless. I fell closer to the latter.

I put it into drive and reentered traffic. I didn't drive much in general and found myself nervous as cars wove in and out of lanes and pedestrians darted into the street or bikes rode too close.

The half hour went by slowly. Afternoon traffic was picking up. It was strange to see all the potential customers meandering on the streets from this new perspective. I spotted dealers right away in their little congregation underneath awnings and in alcoves. The fog of weed was strong in Westlake as everyone took advantage of the state marijuana laws. I watched the demographic shift as I went up streets. College kids and business workers mingled with street trash. People from every walk of life in massive groups waiting at bus stops, all of them going about their daily lives.

It was a different world out there. Not long ago I was in the daily grind, moving through my life like it was a dream. I'd never be able to go back to that exact place, but I had no doubt wherever I drifted to next would be much the same. Suppliers needing dealers, customers needing a fix. The people changed but the game was the same.

By the time my half hour was up, I'd relaxed into the car. Beside a few thumps, Holloway hadn't made a peep. I made my way back to Julie's and found Olivia waiting at the loading zone with her arms folded tightly across her chest. She'd unpinned the lace over her eyes and her hair was loose. As soon as the car stopped she was in.

"You look like hell," I said.

"Thanks a lot. That's exactly what I needed to hear right now." She buckled up. "Go to D.P. I just want to drop him off and get home."

So the plan hadn't changed. I flicked the blinker on and waited for a mint green Prius to pass. "Someone needs to stay with him."

Olivia snorted. "Oh yeah? Why is that?"

"If anyone sees us drop him off, they'll see it as information. You can get money or drugs off information. Favors. They might come to us first and we'll need to buy their silence." I tried to keep my tone level. Olivia's mood had shifted from angry, to murderous, to dazed, to belligerent all in the space of a few hours. I had to be careful. "We don't want any witnesses. Also we can't leave him alone. Someone will have to watch him."

I got on the road and drove six blocks before she spoke.

"I have a couple hundred in cash, is that good enough?"

"Should be fine."

"And as for someone staying with him, can you?"

Just as I was going to say no, a little voice in my head reminded me I had nothing else to do. I literally had nothing else to do. I glanced at Olivia then back to the road. "Sure."

She sighed in relief. "Thank you. That's one less thing I have to worry about."

"Glad I could help." The words felt like cotton in my mouth and it took a lot to get them out.

"Did Julie settle in all right?"

"I guess. I helped her take a shower then put her into

bed. Took the patch off her. I don't think I can look at her the same way after this. Fortunately I don't see her too much, but still."

Olivia punched in the address to D.P. on the screen in her console and for the rest of the trip we listened to a soothing robot woman direct us.

We arrived at D.P., still as decrepit as it was when we left it, and parked close to the front doors. I scanned the area for anyone I recognized. There were a few homeless in blankets and layers sleeping near the building across the street, but otherwise the coast was clear.

Olivia and I got out of the car and met at the trunk. I started to wonder how we were going to get him through the narrow hole into D.P. and if his wounds were going to get infected and stink. When Olivia opened the trunk, those questions didn't matter anymore.

Holloway was dead. His vacant eyes bulged out of their sockets, bloodshot. His white dress shirt was almost completely red, his wounds having soaked through. The cuts Olivia dealt were superficial as far as I was concerned. I didn't think he died from them.

The gag sealed his mouth completely and there was snot and blood running from his nose. I figured he'd suffocated. Then again, it didn't matter how it happened. He was gone.

Olivia stared at the body. Her face was slack. She reached out and pressed her fingers to his throat, but her hand fell away quickly.

"He's dead." She sucked in a short gasp of air. "I killed him."

"You didn't." If you wanted to argue semantics, she did. "He suffocated. It was an accident."

"What are we going to do?"

My brain went into overdrive thinking of possibilities. I was elated he was dead, though I didn't show it. One down, five to go. We could use the death to scare the others, but it had the potential to work against us. We needed more bargaining chips against them.

"This is it, Olivia. We have to end all of this now. You need to decide where you stand."

"Where I stand? I didn't know there was anywhere *to* stand."

I closed the trunk, hiding her father. "From where I am, there are two options. We take out everyone involved or we expose all of them. We know three of the people involved. It's only a matter of time before we have all of them, and then what? What's the point of finding all this out if we aren't going to do something about it?"

At some point Olivia was going to find out what my goal was. If there was any time to test the waters and see if she'd agree with my plan, it was now. It would be helpful if she was on board, but not necessary.

Olivia clenched her jaw. She rubbed her temples and took a step away from the car. "It isn't black and white, and murdering all of them isn't the right answer. This is complicated now. My dad is dead and I'm involved in it. Whether it was an accident or not I was involved. I could go to prison for manslaughter."

"It isn't complicated. Your dad was a maniac and he's dead now. I'm sorry, Olivia, but he got what he deserved." I walked around her to face her. "I say we move fast. We use your dad's cell to trick Hugh into meeting up and we get him. We can interrogate him, maybe get his dad, too. I still know a few people who could do the deed for us."

She held my gaze and for a moment, I thought she was going to agree. "No, Ethan. I don't want anyone else to get killed. It isn't right. They deserve justice, but not like this."

Dammit. So much for that. She was still being indecisive. It was clear to me she didn't truly know what she wanted out of this, and at this point that wasn't going to work.

"What do you suggest we do now?"

"We still need to find out who else is involved and Hugh is our best chance of getting that information. I'll ask him if he wants to go out tonight. I'll say I'm sorry I had to rush out earlier. He'll believe me. While I have him, you go to his house and look for the videos he mentioned back..." she took a deep breath. "Back in that room. He said he had videos of my dad."

"That's dangerous. He could slip you Whiteout anytime and you know what'll happen from there."

"I'll bring a friend. I'm not stupid, Ethan. I don't trust him anymore. I'm not going to get close to him and I certainly won't go anywhere strange." She glared. "I'm not a total idiot, despite what you might think."

"Fine." I had to take her word on it. "What about your dad?"

She cringed. "Know any good places to dump a body?"

It was hard not to smirk. "Actually, I do."

CHAPTER 31

Hugh Raven's house was in north Seattle and was one of the nicest ones on the block. It was a craftsman style home, something people in the area loved to talk about. I had an interior designer with an Adderall addiction who carried on about the craftsman style for fifteen minutes every time I saw her. Apparently she was famous for renovating and saving houses just like this. The nervous preamble was as predictable as the sunrise and I indulged her because she was one of my devoted, frequent clients.

I remembered the last conversation I had with her. We met behind a Peet's Coffee downtown after I got the usual text. *Coffee at the usual spot? See you in ten.* Shirley was there waiting in her silver Mercedes. She greeted me pleasantly as I slid in.

"I'm working on a beautiful 1970s home in the American Craftsman style. Gorgeous. Still has the original hand scraped wide plank flooring. The exterior is in shambles and the previous owners absolutely destroyed the wood upstairs by covering it with carpet. God, and the bathrooms! Horrific. They need a total overhaul."

"Hmm, sounds like a lot of work," I said.

Shirley continued for a while about the wood the cabinets were made of, the paint color, the staircase she had to have rebuilt. She fanned her flushed face with her hand. "Yes, yes. So much work. I have a tight schedule on it, too. I just need a little something to help me focus. I have a prescription for Adderall of course, but it expired and I don't have time to see my doctor. You know, so busy. Plus doctors are hard to deal with. You know."

"Really hard to deal with. Anything I can do?"

"Oh, just whatever this will get me." She slipped me the cash, checked the rear view mirror and side mirrors. Poor, nervous Shirley.

I counted it, gave her what she had enough for, and got out of the car. Shirley sped away. I hadn't heard from her since, but I imagined she'd need a refill soon.

Now in Hugh Raven's back yard, I wondered if this was a house Shirley worked on. The backyard had landscaping of moss, red beauty bark, and little evergreens that were all perfectly uniform. There was a pond of koi with benches flanking it. Shirley loved koi. Why the fuck did I remember that?

Anyway, it was a charming place for a snake like Hugh to live.

Lucky for me, he also had tall fences to protect me from the neighbors. I was crouched beneath a small window in the back yard, praying no one saw me before Olivia let me in.

The plan was simple, but perfect, and so far we'd managed to execute it without a hitch. Surprising, considering how our plans had gone in the past. Olivia made the call three blocks from his house. Hugh answered on the second ring and agreed to meet up for an early dinner. Just hearing his voice made my blood pressure rise. Olivia told him she was in the area and would pick him up. He almost didn't agree to it, but Olivia was cutely persistent and he caved.

She dropped me off a half block away then drove to his house. We were now at the riskiest part of the plan. I slipped into the back yard, waiting for her to let me in through the bathroom window. If there was any time for Hugh to drug Olivia, it would be then.

My thighs were on fire and my knees felt tight as I waited. I heard the doorbell ring inside and faint voices. Minutes later the window above me opened and Olivia stared down.

"Quick, come on!"

I climbed through the window into the tiny bathroom. It was cramped. Just a toilet and sink.

"I'll text you when we're on our way back. I'll keep him as long as I can." Olivia flushed the toilet and turned on the sink, keeping up the hoax. "Good luck, okay?"

She slipped out of the bathroom, turning the light off at the same time. I held my breath and prayed Hugh wouldn't stop in before they left, too.

Hey, nice to see you again. Great craftsman house you have here.

In moments I heard the two leaving and the shrill beeps of an alarm being set from the front door. I waited five minutes just to be safe before I exited the bathroom.

The house was something out of a magazine. As I traversed the hallway leading to the bathroom, I came into a living room. The woodwork gleamed. Colors were masculine but thoughtful. Nothing was out of place. I wondered if my Adderall renovator worked on the house. There was comfort in thinking about the familiar in a place like this.

I walked the first story to get a feel for the layout. It was about what I expected; kitchen, living room, family room, dining room. I went upstairs, reminding myself there was no one to hear the creaking wood steps so I didn't have to cringe at every sound. Upstairs were four rooms all coming off one open space at the top of the stairs. A master bedroom, bathroom, guest room, and office. All the doors were open.

I searched the bathroom first to cross it off my list, then the guest room. I pulled open drawers, slid my fingers around dressers in case something had been taped underneath. There was nothing between the mattresses or behind the art. I steered clear of the windows on the off chance I'd set the alarm off.

The office was next. There was a behemoth of a wooden desk similar to the one at the law office commanding most of the room. A heavy clay dish full of loose change, which I pocketed the quarters from. More bookshelves.

Fuck. More bookshelves. I realized any one of those books could have a memory card slipped between the pages. It was a great place to hide something that small. It was as close to a needle in a haystack as it could get. If all else failed, I'd start checking them, but I hoped I'd find something before I had to resort to that.

There was a sleek black laptop closed on the desk. I opened it and powered it on. After a second the log on screen popped up. Password protected. It was a long shot anyway and I wasn't about to start typing in random guesses.

Two of the desk drawers yielded well organized office supplies. The other, random power cords and cables. It turned out the last drawer was just right; looking up at me were a digital camera and a video camera. I snatched them up and turned them on, relieved I'd found something so quick.

That relief died out as fast as it came. Both cameras flashed an angry warning that there were no memory cards.

And so the hunt continued. I'd already been looking for an hour. I didn't know how long Olivia could keep him for, but the sooner I was out the better. I hated the idea of her having to play nice with Hugh knowing what he did.

I left the bookshelf untouched and went to the bedroom. Throughout the house I noticed the lack of personal photos. He had art on the walls, but not a single image of himself, or with anyone else. If I were a sadistic fuck like him, I'd put that kind of stuff up. Better cover.

The master bedroom was slightly bigger than the guest. Unlike the hardwood in the rest of the house, it had thick tan carpet. The bed was made and boasted at least a dozen decorative pillows. Nightstands on either side. I hit those first and tried to keep my hopes at bay. The more I searched the more intense my anxiety became. I might discover what I needed at any time, but the chance of finding something seemed slim.

A tablet, reading glasses, condoms. The other nightstand drawer was empty. I searched between the mattresses and all around the bed frame, behind dressers. Nothing. I crossed the room to the walk-in closet and flicked on the light. More organized, overpriced shit. I rifled through the clothing. Checked coat and pant pockets. Reached inside shoes. Nothing.

This was ridiculous. I shouldn't have agreed to search the house. Not when the option of abducting and interrogating

Hugh was right in front of me. Once again I was caught between wanting to take the sure route and going along with Olivia.

I rubbed my face and temple. Self-soothing techniques. Fucking self-help books. What I needed was a cigarette.

Then I saw it. If I hadn't been staring at the ground wallowing in my own misery I wouldn't have spotted it. At the end of the closet the carpet turned up onto the baseboard. In a house where everything was immaculate— and true to the craftsman style—why would there be carpet? To hide something.

I dropped to my knees there and pulled at the loose edge. Beneath it was hardwood like in the rest of the house. It was as though the carpet had been tossed over it, not secured in any way. I kept pulling at the edge until an entire piece of carpet, about a foot square, came free. The edges were so thick it blended almost perfectly with the rest.

My hands were sweaty. I wiped them on my jeans as I looked at the hardwood and saw a loose floorboard right in the center. I retrieved my knife and used the edge to pry up a corner. It came free. Beneath was a plastic baggie full of memory cards. There were at least fifty, each labeled with the code names from the log. Beside the bag was another small video camera and a sealed bag of patches like the one Hugh used on Olivia. Where were they getting the patches from, when Whiteout in pill form was on the streets?

I lifted the camera out and turned it on. Unlike last time, there was a card in this one. I found the gallery button and hit play on the most recent.

The familiar sight of the torture room came into view. A girl lay on her back, both wrists hoisted over her head and chained to one of the rings on the wall. She was blindfolded and gagged, her body naked and covered in red marks. A man came into the frame and knelt beside her face, rubbing himself against her. He held a riding crop in one hand.

It was Hugh. I turned the camera off, sickened by the sight of him and what he was doing. I plucked out the memory card. Herring was written in neat permanent marker on it.

I picked up the baggie and sorted through the cards, taking one for Eagle, Captain, and Bolt. I knew Olivia's father was Azure, and assumed Eagle was Hugh's father, but I had to check. If I saw their faces, it put me closer to knowing their identities for myself. Closer to getting what I wanted.

Eagle was old. His hair was completely white, thick tufts of it on his chest trailing down to his groin and legs. He forced himself on a girl that was probably no older than fifteen. I watched long enough to get his face into my mind then switched memory cards.

Bolt was a middle-aged man with charcoal black skin. He had two girls. One was from the streets. I saw it in her ratted hair, her skin and bones physique. He murdered her in front of the other one. Strangled her and raped her corpse while the other girl sobbed hysterically. Every time she tried to look away he ordered her to watch or die.

My chest was tight. I tasted bile in my throat and felt dirty for watching the videos, even with my intent of having the men in them killed. There was misery, pain, and unfairness in them like nothing I'd ever seen before. I took no comfort in knowing the girls wouldn't remember what happened to them.

I told myself it was almost over, just one left, but my body shook and my skin crawled. My eyes burned from what I'd seen and I knew I'd never forget it. Decades from now I'd still see them in my mind.

Captain was heavyset. That's all I noticed before I saw the girl on the bed, blindfolded but not gagged. I saw her auburn hair, the pale skin, and knew it was Olivia. The tiny speaker on the camera made her voice sound distant as she begged for mercy, asked over and over why she was there.

"Are you a good girl? Your daddy says you're a good girl."

"Please don't do this, please let me go."

I felt my stomach seize. I dropped the camera and made it to the toilet in time to wretch until I vomited what little food I had. It took ten minutes before I could return to the closet and pick up the camera. Without looking at the screen, I turned it off and pocketed it and the memory cards.

The alarm was deafening as I walked straight out the front door and headed down the street. I didn't care. I had to get as far away from the house as I could.

Only I couldn't escape it. It was with me. It would be with me forever.

CHAPTER 32

I wanted to wait until I'd gotten myself together before I sent Olivia a text to come back, but it seemed wrong. I didn't want her around Hugh, or anyone else who put her at risk. Yet how could I face her after seeing that? Should I lie about what I found? Dealing with Whiteout was all about withholding information for the greater good. Or personal gain. Or to protect yourself. I liked to think I didn't support any of those things. Hypocrisy at its finest.

Using the change I'd scrapped from Hugh, I hopped a bus to get back downtown to Olivia's apartment. Just as I sat down, my phone buzzed with a text from her.

Are you okay? The alarm went off, we're headed back now.

My thumb hesitated over the ancient keys as I gathered a response. *I'm fine. Meet me back at your apartment.*

The bus felt worse than usual. As my gaze shifted around the other riders, I imagined they all knew my secret. They could see me replaying what I'd seen, a projector in my mind displaying the girls and their assailants.

It was natural to replay traumatic incidents. Avoid judging yourself. Fucking self-help books.

As soon as I got into Olivia's apartment I was going to raid the vodka bottle in the freezer. I would come clean; I did find something, but it was graphic. If she let me describe the men in the videos to her, maybe we could find them off that alone. Then no one would have to see them.

A cool automatic female voice announced my street was coming up. I made my way to the center of the bus and was out the moment the doors swung open. The two block walk to her building felt good. If I focused hard enough on my footsteps, the nipping cold on my face, I had brief seconds of emptiness in my mind.

Someone was just entering the courtyard when I arrived, and I slipped into the complex before the door swung shut. I sat on a bench in her courtyard while I waited. The bag of memory cards was necrotic in my jacket pocket. It ate away at me. I wanted them gone. I needed this to be over.

"Ethan?"

"Fuck, I didn't expect you so soon."

A healthy, albeit stressed, Olivia crossed the courtyard towards me. Not tied up and sobbing. Not being used up like she was nothing.

"How did you get in here?" She sat next to me and folded her arms across her chest. "Never mind. What happened? I thought you were going to wait until I got back?"

"I couldn't," I managed, my voice meek. It was time to tell her. But not until I had a drink in me. "Can we go up to your place?"

She frowned and looked at me skeptically. "Sure. Come on."

Neither of us spoke as we made the trek up to her apartment. Once in, I headed straight for the freezer and guzzled the burning liquid straight from the bottle. The ice cold glass felt good against my lips, the warmth spreading throughout my body even better.

I took the bottle to the stools by the kitchen island and

sat next to Olivia.

"What did you find?"

"Olivia, first of all I want to—"

"Cut the bullshit. I know you found something. I don't want a preface or your fucking interpretation. I want the truth."

My jaw hung open. I looked away from her enraged face at the bottle. This was it. "I found memory cards under the floor board in his closet."

"Did you take them?"

"Yes." I reached into my pocket and dropped them onto the counter.

Olivia barely glanced at them before getting up and retrieving her laptop. She plugged a small silver box into it and went for the baggie. I put my hand over it to stop her. Her skin was cold.

"Listen to me." She tried to push my hand away. I clenched the bag. "You fucking listen to me. Once you see what's on here, there is no going back. You will never forget it. It will only bring you pain."

"You can't decide that for me," she shouted.

"I'm not deciding for you. I'm warning you. We can still figure out who's in these without you having to see them. Let me describe the other three to you. Find them on the internet and show me their faces and we'll know."

"Am I on one of those videos?"

My mouth went dry. I couldn't stand looking at her and focused on the condensation on the vodka bottle instead. "Yeah."

"It's my life and I'm missing pieces of it. I don't care how terrible the experiences are; it's my right to know. If you could get video of all your missing life during the trials, wouldn't you?"

"No," I said honestly. I was unsure before, but now, it was clear. "After remembering what I did to Andrew Cole, after the nightmares I have? No. Seeing what happened to me won't change who I am. It's too late for that."

"Well, I'm not you. I want to see."

At least I tried. When all else was dark and I was tearing myself apart for letting her watch it, I could at least remind myself I tried. I took the bag and retrieved one of Eagle first.

I was a fucking monster. I didn't want Olivia to watch any of them, but if she was I was going to get the information I needed from her. If that meant showing her the one of her and Captain last, so be it.

She popped the memory card into the silver box and clicked away on her laptop. A loud burst of audio began of a girl crying. Olivia hit mute.

"That's Hugh's father." She turned it off immediately and tossed the memory card aside. Her face was always pale, but it looked gray now. "Next."

I gave her one of Bolt. The memory cards got jumbled in the bag. The video she watched now was different than the one I saw, but it was the same man. He was tying cord around each joint on a young boy, one that looked about Skid's age. Olivia waited until she saw the man's face when he lay next to the boy, then shut it off.

"Lincoln Johnston. Captain of SPD. Next."

I set a memory card with Captain written on it in front of her. I knew it was the same one I watched. I recognized a smudge on the upper right corner of the label. She opened the video.

Captain's face came on screen as he neared her. Olivia started to speak, coughed, then said, "That's the mayor. That's Lewis Ward."

She didn't turn off the video. She kept watching, her face surprisingly blank. I got off the stool and took my bottle of vodka to the couch, far away from the laptop. I couldn't imagine what drove her to keep watching, or what horrors were in the rest of the video.

But I had my names. Despite all the fucking terror of the day, I knew all the men behind it and one of them was already dead. Ward, Hugh's father, and Lincoln Johnston.

A half hour later she closed the laptop.

"I need you to leave."

I sat up and turned to see her. Olivia's eyes were deadened. Her voice was hoarse. "I'm sorry you had to see it."

She shrugged. "I wanted to. Now I did and I want you to leave. I want to be alone."

"What are we going to do? I can't leave you now, not after this."

"*We* aren't going to do anything. You are going to leave my apartment because I need to be alone right now."

I set the nearly empty bottle on the coffee table then stood. My body swayed. I'd crossed being buzzed and was almost drunk. "This is it, Olivia. We're at the eleventh hour. Hugh probably already knows the memory cards are gone. They're going to realize your dad is missing. They aren't stupid. They probably have a backup plan on how they're going to deal with something like this. Maybe they're going to leave the country."

She laughed. The sound was so harsh I stopped talking, stunned. She crossed the room and came up to me. "They aren't going anywhere. Whatever we do, they will make us disappear. Like Kaylee and Laurel, like all the people in those videos. Hell, the mayor's gala is tomorrow. I've spent months planning a fucking party for the man who has been raping me for God only knows how long."

Olivia's expression became distant as she delved into her own mind. Something shifted in her. I didn't know exactly what, but something had.

"Get out, Ethan. This is over." Tears finally welled up in her eyes. "I can't do this anymore."

I didn't bother arguing. I had my names. I was going to find one of the Melnikov family's exiled hitters, scrounge up some money, and have them killed. There was nothing I could do to reverse what Olivia had seen. Like she said, it was her decision.

An impulse to embrace her came over me so strongly I couldn't resist. I wrapped my arms around her and squeezed once. To my surprise, she returned it.

"I'm sorry," I said. "Goodbye, Olivia."

CHAPTER 33

I felt Olivia's absence. It was as though a part of me was left behind in her apartment. There was no follow up. There was no plan. We were done. I knew our friendship—or whatever it was we had—was over. I'd hoped it would be under better circumstances, but realistically knew it went down the only way it could.

The weight of my backpack and duffel bag felt heavier than usual, because I knew I truly had nowhere to put them. I exited the apartment complex and found myself standing on the street.

Deep breath. Plan. I needed a plan. Anything to anchor me in the floating bleakness of my life.

I knew the names. I had a gun. I bet most of the men would be at the gala tomorrow, assuming they didn't leave the country. Where the gala was, I had no clue, but I'm sure I could find out. Maybe I did have it in me to kill them.

Then my old plan for Hugh came to mind. I knew exactly where Hugh was. From there it would be easy to get his dad. Fuck, maybe I could even bait Captain and Bolt, too. One tidy execution of justice in the craftsman house.

My stomach churned. There. That was the plan. I needed to do it before doubt crippled me. I headed for the bus stop, intent on capturing Hugh as soon as possible.

"Sorry, E."

A sharp pain started from the back of my skull down

my entire body. Then everything went black.

Donovan's cologne was the first thing I smelled. I'd recognize it anywhere. He wore too much of it and it wasn't that great even though I knew it cost a couple hundred bucks.

We were in his Hummer. As I opened my eyes I saw two of his men on either side of me. Donovan was in the front seat. A cigarette hung limply from his mouth. The smell of it made my skin crawl with need. Handcuffs dug tightly into my wrists. It was almost dark outside, but the ambient floor lighting in the Hummer provided enough light for me to see.

"You been avoiding me?" He laughed. "I thought I wasn't going to find you, but then, look! We were driving up to the club and there's Ethan, standing like a dumb fuck on the sidewalk. Bad luck."

The back of my head ached dully where someone hit me. I tilted my head down in search of my bags. They were nowhere in sight.

Donovan always liked me, but not enough to keep me alive after what I'd done. To them, I tried to disrupt a delicate hierarchy and that didn't come without consequence. Even if Donovan didn't want to kill me, his father and uncle would make him. Really, I was surprised I'd lasted this long.

"So, elephant in the room. You killed uncle Cheslav." Donovan twisted around more so he could see me better. "And I'm sorry, E, but you know what we have to do."

"I didn't kill him!" My head jerked as I said it. The world was shimmering black before my vision returned to normal. There was a wisp of hope now. Someone else had killed Chuck. Not me. "I shot some other guys, but when I left your uncle was fine. Hysterical, bleeding out a bit, but fine."

"You shot him in the leg. It hit a vein or some shit. He bled out before we could do anything."

"Fuck. It was an accident, Donovan. I swear I didn't mean to kill him. If I'd known who the girls were ripping off, I would've said no. I would've told you about it."

"You know it doesn't matter. You pulled the trigger. We all watched it on his security cams."

That smudge of hope faded. "Okay."

"I have to say, I'm not just killing you because of that. You know I didn't like Uncle Cheslav much. It was Trisha, you know? You always liked her too much. She told me you two were sleeping together, that you gave her your Whiteout so she could get away from me. I don't know how much of it's true, but some of it must be."

"You found her, then?"

"She didn't make it far after that night with Chuck."

I didn't feel sorry for her. Like everyone on the planet, she had what was coming to her. You don't screw over the Melnikov family and get away with it. Trisha knew the risks going into it.

Fuck this. I was so close to revenge, justice, whatever you want to call it, and in the blink of an eye it was over. Now I was going to be killed in one of four ways Donovan favored. They'd tie chains around me and drop me in the Puget Sound, throw me to their dogs in the fighting pits, get me jacked on acid and drown me, or dismember me. For someone who seemed almost goofy at times, Donovan was truly cruel when he wanted to be.

Fuck *that*. I wasn't giving up. I felt fire welling up in my stomach and chest. Maybe it was the vodka, or maybe it was courage. I hadn't come this far to sit back and take it. All this time I'd told Olivia we'd come too far, we were in it. I was in it now and I was going to figure it out.

I ran my tongue over my teeth, worked up some saliva and swallowed. The only thing that would save me now were words and cleverness. I could do this.

"For what it's worth, I wasn't in on that thing with your uncle," I said, trying honesty for once. The fit was uncomfortable, but it was all I had. "Trisha told me she would take me to a Whiteout supplier and I could ask him some questions. She tricked me to get the Whiteout you gave me. She and Chastity ran off together."

Donovan sucked on his cigarette and tapped ash into an empty Starbucks cup. "Oh yeah? Why'd you want to talk to a Whiteout supplier?"

Crystal clear, right in front of me, was the angle I needed. Donovan's daddy issues. Donovan's need for power and control.

The driver turned onto the ramp to the freeway. I knew this route. We were going to their warehouse in south Seattle. Dismemberment it was. At least it bought me some time to talk.

"This is going to sound crazy, but give me a chance. Remember when you found me on Alki? How jacked up I was and couldn't remember most of my life before?"

Donovan nodded. I had the attention of his henchmen now, too, who watched me with curiosity.

"I was part of a drug trial for Whiteout. It messed me

up. They were doing a bunch of illegal testing and once they were done with me, they tossed me aside knowing I wouldn't remember any of it. I had all those conspiracies about it, the blog. Then, seven years later, Whiteout pops up on the streets. I started digging. I had to know if it had anything to do with my lost time." I let it sink in for a moment. "So I was looking for the suppliers because I was trying to backtrack. I wanted to know who invented the stuff, who was dishing it out. I wanted revenge against them for ruining my life."

I omitted Olivia. There was no point in dragging her into what was already a serious clusterfuck of a situation.

Donovan dropped his cigarette butt into the coffee cup and retrieved another. He saw me looking at it with longing and handed it to me. I brought my bound hands up and took it awkwardly, sucking the thing down like my life depended on it. He fixed himself another one. Sharing; this was a good sign.

"Did you find the supplier?"

"I don't know where they're getting it made, but I do know who's behind it." I had to tread carefully. My only bargaining chip was knowledge. "I know the names of all the men behind it."

"Tell me, then," Donovan said. His face was neutral but his eyes bore through me. One of the henchmen rattled off something in Russian. Donovan shook his head.

I cleared my throat and met his gaze. "Why should I? You're going to kill me."

"I know what you're doing, E." Donovan grinned. It was menacing. "In the face of death, people do the same shit every time to save themselves."

"But I have something you want. I have your key to the source of Whiteout."

"That's where you're wrong. I have a middleman that bring me Whiteout from the source. I get a good cut. It works."

I felt my grasp on him weakening. I had to push harder. "I know you're sick of being beneath your father. Without Chuck in the picture, you're one step closer to owning this city. Imagine if you were the only Whiteout dealer, if you had every part of the operation under your thumb. Imagine that power. Imagine the money."

"Okay. Say I believe you. How's this gonna happen? How are you going to get me all that?"

Good things don't come to those who wait. Good things come to those who manipulate the fuck out of life and don't wait for it to grind them down.

"The men behind it are high class. They have a lot to lose and we both know those are the best kind of people to deal with. But they won't go down easy. You gotta get all of them at once or they won't talk. They've got a pact to protect each other. If you get all of them, I guarantee you can break them."

"All that if I let you live, huh?"

"Yeah." I took a drag on the cigarette and smiled. "One last thing."

"What's that?"

"Once you get what you want out of them, kill them. Kill every last one of them."

Donovan chuckled. "Wouldn't do it any other way, E."

CHAPTER 34

Donovan had someone drop me off at my apartment as a gesture of 'good faith' after our talk. It felt like I hadn't been there in months even though it hadn't even been a week. The place didn't feel right anymore. My life was morphing and the apartment symbolized a different version of me.

They'd trashed it at some point. I imagined after they found out I was involved in Chuck's death they came looking. As I wandered around I found all my drugs were gone. Some dredges of liquor were left behind, all of which I finished off as I found them. The mattress was overturned. My easy chair had a gash down its center. I tossed my bags by the chair as I mourned the loss of one of my nice things.

I took in the state of the place quickly while I searched for my phone charger. I plugged it in and saw I was out of minutes. Stupid fucking burner phones. I found Olivia's phone number and scrawled it on my hand, then rushed downstairs to the pay phone in the lobby. I used more of the change I scavenged at Hugh's to call her.

No answer.

I called again and the number went straight to voicemail. She was ignoring the calls on purpose. I guess I shouldn't have expected her to do anything else. When she said she wanted me gone, she meant it.

"Olivia, it's Ethan. I know you don't want to talk to me but please listen. Don't go to the gala tomorrow. Just don't go." It was too ambiguous. Without a solid reason not to, she would go. "I told Donovan about the mayor, about everyone. They're going to get them tomorrow. I don't want you to get hurt. Please."

I hung up. A feeling of hopelessness washed over me. Donovan was going to kill the men after he got what he wanted. That was fine with me. But it was going to be messy. There would be casualties.

A day sat between me and the gala. There was nothing I could do, no more answers to find. I returned to my apartment and went straight to the kitchen where I retrieved some coffee grounds from the freezer and got a pot brewing. At least they hadn't destroyed the second nicest thing I owned. I searched the fridge and found an opened package of saltine crackers. Better than nothing.

I sat in my abused easy chair and listened to the sounds of nightlife in the city while the crackers leached all moisture out of my mouth. Waiting wasn't my thing. It put me in that place where I had nothing to do but reflect.

This time, the end *was* close. Where was I going to go? Who was I going to be once it was over? I wondered if Donovan would truly let me go. If he got what he wanted from the men, he'd stay true to his word. I bet he'd even give me my old job back.

I looked around my bleak apartment again. The thought of resuming my life was horrifying and impossible. For so many years I'd been making stipulations. If I knew my past, then I'd make a life for myself. If I could figure out what happened to me, then I could move on. Now that I was meeting those requirements, it was daunting. Easier said than done.

Instead of wallowing I got up and forced myself into the shower where I stayed until my skin was pruned and the water went lukewarm. There were no towels, so I used a semi-clean shirt to dry off. I gulped down the first mug then sipped the rest of the pot.

It was almost eleven. The beginning of the day was distant. To think last night Olivia and I were eating noodles. My chest ached as I recalled it.

What if I'd lied to her about the videos? I was beginning to think that was the right thing to do. Sometimes the truth was the last thing a person needed. I would've saved her the horror of seeing herself.

A memory came up, one from my childhood. I was with my mother and father sitting on a couch. Their faces were always blurred and when I dredged up the image. Our dog died and they told me she'd gone to heaven and that all things died eventually. It was sad, but part of life. I cried and yelled at them. How dare they tell me that? Didn't they know how much it hurt me? I sensed the finality of life, but there was something about them saying it out loud that made it real. It was as though if we could just ignore it, it wouldn't be true.

I looked over my apartment at the stacks of overdue library books, each one an emblem of my failure to change. Their messages went ignored because if I believed them, if I actually applied them, it would be irrefutable evidence that I was broken. Belligerent and angry, I could talk about how fucked up I was and use it as an excuse.

But the right thing? The right thing was to look straight at the mess and say, I'm done.

I found every book I had and stacked them by the door.

When this was over I was going to return every last one of them and never look again.

I was done.

CHAPTER 35

It was almost noon when I woke up feeling groggy and disoriented. It was hard to believe I could sleep nine hours straight without the aid of drugs or a fuck ton of booze. I dressed and left the apartment to the library where it took all of two minutes to find the location of the mayor's fundraiser gala. There were numerous articles on it, and how it was planned by one of the cities most renowned campaigners, Olivia Holloway. Not to mention it had an official website with a fancy donation page.

Without any money, not even enough for the bus, I was left walking for the day. I stopped at Olivia's office and waited for two hours outside. She never came. At one point I even went upstairs and dealt with her snobbish receptionist who informed me she wasn't coming in the office at all due to an important event.

I hung outside her apartment—turning down multiple solicitations from some usuals that spotted me—but left when a police car circled me twice. After that I headed to the location of the gala. It was due to start in an hour. It was at the Fairmont Hotel in downtown Seattle. Trucks of all kinds lined the loading zones; flowers, catering, rental services. Security was posted at every door. I circled the block and found a parking garage entrance that also lead to an underground loading dock. Security there was at a reduced level. It looked like everyone was wrapping up their deliveries.

Now was my time. While most of the delivery people outside and in the garage had uniforms on, there were a few in plain clothing. The bored guards didn't even bat an eyelash at anyone walking into the service entry if they had a box in hand. Even when a new crew of people arrived, they only looked at their boxes and ushered them forward.

It took fifteen minutes of waiting behind an Escalade for the right moment. A seafood truck was parked just out of immediate sight of the guards and was abandoned, all of its inhabitants already inside delivering their first boxes. I ran a hand through my hair and took a deep breath.

Act natural.

I strolled up to the back of the truck, which reeked of saltwater, freezer burn, and fish. There were a dozen crates of salmon on ice. I slid one towards me and carried it to the entrance.

Mimicking the actions of the people I'd seen before, I went to move by the guard and into the service entry.

He raised his hand and put it in front of my box. I stopped and looked at him. "What's up?"

"Where did you come from? The rest of the fish guys are already upstairs."

Shit. Here we go.

"I was in the back of the truck. Was moving the rest of the boxes so we could unload faster."

The guard shrugged. "Okay. Head up. Miss Holloway is going to lay into you for being so late. Trust me, I know."

"Yeah, figured," I grumbled, not having to feign the camaraderie. I nodded curtly and moved into the service area. There were stairs and two elevators. One elevator had

'Kitchen' emblazoned in yellow letters across the doors.

That's where I was supposed to go. Behind me I heard the security guard strike up a conversation with his partner about food, and whether or not they'd get dibs on any of the leftovers. Their attention was elsewhere.

What to do with my fish? If I ran into the delivery guys I was screwed, but I couldn't carry around a crate of fish while I looked for Olivia. At the opposite end of the room a hallway stretched to the left of the elevators. It led to a laundry room and a janitorial closet. I went straight to the closet, which ended up being a huge room filled with bulk cleaning supplies, and set the fish under a shelf of bleach.

Step one complete. It wasn't until I rubbed my neck that I felt the sheen of nervous sweat I'd developed. My pulse throbbed in my throat. I'd kill for a cigarette or anything harder.

I tore open a package of paper towels and wiped down my exposed skin while I thought of my next move.

Olivia was upstairs somewhere and I needed to get her out. I'd told Donovan all the men he wanted would be at the gala—a safe assumption on my part—and there would be security. After I divulged all the information I had, he had me driven back home. I didn't know his plans for certain, but I knew Donovan. He would make a show of it. He wanted to show he was in charge and a force to be reckoned with. A public display of power would achieve that.

Right then, Olivia could have been anywhere in the building getting preparations in order for the party. But once it started, she had to be in the main ball room. I needed to time my entrance perfectly; right when the party would be in swing, I had to get up there, grab her, and get her out.

That was assuming security didn't nab me first. I doubted my jeans, torn and sweaty t-shirt, and dull leather jacket counted as black tie.

I waited an hour in the janitor's room. It was the longest hour of my life. The small hand on the clock, covered in a metal cage on the wall, moved fluidly instead of ticking. It bothered me so I sat facing away from it against a tower of boxes of hand soap, checking only so often. There was a giant laminated map of the building layout on one wall, I guessed for the staff's use, that I used to memorize my route.

When the time came, I was in motion. I left the janitor's room and headed up the stairs I spotted when I arrived. As I climbed out of ground level, I started picking up on the faint sound of string music.

At the top of the stairs a set of swinging double doors lead into a long, harshly lit corridor with checkered tile. There were food carts flanking both sides of the hallway. Men and women in black and white waiter attire were prepping carts of tiny appetizers. No one noticed me. They were too absorbed in their work to pay much attention. Besides, if I was already up here I must belong, right?

"Janice, you need to be on drinks not amuse-bouche! Ward is delivering his introductory speech in 5!"

"On it! You guys with me!"

The people were a whirlwind, all headed in the same direction towards the music.

I walked behind them with more confidence now, all the way down the corridor. To the right was another set of swinging double doors that opened into the grand ballroom. The waiters held platters of thin champagne flutes over their heads.

Once they were in and the doors stopped swinging, I peered through the port window. The crowd was massive. The women wore lavish gowns of all colors while the men seemed to be wearing the same kind of tuxedo. I tried to hone in on one area at a time, searching blocks of people rather than scanning the whole crowd.

I spotted Hugh and his father almost immediately. They were surrounded by a handful of tuxedoed men near a bar erected in the corner of the ballroom. Each had a glass of amber liquid, something I bet cost a fortune and had a taste to match.

My gaze kept traveling. Waiters darted around the group making sure people had drinks. A pretty black haired girl handed a flute to Donovan.

Fuck. There stood Donovan with one of his usual buddies, dressed to the nines in a tailored suit. I didn't expect him to be in on the action this closely. How did he get in? Had he paid someone off?

I took a deep breath. This didn't change anything

"Hey, are you kitchen or waitstaff?"

The voice startled me. I turned and was face to face with a young man in a suit clutching a clipboard for dear life. His face was delicate and I think he had on eye makeup.

My answer came off more as a question than anything. "Kitchen?"

He ran his finger down a page. "Oh, late shift? Where's your uniform?"

"Yeah, late shift. It's in my car. Haven't changed yet,

still have a few hours." Damn, I was getting good at all this undercover shit.

"Why are you here so early?" He looked through the porthole and gave me what I imagined was a sympathetic smile. "Came to watch the rich and famous a bit first? We've all been there. No worries. Just get to your shift on time and we're good, okay?"

"Got it. Thanks."

The guy pushed by me into the ballroom. Music swelled louder then dampened as the door shut. I continued my search for Olivia and at last found her at the center of a group of people. She wore a sleek emerald green ball gown that brushed the floor. Both hands rested in front of her clutching a small purse. She had her mask on. That brilliant smile flashed as she spoke. I knew it now and I knew she was nervous. When she wasn't speaking her jaw tensed. Her gaze never stayed on one person too long. She kept looking at the front of the room.

It was a narrow stage she kept looking to, about twenty feet away. A microphone was in the center. Behind it a string quartet played. Above them a giant picture of the mayor hung with patriotic banners and bows. His jowly face looked friendly enough. But I knew what he really looked like, at his most vile.

Overhead, chandeliers dimmed. The quartet finished the last note of their melody and rested their instruments. A spotlight lit up the microphone. A handful of men walked up onto the stage. I recognized two; the mayor and Bolt, the SPD captain.

Bolt went to the microphone and tapped it. "Is this thing on?"

The crowd gave him an obligatory laugh. It was worse than the canned laughter on TV. This was even more fake.

"I'm away from the station tonight with you all because tonight, we're here to celebrate and promote a man known for his honesty, devotion, and compassion. My dear friend, Lewis Ward, has dreams to help make this city, state, and country a better place."

Fucking murderers. The words kept running through my head. I wanted to puke. Bolt had the crowd's attention. They beamed at him. They thought he was great, and so was the mayor.

I tried to step outside of my rage. I was here to get Olivia, not to dwell on the monsters on stage. With the lights being dimmed, now was the best time to grab her.

I gently pushed the door open and worked my way around the perimeter of the room to where she still stood. As I neared one of the exits, it swooshed open nearly hitting me in the face. One of Donovan's lackeys from the previous night came out.

"E, I suggest you get outta here."

Behind him in the hallway were ten of Donovan's men. They carried sub machine guns and a few shotguns. Further down I spotted two security guards slumped against the wall, their throats slashed.

Fuck. *Fuck.* I pushed by him into the crowd. I had to find Olivia. The crowd was fixed on the police captain who was doing a piss poor job of using a boating story as a metaphor for how great Ward would be as Senator. They had no idea what was coming.

Bolt finished his story. "Now, without further ado, let me introduce you to Lewis Ward, the man of the hour!"

The mayor sauntered up to the microphone. He gave the crowd a sheepish grin and opened his mouth to speak when a stream of gunfire shredded the man standing to his right.

A split second of shock, then screams. People turned to run for exits. It was chaos. Security guards pushed through to get to the mayor. One by one they fell as Donovan's men shot them. Already on the outside of the group, I spotted two exits already blocked by men with assault rifles pointed at the crowd. Donovan's men.

"Get down on the ground now!"

I wasn't sure who was yelling it but as people began dropping onto their stomachs on the ground, I followed suit. Those who were left standing were Donovan's people and the brave security guards who fired back, but were overwhelmed and dead in an instant. On my initial count there were over twenty of Donovan's men. Most were dispersed at the exits. Three, including Donovan, were at the stage. It was Donovan who'd been ordering people to get down on the ground.

Shit. My plan went out the window.

"Ladies and gentlemen, we will be out of your lovely party in a minute. I'm here for four men. Two of them, I already have." He kicked the mayor who was now on his knees, hands tied behind his back with two wraps of duct tape around his mouth and head. Beside him they were in progress tying Bolt. "But I need two more. I want Hugh and Stanley Raven. Stand up now."

I lifted my head to try and get a better view of the bar where I'd last seen them. No one moved in that area. I scanned for Olivia. Someone jacked the lights back up to full blast.

She was looking right at me. Her face was blank as our eyes locked. She was on her stomach about fifteen feet away from me, her chest propped up slightly as she rested on her elbows.

"Nothing?" Donovan laughed. He raised his gun—a shotgun I knew he thought made him look like a badass—and fired at one of his nonessential hostages. The man's head exploded, gore slapping against the stage.

Around me were frightened moans and screams. Donovan pulled a woman from the crowd, and without making his request again, fired point blank into her chest.

"How many more have to die?" Donovan pointed the shotgun at the crowd. "Tell me where the Ravens are."

"He's over here!"

It was a man's voice. There was a scuffle and a yelp in that area. Donovan's men navigated their way through the lying bodies to the bar. They yanked Hugh and his father up then lead them to the service doors I'd come through earlier.

"Thank you. See how easy this was? The key is cooperation." Donovan tapped the mic, saluted the crowd, then headed off stage. His men hauled Bolt and the mayor up by the shoulders and forced them from the stage.

They were walking straight towards us. I wasn't sure what Donovan would make of me being there, so I kept my head down as much as I could. I watched from the corner of my eye as they passed Olivia, then were almost beyond me.

That's when Olivia stood. I wanted to scream at her to get down, what the fuck are you doing, when I saw the gun

in her hand and my mind went blank.
     She fired.

CHAPTER 36

The mayor went down around the same time every one of Donovan's men turned and fired at Olivia. Her body jolted as dozens of rounds hit her. Blood burst from her body, soaked her emerald dress and splattered her skin. Donovan screamed in Russian. They went into double time and hauled the mayor and Bolt through the service doors. The rest of his men left, too.

We were alone. Nothing but fear and ragged breath. Somewhere in the distance I heard sirens.

My body and mind were numb. I crawled to Olivia's body. The people around her had pressed themselves away, leaving her sprawled in a circular opening. I cursed them for their ignorance.

Olivia was still alive, but not for long. Blood gushed from bullet holes across her body. She gasped for air. Her gaze was distant. Against the splatter of red on her face, her eyes were bluer than I'd ever seen them before.

"Did I get him?"

"Jesus, Olivia. Yeah you did," I said. I cupped her face in my hands. Her skin was incredibly soft. "You got the fucker. You killed him."

I didn't know if he was dead, but that's what Olivia needed to hear. She needed to know what she'd done wasn't for nothing. If there was one thing I could do for her, it was to give her that.

Tears welled in my eyes and dripped onto her face. "I wish I could've stopped you."

I wanted her to deliver some line that would fix it all. Something to reassure me she'd die happy, that it was all going to be okay.

Instead, she stared into the blinding chandelier without saying another word. Her chest stopped heaving. Whatever made us alive, who we are, seeped from her body leaving her just that; a corpse.

Around me people were standing. They stared at Olivia with repulsion and shock. To them, Olivia was a murderer. They saw her shoot the mayor. Their precious fucking mayor.

The front doors to the ball room burst open as police entered the room.

This wasn't justice.

I snatched up her purse, fallen and blood smeared beside her foot. I took one last glance at Olivia before I used the few precious minutes I had left to escape.

CHAPTER 37

My body was on autopilot as I jogged. It seemed every emergency vehicle, including S.W.A.T., was headed to the scene. Part of me wondered if Donovan could really make it out of there alive with his hostages. I could very well have set him up for a brutal death from police chase or shootout. Then again, he knew what he was getting into. That wasn't on me.

The city was louder than usual. Everyone was buzzed with curiosity as the vehicles sped by. Lungs on fire, I darted into an alcove of a restaurant to escape the rain that had picked up while I was inside. It was a taco joint. The greasy smell of meat and spices made me nauseated. I still took huge gulps of air that felt hard going into my lungs.

I withdrew Olivia's purse from my inner jacket and popped the clasp open. Inside was her cell, some makeup, a couple twenties, her apartment card and her keys. I pocketed the keys and security card and considered what I should do with the bag. My head swam and I leaned against the wall for support as I smelled her too-sweet floral perfume on the fabric.

Olivia was dead because of me. I shouldn't have listened to her when she told me to leave. That was stupid. So fucking stupid. No one could've walked away from what she saw unscathed. When her attitude shifted, I should've known what was coming. I'd seen it before in addicts. That moment where the fine line keeping them tethered to any sense of morals and self snaps. When what we should do and what we want to do are in opposition, and we shut ourselves down to do what we need to in order to get what we want.

It starts out small. A father skims funds off the kid's college account for his coke habit. A woman gives up her wedding ring for another bottle of Valium. The need grows, and so does their willingness to betray themselves. Someone offers their partner for sex in exchange for drugs. They have nothing to pay with, so they turn to murder to get what they want.

When they check out, I see it in their eyes. I saw it in Olivia that night. I saw her tether begin to fray when she tortured her father. I saw it snap as she watched herself on that video. I left Olivia drifting away from herself.

I was too angry at her, too consumed with my own plan to kill the men, to pay any serious attention to what she was going through. I had no one to blame but myself. And I sure as fuck would blame myself forever.

I patted my jacket for cigarettes. None. Cursing the world, I left the protection of the alcove and kept heading downtown, Olivia's purse clutched tightly against my chest. I made myself slow the pace. People jogging in plain clothes when a massacre just occurred looked suspicious.

Her apartment wasn't far. After a half hour I was at the gate to the complex. I let myself in and headed straight for her unit. The place was exactly as it was from the last time I saw it. The same dishes, same stacks of junk.

But it lacked life. It lacked her. The heater was off, leaving the place uncharacteristically cold. Only the light over the oven was on. Her laptop was where it had been. The baggie of videos was empty now, each of the memory cards stacked in rows. There was a slender wooden box open beside it with gun cleaning supplies inside. Six shots had been removed from a box of ammo beside it. For all the distaste Olivia had for my gun, it looked like she had one of her own.

I set her purse on the counter and shoved the memory cards back in their baggy, then grabbed two plastic bags from under the kitchen sink. There were stacks of documents from D.P. littered about the apartment. I took all of them, shoved them into the bags and piled them by the door. All the evidence we had against the mayor and his cohorts. I grabbed the forty bucks from Olivia's purse—not without a hundred thoughts against myself for stealing from a dead girl—and dragged my evidence out to the curb.

I flagged down the first cab I saw and stowed my luggage right by me. I was going to get true justice for Olivia if it was the last thing I ever did.

CHAPTER 38

"Jesus, get away. I told you not to come back here!"

Rupert Fearnley's face peered out from behind six inches of open door to his studio. He seemed to think that would stop me from getting in. The only thing stopping me was the group of people walking towards me from less than a half block away.

"And I didn't listen. You need to let me in. We have to talk."

"No. I'm going to call the cops."

The group passed by and were headed down the street. Their colorful umbrellas bumped against one another as they moved. Umbrellas? Definitely from out of town.

I gave the door one hard shove sending Fearnley back onto his butt. In one swift motion I plopped my plastic bags of documents in the entryway and turned to shut the heavy door.

"I'm not going to hurt you. You're not going to call the cops. We're going to talk." I found the bolt locking mechanism on the bottom of the door and slid it into place.

"I don't have anything to say to you."

"You will. Let's go upstairs, okay?" I bent down and offered him my hand. "We can have some of your fancy tea and work a few things out."

Fearnley stared at my hand for at least a minute before he took it and let me haul him up. It took everything I had to focus on what was in front of me.

He led me upstairs. My bags thumped against the staircase as I brought them up. Soon I was sitting in the same chair in his den. This time Fearnley didn't offer me any tea or cookies. I guess my welcome didn't go that far.

"Lewis Ward, Lincoln Johnston, Eugene Holloway, Hugh and Stanley Raven. All Whiteout users. Ring a bell?"

Fearnley's face distorted into something between a frown and pain. His one word held relief and frustration. "Yes."

There was something uniquely satisfying about having your suspicion confirmed. I gave myself a second to enjoy it. "Holloway told me about you and Draper, how you wanted to reintroduce your off-the-record Whiteout test subjects back into the world. It was good intent, only fucking terribly carried out."

"I know." Fearnley leaned back in his chair. His shoulders slumped forward. "It was difficult and messy. We didn't do it right. Did you ever remember your name? Or do you still go by Ethan?"

Nothing could surprise me at this point, but I *was* interested. "Ethan. I know my name was William, though. I've filled in a lot of blanks. You remember me?"

"Of course. I remember all of you. I've never forgotten. Ethan was my late son's name, and Knight my now ex-wife's maiden name. You were the only one I gave a special name to. I felt the worst about you."

"Great."

Fearnley gulped. His bulbous Adam's apple bobbed. "When Draper came to me with Holloway's demand, I tried to stop him. It was unethical, outrageous. But I was young and working for Draper was as good as I'd ever do. He threatened to destroy me. Draper also promised none of you would be hurt badly and that we'd let you back into the world when it was over."

"When my friend and I came here, you recognized me?"

Fearnley nodded. "Instantly. I've always suffered for what I did to you and the others. You're in my mind every time I wake up and go to sleep."

Under different circumstances, I would've gloated. My suspicions when we first met were true. He couldn't stop staring at me because he knew me. I was a ghost come back to life. With the weight of Olivia's death still crushing my heart, gloating was impossible.

"You have to believe me, I wanted you all to get your lives back. When we put you in that apartment in Ballard, I gave you a photo of you and your girlfriend. I stole it from the personal belongings that were locked away. I hoped it would trigger memories and help get you back on your feet."

I couldn't stop myself from laughing. "You had to have known how dangerous it would be to let me free. You didn't even bring me down off Whiteout in a safe place. You threw me into the world, addicted to painkillers and downers, and hoped for the best."

His hands shook. When he noticed, he put them over his face and took a slow breath in. His narrow chest expanded then collapsed as his stature crumpled even more.

"I know. Well, I didn't know what would happen at the time. You'd been on Whiteout too long, on too many variants of it, and that made your situation particularly bad.

Listen, there's nothing I can say that will make up for what I did. Nothing will explain our inhumanity, our cruelty." Fearnley choked back a sob. "All I can say is I'm sorry."

"That's not all you can do. I have questions that I want answered. Can you do that?"

Fearnley nodded. "Whatever you want. Ask."

"Why didn't you blow the whistle on it?" I asked. "You obviously don't agree with what's going on."

"Holloway pays me off. For the first few years I ignored what we were part of. I didn't know exactly what Holloway was doing with the Whiteout Draper supplied him with. Once Draper died and manufacturing was in my hands, I still never asked. I was able to follow my dream of being a sculptor. I had a beautiful home, security. It could all vanish in a second. In the end my greed won over my conscience."

My heart skipped a beat at one sentence Fearnley offered so casually. "You're in charge of manufacturing?"

"Yes. I use my offshore drug manufacturing connections to get them done. As long as they get paid, they don't ask questions. It protects the mayor and his friends if I'm the middleman. Even if I'd wanted to come forward, I'm the one making the drug. I'm the one distributing it. There's no record of them taking it from me."

"What about Whiteout on the streets?"

"It was Ward and Holloway's idea. They got greedy. Ward saw profit in it and Holloway jumped at the dollar signs. Holloway had a few connections with small time drug dealers. They just started distributing it a few weeks ago."

I remembered the Whiteout pills I encountered, but also the patch. "What about the patch they were using? I'd only seen pills until Hugh Raven used one on Olivia."

"The patch was developed years ago per Ward's request. Another offshore venture. The pills are cheaper to manufacture and Ward wanted access to the patch exclusively." Fearnley smiled, forlorn. "I guess it doesn't matter now. I'd imagine they'll be dead soon anyway."

"What?" I tensed. "How do you know that?"

He leaned forward and picked up a remote from the coffee table and used it to turn on a narrow flat screen in the center of the bookcase. It was on a news channel. I recognized the outside of the Fairmont. A stream of text on the bottom kept repeating the names of men abducted from the gala. A petite Asian woman came on screen and started to list the events that took place.

As far as they knew, gang members abducted four men and nearly sixteen were killed during the gunfight, most of them security guards. The criminals involved are nowhere to be found.

"In a bizarre turn of events, campaign manager Olivia Holloway is reported to have shot the mayor. While police have not commented on her involvement, there could be a possible connection between her and the gang involved." The woman's face was carefully stoic. "Please be aware, the following footage is uncut and extremely graphic. Phil, what you're about to see is cell footage of Holloway shooting the mayor. Again, this is graphic and not recommended for sensitive viewers."

It cut to vertical footage of Olivia standing and shooting the mayor. The shot ended just as the Russians began shooting Olivia. That moment took forever in real life. The video showed it for what it was; seconds.

"The location of the kidnapped is still unknown. We are hoping for their safe return. Back to you, Phil."

The shot cut back to two news anchors who began discussing Olivia's involvement and rehashing what took place again. I watched until it cut to a commercial. Fearnley muted it.

"I was watching it before you arrived."

"Turn it off," I told him. "I was there. I don't need to see this. But that is why I'm here."

Fearnley turned it off. There was something different about him now. He wasn't trying like he had been when I first met him. His guard was down. Instead of vibrant and showy, he seemed flat yet more aware of what was going on around him. I wondered if he'd been waiting for the day when someone called him out. I would've been, if I were him.

"You're the only one who gives the product to the mayor, right?"

"That's correct. I receive a shipment of about two hundred pills and a hundred patches once a month. I deliver them to Ward or Holloway." Fearnley winced. "They sometimes invite me to participate in their…their club. I've never accepted."

"Good for you. Do the others know about you?"

"Not that I know of. I only deal with those two. They keep it that way to prevent mutiny."

Holloway was dead. The mayor was most likely dead. Knowing their need for control through knowledge, I doubted they'd told the Ravens or Johnston about Fearnley. If the mayor was dead, that was the end of Whiteout. Donovan wouldn't be able to get his hands on it.

"Good. Here's what I want you to do, Fearnley. I think it's something you've wanted for a long time. I want you to come clean. I want you to find the right people and tell them what Ward and his buddies were up to. Tell them about your involvement if you want, or tell them you were forced the whole time. I want those men's lives ruined. I need the world to know they weren't the victims here." I rubbed my fingers against my temples. "I would do this myself, but who would believe me? I'm just a drug dealer who uses too much of his own product. They'd look at my involvement with the Russian's who abducted them and never see beyond it."

There was no argument, no resistance. Fearnley nodded. "I'll do it. None of what I have is worth the agony I live in. I'd rather go to prison knowing I came clean. But we have nothing against them but accusations. *I'm* the one getting the drugs made and distributing them. I have no evidence. Hell, I don't have anything going back to Draper or the trials or *anything.*"

"I do." I pulled my plastic bags towards me and untied them. I began to stack the documents I brought from Olivia's on the coffee table. "We retrieved these from the old D.P. building. Patient forms, financial records, information on Whiteout. That should help. But this is what no one will be able to deny."

The plastic bag of memory cards didn't look like much, but it was undeniable proof of the men involved.

"Each one of these has videos of the men raping, killing, and torturing. They kept them to use as blackmail against each other. I'm willing to bet there might be more, but there's videos of every man involved. In a building beside the Holloway & Raven office, in the basement, is a soundproofed room they did it all in."

I told Fearnley everything because he was the only person who could do anything about it. I told him about Olivia, her sister. About her father killing Kaylee, the log book. Barring what I convinced Donovan to do, I gave every detail I had. The more I spoke to him, the stronger his conviction to redeem himself grew. Fearnley severed himself from what was right years ago. Now he was ready to reconnect.

CHAPTER 39

A week later, when nothing happened after talking to Fearnley, I went back. His studio was empty. There was no sign of him. I hung out at electronic stores watching the news for any breaking developments on the mayor. It was the same story over and over; people were convinced Olivia Holloway was involved with the Russian mob. She was offered money to kill the mayor. She was in love with one of the Russian mobsters. The list of angles was endless.

I wanted to hate Fearnley but even that took too much effort. I was drained and depressed and couldn't muster up the energy to try and hunt him down or do much about it. I tried to get Olivia the justice she deserved and failed. I failed at everything I did. It was in my nature.

Donovan quickly discovered the men knew nothing about how to get more Whiteout. He came by my apartment and sat on my easy chair, his head dropped in his hands and spoke quietly. His father might kill him for the stunt he pulled at the gala. He was going to move to Italy to avoid his wrath. He hated himself for failing. No one would keep me in the game anymore since I was so close to him. I should go to Oregon where his cousin was. They'd help me out.

I was surprised he didn't blame me. I was the one who told him the men would tell him everything he needed to know. As it turned out, Bolt and the Ravens said the mayor was the only one who knew anything and he was dead from a bullet through the brain. Donovan hated Olivia, not me. I did everything I could.

He told me he was sorry he couldn't be there for me anymore. He gave me a wad of cash and a shitload of drugs as a parting gift, with regretful words on how sad he was he had to leave.

After that, time didn't exist anymore. I was in and out of consciousness, my body pumped with a cocktail of drugs and booze that would intimidate the worse of the worst.

Some days I lay on my bed and saw Laurel and Olivia smoking cigarettes on my apartment floor. They smiled and laughed. I crawled to them and they were gone. Sometimes they stayed and told me I was a fuckup.

I got jacked on cocaine and Adderall and used a comb to vacuum my floor three times. When I finished my hands shook and I couldn't form a fist. I had basketball sized lumps of dirt and carpet fibers stacked by the front door next to the library books I still hadn't returned.

When I crashed from exhaustion I stared at the mold on the ceiling and saw a riveting Shakespearean play that brought me to tears. I shouted *Encore! Encore!* from my soiled mattress.

Eventually the drugs ran out and my binge came to a hard, bitter end. I realized I should've saved some to sell. I used all the money Donovan gave me to buy more, to keep the rampage going. Now I had nothing.

I panhandled for a while. Or tried to. I was going through withdrawal. Withdrawal for me meant frantic eyes, mumbling, and lots of foul smelling sweat. I was the kind of person people crossed the street to avoid, or pretended to make a call so they could feign distraction.

Penniless and months behind in rent, I got kicked out of my apartment. I knew it was coming and left before the landlord could make me clean up the place. Packed my duffel bag with all the clothes I owned. The easy chair and coffee machine had to stay. Maybe the next owner would love them as much as I did.

I went to Lucya's first, hoping Artur would convince her to show mercy. No luck. Both had been good friends of Chuck's. Accident or not, I murdered their buddy. There was no place for me there. A few people under the overpass took pity on me and helped me for a while. Of course, they didn't spare any of their own drugs for me, but they gave me food. Let me sleep in their tents when they weren't using them. I'd been through hints of withdrawal before, but this was real. My body punished me for what I'd done to it.

For weeks I kept checking the library and TVs every day, waiting for Fearnley. Hoping he hadn't given up. Hoping he would do what was right.

And finally, he did.

EPILOGUE

4 Months Later

Happy endings and getaways are sunny. Everyone is smiling and sipping a frosty beverage on the beach or in their villa. They're driving a fast car on the open highway. A beautiful woman has her hair whipping in the wind while a roguish man grinned in triumph. Whatever it was that held them back was gone.

That's not what my happy ending looked like because this is real fucking life. My happy ending was misty and cold because Portland weather was almost the same as Seattle. Mine was made up of the same things as before, because the people there might be stranger but were still just as willing to buy drugs. A good apartment still cost more than I could afford and the endless self-help knowledge I'd accumulated could never dissolve the trauma that held me back.

At least, not completely.

My shitty apartment wasn't as bad as the one in Seattle. The walls weren't moldy and I got a corner unit, making the place quiet. There was a donut shop downstairs and every morning I was graced with the delicious smell of carbs, sugar, and fat. At night I got the donuts that were going to be thrown out. I still dealt drugs for the Melnikov family, but hundreds of miles away from the scene of my misery. I had no education, no skills, and my blood was still primarily made of nicotine.

But I hadn't done a single drug since I came down off the binge. Since it all ended and I moved, my nightmares weren't as frequent. Not all my income came from drugs; I worked security at one of the Melnikov strip clubs downtown. And I had my own damn computer, sitting neat and pretty on a desk. It was one of five nice things I owned and I spent a lot of time on it.

For a while after Olivia died, thoughts of Skid came with guilt. I let my remorse and mourning take its course, and over time I let myself acknowledge Skid would've been proud of what I accomplished with my new life.

I scrolled through another article, this one on CNN since the story of the 'Ward Sex Club' scandal hit it big. The title didn't do the horror justice. It made it petty when it was anything but. Two girls had come forward claiming the mayor sexually assaulted them and paid them off not to say anything. There were dozens of these stories between the mayor and his friends; some were proven legitimate while others remained only claims.

More articles had popped up over the months about people who played small roles in the operation. Lincoln Johnston had numerous officers on his payroll. He had unauthorized taps on dozens of girl's phones, which he and his buddies used to monitor them. The Mayor had ties to a coroner's office and doctors to forge death certificates. The network of people involved in the Whiteout ring was bigger than I thought. The public was shocked at how deep it went. Olivia and I had already known; we just didn't have exact names.

Fearnley's confession and evidence was kept under

wraps for months. It wasn't that he'd bailed; the accusations were so severe it took longer to make things public. I know because I visited Fearnley shortly after the news aired. He was on house arrest in Seattle until trials began. He gave me his fancy tea and bitter healthy cookies and gave me every last detail.

He also gave me the name of the cemetery my parents were buried in. Both died in a car accident two years earlier. He gave me Sarah's last name. He apologized again for what he'd done and offered me help in any way he could. I thanked him and meant it. I also asked for one of his sculptures to sell on eBay since they were going for fifty grand a pop now that he was famous from being involved in a high profile case. I guess you could make a living off art.

News coverage went from portraying Olivia as a deceitful bitch to a true hearted vigilante. Yeah, she murdered Lewis Ward. Who wouldn't considering her circumstances?

It wasn't for me to decide if what I did gave Olivia the justice she deserved, but that didn't stop me from hoping it was what she would've wanted. All the men were dead, their evil exposed, and the reputation of the girls involved was upheld.

I closed the articles I'd been reading and put the computer to sleep. In a few hours I was due at the club.

I went to the kitchen and started brewing a pot of coffee on my newer, better machine. A box of the previous night's stale donuts were piled high in a pink cardboard box beside it. I grabbed a bacon maple bar and ate it as I leaned on the counter watching my coffee drip into the pot.

It took a while to get used to the idea I was just a victim

in a drug study gone wrong. There wasn't a grand plot against me. I wasn't the center of the universe. Making myself and everyone around me suffer wasn't going to fix anything. Wanting to fill in the blank spots in my memory wouldn't, either.

If I really wanted to say fuck you, I had to control my life.

The thought came so clearly that it startled me. My gaze fell on the photo on the fridge. Beneath it was her phone number. I hadn't moved to Portland because I wanted to. The job offer had something to do with it, but it was because I'd found her after months of searching. I thought moving there would help me build up courage. I hoped one day I would run into her. It had been two months and I hadn't.

Everyone has to live and die for something. You decide what that something is.

I swallowed the bite of donut and washed my mouth out with a gulp of water from the faucet. Cracked my neck and rolled my shoulders. I got my cell out and typed the number in, hitting send while I still had it in me to do it.

It rang.

It rang.

"Hello?"

"Sarah?"

"Oh god." Her voice was meek, shocked. "Will? Is that you?"

I took a deep breath. I wasn't Ethan anymore. I was whoever I chose to be.

"Yes," I said. "It's me."

ACKNOWLEDGEMENTS

When I first decided to write Anamnesis, I thought, "This isn't zombies. This isn't post-apocalyptic. What am I doing?" I threw self-doubt to the wind, buckled down, and wrote it because it was something I needed to do. The concept had been in my mind for over a year. It was one of those ideas that will never leave you alone until you do what it wants.

Huge thank you to all the people who supported me and encouraged me to pursue Anamnesis even though it was outside of my usual genre, especially the handful of beta readers who gave this book a shot.

Thank you to Jonathan Lambert, who has been one of the most amazing readers, fans, editors, writers, and friends I could ask for.

To all my fans who made it this far, *thank you*. I cannot do this without you.

ABOUT THE AUTHOR

Eloise J. Knapp hails from Seattle and never complains about the rain. She is a graphic designer by day and author by night. Knapp's work includes The Undead Situation trilogy and Anisakis Nova series. When not writing you'll find her hiking the Pacific Northwest.

Connect

www.eloisejknapp.com
www.facebook.com/eloisejknapp
@EloiseJKnapp

22938151R00224

Made in the USA
Middletown, DE
13 August 2015